Her Forgotten Life

Debbie Volf

Her Forgotten Life

This is a work of fiction. Names, characters, places, and incidents are products of the author's imagination or are used fictitiously and are not to be construed as real.

ISBN: 978-0-9950499-0-1

Cover design by: JD&J Design

Printed in the USA
Published by Debbie Volf
www.debbievolf.com
debbievolfauthor@gmail.com

In loving memory of my mother—a truly remarkable woman.
I will never forget her stories of the past. They will stay with me forever.

Our past cannot be changed, but we have the ability to choose how we interpret our memories. Perhaps we look at them with fondness or possibly with disdain. Maybe we effectively block some memories from our conscious mind because they are too painful to recall. Regardless of how we perceive our history, our memories, conscious or not, make us who we are. Not only can they mold our future but possibly those of our children as well.

Part One:
A Family's History is its Legacy

Chapter 1: The Longest Day

A VEIL OF confusion and fear suddenly covers her ancient face. "I want to go home now!" demands the woman. "Where am I? I don't like it here! Who are you people? Can you take me back to my home?"

Standing in the small hospital room, we look sympathetically at this petite, frail body that seems more like a skeleton covered with wrinkled, sagging skin than that of an elderly woman. We speak in low, soothing voices to avoid causing her any further upset or confusion. The end is near for this mother, grandmother, and great-grandmother—the end of a life to which most of us could not begin to comprehend or relate.

"It's okay, Mom, you'll be going home soon," I say in a tone that I could almost believe as being true. She closes her eyes once again and falls asleep.

My mother and I have been best friends my whole life. To see her this way is torture, but there's nothing to do now except wait and pray for a speedy end. My husband and children are with me today to say goodbye and to support me in what I know will be difficult for all of us.

Alzheimer's disease is probably one of the worst diseases for loved ones to face. In most cases, as with my mother, the person with the disease is in his or her own world and not able to understand what is happening to them. Mom's diagnosis came when she was eighty-four years old, so it wasn't early onset, but it was a blow to us nonetheless. Since then, I've had to make some of the toughest decisions of my life. My grief over the loss of my mother and best friend has long since passed. The person she was is gone, but even though she may no longer know me, I won't stop being there for her. I know, had the roles been reversed, she would never leave my side.

This disease not only destroys a life but also a lifetime of memories—both good and bad—leaving a person unable to recall the simplest things. It's not selective. Like a robber whose greed is unfulfilled, it refuses to be satisfied until it has claimed the physical being. From the onset, it slowly reduces a person in the most undignified fashion.

Family is most important for someone afflicted with this horrible disease. Although it's tough, we always try to look for the positives in this slow and painful journey. It's never easy to find things to smile about, but in some instances, we find ourselves looking at certain situations in a more light-hearted fashion as a way to deal with the sadness we face.

When Mom turned ninety, I went to visit her with the gift of a balloon and some flowers. Not realizing it was her birthday, she stared at the number ninety on the balloon with shock.

"Ninety? *Am I ninety?*"

After I had confirmed this, she looked at me and shook her head in disbelief.

"When did *that* happen?" she asked incredulously as a frown formed on her face.

"Today, Mom. It happened today," I told her while trying to hide a smile.

Sad, I know, but slightly humorous as well. I think unless you go through this situation, you could find it difficult to understand, but for me, times like this help to keep me going.

"DO YOU THINK she's in pain?" Cathy asks.

"No," I reply. "The doctor prescribed some pain medication so she's comfortable."

My daughter, Cathy, is the younger of my two children and is a sensitive, caring person. She has always had a special bond with my mother, and although her diagnosis hit her very hard, she has tried to do what she can for her. My son, Mike, is much like his sister, but like most men, he tends to hide his emotional side.

Mike looks over at me for the first time in hours and asks about the funeral arrangements and his Oma's final wishes. "Would it be okay for me to do the eulogy? I'd really like to, Mom," he whispers as we sit in the silence of the hospital room.

I contemplate it briefly and agree to let him do it since I doubt I will be in any condition to do it myself. *At least one thing is off my plate.*

Suddenly, one of the most solemn expressions I've ever seen my son wear crosses his face. "Okay then, I'll need you to help me with it so I get the details right."

Ah, yes, the details—I guess this isn't off my plate after all, and I feel a sense of dread wash over me as I think of the past.

"Let's get a cup of coffee," I suggest to my son.

Cathy looks up from her book. "I'll go with you. I need a break, too."

"You guys go ahead, I'll stay here," my husband Jack tells me as I look in his direction.

"Okay, we won't be long," I say appreciatively. "Did you want anything from the cafeteria?"

"No thanks, you go on and take your time. I'll come and get you if something changes, so don't worry."

Jack has been my rock. Throughout the years, he has kept me grounded even when I've been at my wit's end and feeling as though I couldn't go on another day. Without his support and constant reminders that I've done everything humanly possible for my mom, I probably would have had a breakdown long ago.

As we walk to the cafeteria, my mind goes back to the many stories Mom told me over the years—some funny—others disturbing. *How much should I tell them? Would Mom have wanted me to tell them both the good and the bad? Do I owe it to her to speak of the horrible times she went through?* My heart and my head battle it out until I finally come to a decision.

"I'm so proud of the woman your Oma was even if she can't remember her life. I think she would want me to share what I know so that you can tell others what a special person she was."

After we get our coffee and find a spot to sit, I look at my children and think about what I want to say. "Your Oma's story may not be that remarkable when compared to others from her era born in Europe and who lived through the war, but to me, her story is just that—remarkable. Maybe it's because I can't imagine what it must have been like to live during those years and under those circumstances. I often wonder how I would have handled my life had I lived back then."

Both Mike and Cathy look at me with interest, patiently waiting for me to continue. *Where do I start?* There are still so many things I don't know myself, things that my mom didn't want me to know or that were just too painful for her to recall. *Maybe it's for the best anyway.* I take another moment to organize my thoughts and find the right words to convey the stories I was told as a child. At the time I heard them, they held little meaning or interest to me. I wish I had paid more attention and asked more questions, but I suppose my immaturity was to blame. Well, as they say, hindsight is twenty/twenty. Unfortunately, there's no going back in time to change things.

"Oma is one of three children who survived to adulthood. There were seven in total, but the rest of them died either at birth or as toddlers. She's the youngest of the three. Her sister was the eldest with sixteen years between them, and she had a brother who was eight years older."

"As you know, she was born in Hamburg, Germany in November of 1923. Around that time, the Communists made an attempt to overtake the country, and the economy was on the verge of collapse. Oma once told me that back then, people used money to wallpaper their walls since it was almost worthless. From what I understand, this was because the country had to reimburse loans used to finance the First World War. Many people starved to death back then so it was a small miracle that Oma even survived infancy." I stop for an instant, thinking about what I had just said. I knew these facts, but never truly gave them much thought. *How difficult must it have been for my grandparents to raise a family in those years? How did they deal with the ravages of the First World War—a war that conscripted my grandfather—a war that left its indelible mark on the man?*

"Hey, Mom, are you still with us?" Mike asks.

I look at him and bring myself back to the present. "Sorry, I just haven't thought about this in such a long time."

I tell my kids about my grandfather suffering from shell shock, known today as Post-Traumatic Stress Disorder, after fighting in the First World War. My mother told me stories about how he could sometimes be so mean and hurtful. My adult mind can now understand and link that behaviour to the condition, but when I first heard those stories, I formed a negative opinion of the man.

"He wasn't all bad," I say in his defence. "He used to dress up as Saint Nicholas on Christmas Eve and go door to door in the apartment complex where they lived. He was so good at it, in fact, that none of the children recognized him. They didn't believe Oma when, in later years, she told them that it was her father." As I sit there, I try to envision the man I only recognize from photographs dressing up as Santa Claus. It's difficult for me to imagine since every picture of my grandfather depicted a stern man without a hint of a smile. *I guess there wasn't much of a reason for him to smile.*

"What about your Oma?" Cathy asks.

"You mean Oma's mother?"

"Yeah, what do you know about her?"

"Well, again, not that much really. My grandmother had a twin sister who lived in Berlin, but your Oma rarely saw her. Oma's parents married in 1908 when her mother was twenty, which in those years, was considered old for marriage because life expectancy was so much lower than it is today. They had another daughter, before she was born, who, at two years of age, fell from a second story window to her death. Oma told me that the accident caused her mother's hair to turn snow-white overnight. She always believed she was conceived as a replacement for the child they lost."

"Wow, how sad!" Cathy says with a shake of her head.

I nod in agreement. "Well, if that hadn't happened, we wouldn't be here having this discussion. You both know I'm a firm believer that all things happen for a reason, even if it isn't always clear to us. Although it was a terrible thing, it obviously was how things were intended to be."

Looking at the clock on the wall, I decide it's time to head back to my mother's room. When we approach the nurse's station, a nurse looks at us and smiles sympathetically.

"Things are status quo right now, so why don't you head home and get some rest? We'll contact you if there is any change."

I stare at the woman through exhausted eyes that burn as if they were on fire and nod my reply.

Mike looks over at me with compassion. "Go home, Mom, I'll stay. You need to get a few hours sleep. I'll call if you need to come back."

"Yeah, Mom, go home," agrees Cathy. "I'll stay with Mike to keep him company."

"Are you sure?" I say with some reluctance.

"Yes, go on now, you won't do anyone any good if you stay," my son says reassuringly.

I embrace my kids gratefully. *When did they change from those needy little children into the adults standing before me?* I look back at them with pride as Jack and I leave the hospital.

ON OUR WAY home, I think more about the stories I heard as a child. My mind floods with different memories, none of which I can make sense of due to my fatigue. I'm in desperate need of a good night's sleep to sort through the thoughts that plague my brain.

"You okay, Laura?" Jack asks.

I snap out of my daydream and look at him. "I'm sorry, what?"

"You looked like you were a million miles away. Are you alright?"

"I'm okay. I just need to get some rest."

For the first time, I find it difficult to express my feelings to my husband, but he knows me well enough to know when I'm holding something back. Jack is aware of some of the things my mother told me, but others I've always kept to myself. Those unspoken details have opened old wounds and now make me second-guess my decision to reveal them. *Maybe it's a mistake. Maybe it's best to have Mike do a simple eulogy and not stir up the past.*

After parking the car, we make our way to the house, and I feel like a drunkard unable to walk a straight line. I wobble my way along and focus intently on placing one foot in front of the other. Jack notices my difficulty and rushes to my side, wrapping his arm around me. I lean against him and immediately appreciate his support. I don't think I've ever felt this exhausted.

Once inside, Jack helps me to change and tucks me into bed.

"Thanks, Daddy!"

"It's good to see you still have a sense of humour," he says as he bends down to kiss me. "Now, get some sleep. Goodnight."

HOURS LATER, AND to my chagrin, sleep eludes me yet again. I quietly get out of bed and head to the kitchen for some water and guzzle it down as though I had walked through the desert for days without it.

I can't seem to turn off my brain, so I go to the basement and make my way to the storage area. It isn't long before I find what I'm looking for—a box with my mother's name on it. I pull it off the shelf and carry it to the basement family room. Sitting on the sofa with the carton beside me, I take a deep breath and open it. Inside, I see items I've long since looked at and try to remember the last time I went through this box of memories—it has to be five years or more.

As I stare into it, some childhood memories resurface from the murky depths of my mind—almost as though they happened yesterday. Many of those memories are unhappy, yet a precious few make me smile.

When I packed this box all those years ago, I carefully selected each item I thought should be saved. Some of these things mean little to me, but I kept them anyway. They meant something to my mom, so it was important that I held onto them. Maybe some part of me hoped that if I showed her these things, it would trigger her memory to come back. A silly notion at best, but sometimes it's these silly ideas that give you hope. *If only these things could talk.*

I dig through the musty-smelling box and come across the one thing that could possibly unlock the secrets of the past—a black notebook. *Do I dare look through it?* Before my brain has a chance to respond, I find myself opening it instinctively to see handwriting I easily recognize—it's that of my mother. When she would have written it, I have no idea. I've never told anyone about this book since I'm sure it holds many facts, memories and feelings too painful to recount. Perhaps Mom wrote as a therapeutic release, or because she wanted to tell me these things but could never bring herself to do it. Whatever the reason, I hope it helped her to deal with her past.

This notebook was unknown to me until we cleaned Mom's house after her move to the nursing home. During my final inspection, I opened one of the kitchen cabinets, and there it was. I was certain everything had been packed up and failed to understand how it could have possibly been missed, but somehow it had. Maybe I was meant to find the book, yet at the time, I just threw it into the box and forgot about it. It wasn't until much later while sorting through things that I once again stumbled upon it. I read the first few pages but just couldn't continue. *Was it because I felt guilty for taking Mom from her home and placing her into long-term care? Was it because I felt I was invading her privacy?* I don't remember what went through my mind at the time. All I know is that it was too difficult for me to read on, so I took the notebook and placed it in the box with the other keepsakes and put it on the shelf in the basement.

Looking at it now, I once again have doubts about whether I should read on. "What should I do?" I say aloud, and the sound of my voice startles me. Suddenly the notebook falls from my hands, and an envelope pokes its way through one of the pages. I pick it up and see my name on the front. It brings a chill to me yet I'm compelled to open it, and as I do, the first thing I notice inside is a black and white photograph. Despite my exhaustion, it instantly brings a smile to my face. It's a picture of Mom and me at Christmas in 1966, and we both seem so happy. After placing the photo on the table, I remove the letter from the envelope. It takes every ounce of courage I have just to unfold it. I do my best to control my feelings as I look at my mother's handwriting and force myself to read.

Dear Laura,

You've become a lovely young woman. I'm very proud of you and know you'll do well in your life.

I love you so much and even though times were tough for us, I always had your best interest at heart. I'm sorry that I couldn't give you all the things you needed and wanted when you were growing up. My hope was that your life would be so much better than mine, and in many ways, I believe it is.

Dad and I were so thrilled to have you, even if you think you were an afterthought. We wanted you more than you could ever know. The day you were born your father said he was so glad you would be here to look after me when I got older. Maybe he already had a premonition that he wouldn't be around long enough to take care of me himself. We brought you home from the hospital on Christmas Eve and since then you have proven to be a real gift to me. Although I couldn't give you more, I want you to have this notebook as a small token of thanks in return for all you have given me.

Love always, Mom

I finish the letter and dry my tears before once again focusing on the notebook. *How weird is it that I had never noticed that envelope before? Maybe I wasn't supposed to read this until the time was right. Maybe this is the right time.* I flip through it quickly and look at the clock. It's now 2 a.m., and I realize that sleep is no longer an option. I head back up to the kitchen to make myself some tea. It's going to be a *long* night.

Chapter 2: Summer 1927

THE OLD MARE saunters along and gives a snort as she pulls the heavily loaded wagon along the dirt road.

"Will we be home soon, Mutti?" the young girl asks her mother.

"We still have some distance to travel, Elsa. You must learn patience, Liebling."

Three-year-old Elsa looks at her mother, who seems much older than her forty years, with her shocking white hair and deeply wrinkled skin. Hers is a face that has seen much hardship, and yet it remains one still capable of showing compassion.

"I'm hungry, Mutti!" Elsa cries.

Elsa's mother, Frieda, looks at her and turns to her eldest daughter. "Greta, is there still some bread in the basket?"

"Nein, Mutti, we finished it at lunch," she says, confirming Frieda's suspicions.

"Peter, do you still have the apple you found on the road?" Frieda asks her son.

"Ja, Mutti, but it's half rotten."

"Well, give it to me, please."

Twelve-year-old Peter hands the apple to his mother, and she takes it and cuts it in half, giving Elsa the unspoiled piece.

"Dankeschön, Mutti!" Elsa bites into the apple enthusiastically and juice dribbles down her chin. Her smile lights up her small face and Frieda can't help but feel happy despite the long, bone-rattling journey they have endured. *Ah, if only you could always find happiness in the simple things in life, Liebling.*

Frieda knows all too well about losing happiness in life, but her faith in God has brought her through many hard times. She has endured the loss of three babies at birth and dealt with the hardships of the Great War on her own with two small children while her husband was fighting in the trenches. Since the war, Frieda has had to deal with his shell shock and the loss of her baby, Ingrid, after falling from a second story window to her death. Despite everything she has endured, she has remained a strong, yet sensitive, and caring person who lives only for her family—it is her sole purpose in life.

The family made the 255-kilometre trip to Berlin to attend the funeral of Frieda's brother-in-law, Pauli, and to provide support to her twin sister, Ida. The journey back home to Hamburg, however, is taking much longer than anticipated. They have been travelling for almost a week now, and Frieda looks to her weary husband and gently touches his arm.

"Heinrich, what shall we do for food? We still must travel some distance, and I'm worried about the children."

"Ach, you worry too much! We will make it by tonight. The children will be fine!"

Frieda knows better than to argue with her husband as his changing moods can cause unnecessary friction. He is strict and often insensitive toward her and the children. The war has taken its toll on many surviving soldiers, including Heinrich, and Frieda does her best to live with its consequences. She is patient and understanding with him and has tried to teach the children to deal with their father's affliction.

Frieda looks at the road ahead and keeps her opinions to herself. *I pray that you're right, Heinrich. I don't think the children can bear spending another night camped out along the roadside, and neither can I for that matter.*

They ride in silence for some time, when suddenly there is a thud and the old wagon tilts to one side. Heinrich stops the horse and goes to have a look. *"Ach, du Lieber Gott!"* he screams.

Frieda hates when her husband takes the Lord's name in vain, but she doesn't comment. Instead, she says a silent prayer that Heinrich can fix the problem so they can be home by evening.

"Peter, go help Vati, ja?" Frieda says.

Peter nods excitedly and climbs down from the wagon to help. Like most boys his age, he is eager to prove himself useful and receive the much-needed approval and praise from his father.

When Peter reaches the rear of the wagon, he sees the wheel buried to the axle in mud. "What can I do to help, Vati?"

Heinrich looks at his young son, doubtful he can be of any assistance. "Go to the horse, and when I tell you, tug on the reins and have her pull the wagon while I push from behind."

Peter does as his father instructs, but after several attempts, Heinrich tells him to stop. Heinrich is covered in mud from head to toe and stands there staring at the wagon as though doing so would get it unstuck.

"Let me try, Vati!"

Heinrich continues to stare at the wagon as though it were the only thing left on earth.

"Vati! Vati! Let me try!" the boy says excitedly, and he shakes his father's arm, breaking the spell.

Heinrich finally looks away from the wagon and into his son's hopeful face. "Get on the wagon! *Now!*"

Fearfully, Peter backs away and quickly climbs aboard without a word. He knows he must be cautious when his father is in this state and realizes that it is best to get out of his way or risk facing the consequences. All three of the children are frightened of their father, especially during one of these spells.

Frieda reaches out and touches Peter's arm with loving reassurance and a look of empathy as he boards the wagon. Greta and Elsa are both silent, but they can relate to their brother's pain from having been reprimanded for no reason, other than their father's foul mood.

Heinrich leans against the wagon and says nothing more. It is now afternoon and darkness will be upon them soon.

"What are we to do, Mutti?" Greta asks with concern.

"We will camp here for the night and get help in the morning if need be."

This news devastates Elsa and causes her to cry. Greta pulls her onto her lap and hugs her tightly. "Shhh—it will be okay, my little one."

Greta gives her mother a worried look. "We *must* get home tonight, Mutti! I promised Arthur I would see him, and he'll worry if I don't show up!"

Frieda strokes her eldest daughter's cheek and smiles. "You really like Arthur, don't you?

"Very much, Mutti," Greta says with colour rising on her cheeks.

"And what is his family name?"

"Schweiger—his name is Arthur Gerhard Schweiger." Greta enjoys how the sound of his name rolls off her tongue.

"Ja, of course! I remember now. Has he finished his studies at the University?"

"Ja, Mutti, he is now a fine doctor."

"Wunderbar. It is an excellent profession for a caring man like him," Frieda replies enthusiastically.

Greta nods in agreement as her lips form a shy smile.

"Well then, we must see what we can do to get us home so you can meet with your Herr Schweiger, ja?" Frieda says with a wink.

Arthur is Greta's first love, and at age nineteen, she spends most of her time thinking about him. Lately, her mind has been consumed with thoughts of marriage. She hopes that one day Arthur will propose and make all her dreams come true. Although Greta loves her family, her father's behaviour makes living at home intolerable, and she prays for the time when she can leave. Even with the intensity of her feelings, Greta is afraid of sharing the depth of her attachment toward Arthur with anyone in case things should fail to work out between them.

Greta is confident that her mother will do everything in her power to see that they arrive home tonight. She says a silent prayer for help as the waiting continues. To keep herself busy, she grabs her sketchbook and draws the landscape around her. Her artistic talents provide her a way to channel her feelings, giving her a sense of peace.

I must do something, Frieda thinks. After a while, she studies Heinrich's mud-caked face and climbs down from the wagon. She approaches her husband and notices the emptiness in his eyes.

"Come, Heinrich, let's get you cleaned up." She takes him gently by the hand and leads him to the side of the road.

"Greta, bring the bucket of water and a towel, please."

Greta puts her sketchbook down and does as her mother requests. She passes her the bucket and towel while gently squeezing her hand. There is no exchange of words, yet the communication between them is apparent. They will each do what they can to make the best of this unfortunate situation.

After cleaning the mud from Heinrich's face and hands, Frieda hears the sound of someone approaching. She makes her way to the side of the wagon to see if perhaps she can get some assistance. Before her comes a young man on a bicycle, riding on the dry edge of the road. *Please God, let this be the help for which I have been praying.* Suddenly, the young man looks in her direction and stops.

"Guten Abend, gnädige Frau. Can I help you?" the stranger asks.

"That would be much appreciated! Our wagon is stuck in the mud, and we have no means to move it."

Without a word, the man goes to investigate the extent of the problem and returns to Frieda's side as the children look on from the wagon.

Elsa sniffles and wipes her nose on her sleeve, and the young man looks up at her, holding out a handkerchief. "Not to worry, Little One. I'll have you on your way again in no time," he says with a wink.

Elsa quickly grabs the handkerchief from the stranger's hand and hugs her sister tightly.

The man then turns to Frieda and smiles reassuringly at her. "I will get some help and come right back."

"What is your name, young man?"

"My name is Erich Kaufmann."

"Vielen Dank, Herr Kaufmann."

Erich tips his hat to Frieda and climbs back on his bicycle, and with a wave of his hand, he is off to get help for the stranded family.

An hour passes, and Erich returns with two other young men carrying shovels. The family waits by the side of the road while the three of them dig until they free the wagon from the mud. Heinrich then approaches the trio and hands each of them a cigarette.

"I can't pay you for your work, but we are very thankful for it."

Erich takes the cigarette and lights it, appreciating the smoke. "You are most welcome, mein Herr."

Erich then looks at Elsa and winks again, and she shyly hides behind her mother's skirt, still clutching the handkerchief he had given her. Once he and the others have finished their cigarettes, they grab their shovels and are on their way.

"What a nice young man. Wasn't it kind of him to stop and help us?" Frieda says happily. "Will we still get home tonight, Heinrich?"

"Ja, we should be able to make it," he says as he prepares to get underway.

Frieda says a silent prayer of thanks for sending Erich to help them. Although her faith is continually tested, she has learned to keep it strong. It is the only thing to help her get through each day and through every ordeal.

The children are so relieved that they will be home by tonight, and Greta smiles to herself, knowing that she will see Arthur.

The family once again boards the wagon, and with a quick snap of the reins, the old mare snorts and slowly moves forward. Peter and Elsa immediately fall asleep and stay that way for the rest of the trip, but Greta is too anxious to sleep, and she loses herself to daydreaming.

They finally arrive at their apartment in Hamburg at 8 p.m., and as they unload the wagon, Frieda looks at Greta and smiles. "Go and get cleaned up. You don't want to meet Arthur with dirt on your face, now do you?"

"Certainly not, but I still have to help unpack."

"Just go now, Liebling, you mustn't keep your young man waiting, ja?" Frieda says with a wink.

Greta smiles and kisses her mother's cheek. "Dankeschön, Mutti," she replies excitedly before running into the building to get ready for her date with Arthur.

Chapter 3: Dreams Become Reality

ARTHUR BEAMS AS Greta exits the apartment building and makes her way toward him. "I was worried you weren't coming," he says, bending down to kiss her cheek.

She smiles tenderly at him. "We only just arrived home. Our trip was delayed when our wagon got stuck in the mud. We were very fortunate that someone stopped to help us, or we wouldn't have made it back until tomorrow."

"You must be tired then. Have you eaten?"

"Exhausted, and nein, I haven't eaten."

"Well, then let's go have something to eat, and you can tell me more about your trip, ja?"

Together they hold hands and walk in silence to the restaurant. When they arrive there, they sit at a table by the front window, overlooking the park. After placing their orders, Greta is lost in her thoughts as she stares out at the young couples walking arm in arm, enjoying the summer evening and beauty of the star-lit sky.

"Are you here, Greta?" Arthur asks, trying to get her attention.

Startled, she turns suddenly to look at him. "I guess I'm more tired than I thought," she says apologetically.

"Greta, Liebling, you do know how much I care for you, ja?" Arthur asks shyly.

"Of course, Arthur."

"Well... I would like to... I mean... I was wondering if... Would it be okay with you if… if I ask your father for your hand in marriage?"

Greta blushes and a smile forms on her lips. *At last, my prayers have been answered!* "Ja, Arthur, ja!" She looks at him and notices his anxious expression suddenly transform to one of joy.

"Very well then, I will visit Herr Schumacher in the morning to ask his permission."

"WE HAVEN'T MUCH money to help you start your life together," his future father-in-law states after Arthur asks for Greta's hand.

"That's no problem, Herr Schumacher. I make a good living as a doctor."

Heinrich nods and continues his interrogation. "And where will the two of you live?"

"Greta and I will make our start in Schwerin. There are many opportunities for doctors at the hospital there, and I have been offered a position."

"Very good, Herr Schweiger," the older man says before he rises from his chair and leaves the room.

Although Heinrich's abruptness surprises Arthur, he takes his dismissal in stride since Greta had forewarned him of her father's moods. Arthur retrieves his hat from the hook by the front door and lets himself out.

"Auf Wiedersehen, Herr Schumacher," he says joyfully before he departs.

THE NEXT FEW months are busy for Greta and Arthur as they prepare for their wedding and find a place to live. They marry in a quiet civil ceremony at City Hall on October 26th, and families from both sides enjoy a delicious dinner at a restaurant in the city's downtown core to celebrate the occasion. After spending the night in a hotel overlooking the harbour, the newlyweds travel by train to Schwerin to begin their new life together.

Chapter 4: Spring 1937

THE SCHUMACHER FAMILY celebrates the graduation of its youngest member from *Volksschule*—the compulsory schooling that every child receives. It is equivalent to a combined primary and lesser secondary education, spanning over a nine-year period.

"Now that you have finished Volksschule, you must find work, Elsa. It is time for you to earn your keep," Heinrich says sternly after a special lunch to commemorate the event.

Thirteen-year-old Elsa looks at her father and nods. She knows that her family, like others, still feels the adverse effects of the Depression. Thankfully, the economic outlook is much improved, and jobs are now readily available. With her brother, Peter, now in the army, and her father unable to work due to his condition, her mother was forced to find employment and was given a job at a clothing factory not far from their home.

"Herr Mueller is looking for someone to work at the bakery. I have told him about you, and he will see you today at three o'clock. Do not be late, Elsa. *Did you hear me?*"

Elsa quickly snaps out of her anxious thoughts of what the future may hold. "Ja, Vati, I will go, and I promise, I won't be late." Although her father is strict, she always tries to please him.

As Elsa puts on her best dress and Sunday shoes, she once again focuses on her future. *I will get this job and make my family proud. But what happens if I can't do it? What if I fail and let my family down?* The more she thinks, the tighter the knot in her stomach becomes. *I'm going to be sick.* A cold sweat covers her and her hands tremble. Elsa takes a deep breath to try to calm her nerves, and when she feels more like herself, she makes her way to the kitchen.

Her mother looks at her and smiles proudly at the young woman she has become. "You look so grown up, Elsa. I'm so proud of you, Liebling!"

Elsa's voice comes out as a whisper. "I'm frightened, Mutti. What happens if I can't do the job? I don't want to let you and Vati down."

"Don't worry, you can do anything—just believe in yourself, and you will do fine. Once you learn what is expected of you, you will forget your fears. Never be afraid to make a mistake because the mistakes are what help you grow as a person. As long as you always try your very best, you can never let us down." She gives her daughter a look of reassurance as she reaches into the pocket of her apron. "Now, here is money for the streetcar, but don't tell Vati. It will be our little secret, ja?"

Elsa smiles at her mother appreciatively. "Dankeschön, Mutti!"

THE BAKERY IS a ten-minute trolley ride from Elsa's home. As she waits at the stop, her thoughts torment her. *I wonder what my life will be like now that I have finished school and must go to work. Mutti says I'll do fine if I believe in myself, but I still can't help feeling scared. This is silly! I can do this! I will do this for my family because they need me.* Although Elsa tries her best to calm down, the weight of the responsibilities she now faces continues to overwhelm her. *I really have to stop dwelling on this. Come on, Elsa! You're acting like a baby!* After a few more moments of self-talk, her nerves slowly settle. She checks her watch to determine the time remaining until the streetcar arrives.

Elsa still fights to control her anxiety when the trolley finally pulls up. She climbs aboard, pays her fare and takes a seat near the window. On the ride, she gazes at the passing scenery and the crowds of people walking the streets. Elsa wonders where they are going and what their lives must be like. *Does everyone go through this uncertainty about the future? Do others feel fear the way I do, or am I the only one?*

When she arrives at her stop, Elsa gets off the trolley and crosses the street to the bakery. As she walks, her legs turn to rubber, and her heart feels as though it will explode from her chest. Once again plagued by self-doubt, Elsa forces herself to walk up to the front door of the shop. She takes a deep breath and primps her brunette hair as she grabs the doorknob. Upon entering the bakery, the aromas of freshly baked bread and cookies immediately envelop her, causing her mouth to water while also providing some comfort to her frazzled nerves.

"Guten Tag, Herr Mueller," Elsa says with a shy smile to the tall older man standing behind the counter. She tries to appear confident, but she feels like turning around and running back home.

The baker looks at Elsa and smiles back. "Guten Tag, Fräulein. How are you this beautiful afternoon?"

"I am well, Herr Mueller. My papa said you need someone to work at the bakery, and I would like to be considered for the job, please," she says with as much conviction as possible.

"Well then, young Elsa, have you learned to bake?"

"Mutti taught me some," she nervously squeaks.

Herr Mueller smiles kindly at the young girl who looks as though she is ready to faint. "I need someone to be here at 5 a.m. to bake the cookies and assist Frau Schmitt with other duties. The job also includes working at the counter selling. Do you think you can do this?"

Elsa looks at the man wearing the blue apron dusted with flour and gathers all her confidence. "Ja, Herr Mueller, I can do this and more!" She astounds herself with this response but does her best not to show it.

Herr Mueller seems equally surprised by her answer and suppresses a laugh. "Okay Elsa, we shall see how you work out. Payment is weekly, 5 *Reichsmarks*, and you will begin at 5 a.m. tomorrow. Frau Schmitt will get you started, and you will listen to what she tells you, ja?"

Elsa looks at the man with relief and smiles widely. "Jawohl, Herr Mueller! I will do whatever she says! Vielen Dank! Until tomorrow then!"

The baker smiles back at his new employee. "Until tomorrow. Say hello to your mama and papa."

"I will, Herr Mueller! Auf Wiedersehen!"

ON THE STREET, Elsa reaches into her pocket and takes out the money her mother had given her for the ride home. While staring at the coins in her hand, she decides to walk and save the money for herself.

As she strolls along, the city appears as though she were seeing it for the first time. Elsa thinks this is perhaps because she suddenly feels like an adult and can now better appreciate the world around her. After passing many shops and witnessing the beauty of the parks along her way, Elsa makes a brief stop at St. Peter's Church. She stands in front of it and marvels at the Gothic architecture before raising her head skyward to view the enormous bell tower. *There is so much beauty and history here. Why have I never noticed it before?*

Elsa hums a tune as she continues her walk. Although she realizes she only got the job because her parents and Herr Mueller are friends, she experiences a sense of pride, which is a new feeling for her. Elsa promises herself to work hard so she doesn't let her family down or cause them any embarrassment.

"VERY GOOD, ELSA. How much is Herr Mueller paying you?" her father asks after she tells him the good news.

"Five Reichsmarks per week, Vati," Elsa beams.

"Alright then, you will give me your pay each week, and I will give you money for the streetcar."

Elsa looks at her father and feels her happiness drain away like water from a sink after the plug has been pulled. She nods and quickly heads to her room.

This is so unfair! Why does Vati have to spoil such a perfect day? Just stop it! You're acting like a baby again! Didn't you feel like an adult for the first time today? Why are you crying? You knew that Vati would take most of your earnings. Elsa does her best not to let this upset her, but to work all day without some of her own money to show for it bothers her more than she is willing to admit.

As she changes her clothes, she decides to save her travel allowance and walk to and from work, even if it means having to get up extra early in the morning to make the forty-five-minute walk. Elsa is happy with this choice because she feels that she is finally taking some control of her life.

Chapter 5: January 1938

WORK AT THE bakery is hot and exhausting, and having to deal with the head baker, Frau Schmitt, is a challenge. She has worked at the bakery since it opened for business in 1910 and is very unfriendly and quick-tempered when things don't meet her expectations. She gives Elsa all the dirty jobs and berates her when she makes small mistakes. In turn, Elsa has learned to keep to herself around Frau Schmitt and does her work to the best of her ability.

After only six months of working, Elsa has mastered the art of bread making, so Herr Mueller gives her this responsibility, despite the protests from Frau Schmitt.

"It is a mistake to have such a young girl responsible for making the bread, Hans," the old woman tells her boss forcefully. "She is much too inexperienced and will not be able to keep the pace necessary to produce the quota needed each day."

Hans Mueller looks at his faithful employee and smiles. "Hilda, my dear woman, you have complained to me on numerous occasions about how difficult making the bread has become for you since your arthritis began. It's time for you to slow down a bit and let someone younger do the hard work. You said yourself that Elsa is very skilled with the bread, so why not give her the opportunity to ease your workload, ja? If she cannot keep up with the quota, then you will take back the job, okay?"

"Okay, Hans, I do not like it, but maybe you are right, I am getting too old to fight with the dough. I will give the girl a chance, but I warn you, the minute I notice that she is not keeping up, I will take over without any arguments, *agreed?*"

The baker is thankful they were able to come to a resolution. Maintaining the quality of his business is important to him because he has a reputation to uphold. With the onset of her arthritis, Frau Schmitt's abilities have slowly dwindled, making it difficult for her to carry out her duties adequately. Herr Mueller has kept silent about this out of respect for his loyal employee who has given many years of dedicated service, but he had to find a way to handle the situation before it became worse. Hiring someone young and capable was the only answer. To avoid hurting the old woman's feelings, he plans to assign her the task of training his new apprentice. In turn, Elsa will gradually take over Frau Schmitt's responsibilities, making it a win-win situation for everyone involved.

Elsa is thrilled that Herr Mueller thinks well enough of her to give her the job of making the bread. He makes it clear, however, that he expects her to put forth the extra effort to prove that it wasn't a mistake to give her this added responsibility.

"I will work very hard to do what is expected of me, Herr Mueller. I promise I will not let you down," Elsa says with conviction.

"I am sure you will do your best, and with this new duty, you will earn an additional Reichsmark per week."

"Dankeschön, Herr Mueller!" The thought of earning some extra money for her family comes as a surprise and makes her extremely delighted.

Since her promotion to bread maker, Elsa continually pushes herself to affirm Herr Mueller's trust in her. Kneading the dough is a physically demanding task, leaving her tired and with arms and hands so sore, she can barely lift them over her head. Every night Elsa walks home, eats supper, and falls into bed, only to wake up before 4 a.m. to start the routine yet again. She doesn't mind her life. She is content doing her part to help her family and still has time on weekends to spend with her best friend, Petra.

ONE EVENING, ON her way home, Elsa stops to look in a shop window. There before her is a beautiful yellow chiffon blouse, which immediately mesmerizes her. Its beauty draws her into the shop just as a magnet draws iron shavings. She enters the store and carefully removes the hanger from the rack. Elsa runs her finger lightly over the delicate fabric and searches for the price tag.

"Two Reichsmarks," the sales clerk says while making her approach. "Would you like to try it on?"

Startled, Elsa turns quickly and almost drops the hanger. She nods anxiously, and the woman smiles warmly as she directs her to a fitting room at the back of the store.

Elsa gently places her arms into the sleeves of the blouse and slowly buttons it. Once she has it on, she steps out of the room to look into the mirror that hangs just outside the door. She admires the fitted design and how it accentuates the curves of her young body.

A few moments later, the clerk returns and looks at her smiling. "Sehr schön, Fräulein. It is very lovely!"

Elsa is beaming. For the first time, she sees herself as a young woman, and not just as a girl. Suddenly, her happiness evaporates, and Elsa turns to the sales clerk with a frown. "I don't have enough money," she admits timidly.

"How much do you have?"

"One mark-twenty."

The clerk places her hand under her chin and thinks for a moment while looking at Elsa. "Do you have work, Fräulein?"

Elsa nods and tells her of her job at the bakery and explains that it will take her just over a week to save up the rest of the money to buy the blouse.

"Okay, this is what I will do," the woman says. "You give me the money you have now, and I will put the blouse away for you until you have saved the rest. Once you have paid the full amount, it will be yours. How does that sound?"

"Wunderbar! Dankeschön."

Elsa is so pleased she could hug the clerk, but she restrains herself because it would be considered improper. She gladly gives the money to the woman, and in return, she receives a ticket for the blouse showing the balance owed. Elsa carefully places it in her purse and leaves the shop with a feeling of joy unlike any she has experienced in her young life.

Elsa's excitement overtakes her, and each day after work, she stops by the shop to pay the day's travel allowance of ten *pfennige* to the clerk. After a week and a half, she has finally paid what she owes and can hardly believe that she now owns such a beautiful blouse. Before leaving the store, Elsa thanks the sales woman once again and grips the bag tightly as she makes her way home. She has never had any brand new clothes, let alone store-bought ones, and she treats it like gold—her most valued possession.

When Elsa arrives home, she smiles lovingly at her mother. "Guten Abend, Mutti."

"You have been coming home late every evening, Elsa. Have you been working longer?"

"Nein, Mutti, but come with me to my room, I want to show you something," she says excitedly.

They enter her bedroom, and Elsa closes the door behind them. She looks at her mother with an expression that lights up the room, and she pulls the blouse from the bag and holds it up to show her.

"Where did you get this, Liebling?"

Elsa explains how she saved her allowance to buy it. Surprised by her youngest daughter's resourcefulness, Frieda smiles and kisses her cheek. Although she is happy for her, she is fearful of Heinrich's reaction should he find out.

"It's beautiful, Elsa, but please don't let Vati see it, okay?"

"I won't, Mutti," she promises.

When her mother leaves, she hangs the blouse in her wardrobe and changes for supper.

Chapter 6: April 1938

ELSA AND HER friend, Petra, belong to the girls' wing of the Hitler Youth known as the *Bund Deutscher Mädel* (BDM) as required by the Nazi Party. Although both girls would be happier doing other things, they must attend the meetings and summer camps where they are made to take part in sports and train for their future roles as wives and mothers.

"Are you coming to the dance on Saturday, Elsa?" asks Petra after the meeting of the BDM.

"Of course, I've been saving my money for weeks." It will be her first "grown up" dance and Elsa is so looking forward to it. She has already planned to wear her new blouse with her grey skirt and Sunday shoes.

"Good! We can go together then," Petra says, grabbing Elsa's arm, and they slowly make their way to the apartment complex where they both live.

"I'm so tired of these stupid meetings! It's just too bad there are no boys there, at least then it would be more fun!" Petra jokes. "Do *you* like to go?"

"Not really, I only go because it gets me out of the house, and I get to see you!"

The girls giggle as they walk and stop abruptly when they pass a group of soldiers who nod to them and whistle.

"Hey, Fräulein, come with us and we'll have some fun, ja?" one soldier shouts.

The girls stay together and walk by quickly without acknowledging the men.

"Ach, you don't know what you're missing!" another in the group says.

Once Elsa and Petra are far enough away from the soldiers, they both laugh again, the happiness of youth visible on their faces.

"If only we were older! There's nothing quite like a man in uniform, eh Elsa?"

"Ach, Petra, you're just boy crazy!" she says as they climb the steps to their apartment building.

"I'll call on you Saturday night, ja?"

"Okay, Petra. See you then."

ON SATURDAY AFTERNOON, the excitement of the upcoming dance is almost too much for Elsa to bear. She takes a bath, combs her hair, and opens her wardrobe to take out the clothes she is eager to wear. As she gets ready to dress, there is a knock on her door.

"May I enter?" her mother asks.

"Certainly, Mutti, come in."

Frieda comes into the room holding a small bag. "This is for you, Liebling," she says, handing her daughter the parcel. "Every young woman is in need of this."

Elsa takes the package and opens it excitedly. Inside is her first pair of stockings with garters. "Dankeschön, Mutti!"

Frieda helps her daughter to put them on and carefully lines up the seams so they are straight.

Once Elsa is dressed, she looks at herself in the mirror, and the reflection staring back at her is one she barely recognizes.

After a few moments, Frieda takes her daughter's hand. "You're so grown up, Liebling. You turned into a woman when I wasn't looking." She wipes a tear from the corner of her eye and smiles. "You must wear your coat now, so Vati won't see your new blouse."

Elsa nods knowing that if her father were to notice, he would surely question where she got the money to buy it. She fears that if he learned she had saved the allowance he had given her for the streetcar, he would stop giving it to her altogether, leaving Elsa with nothing to show for her hard work at the bakery.

A few minutes later, there is a knock on the apartment door, and Elsa grabs her purse as she hurries to open it.

"Where are you going in such a rush, Elsa?" her father asks.

Before she can answer, Frieda tells Heinrich that the girls have to attend a special meeting of the BDM.

"Well, don't be late! It's important for you to be on time."

"Ja, Vati!"

Elsa and Petra share a welcome hug and giggle as they race down the hallway to the stairs and out into the street. On their way to the dance, the girls chatter away excitedly about the evening ahead.

LOUD MUSIC RESONATES from the bandstand, and it immediately causes Petra to sway to the melody. Elsa's cheeks flush with embarrassment at the boldness of her friend. Petra has always been more self-assured, and actions like this always make Elsa feel uncomfortable. She wishes she could be more like Petra but just can't seem to overcome her shyness and lack of self-confidence.

The girls get some punch and look for a place to sit. A while later, they find a table with some space and ask for permission to join the group.

"Sure, have a seat," one boy answers.

Of the six people seated at the table, four of them are boys and two are girls, ranging in age from fourteen to eighteen.

A blonde, blue-eyed boy with a handsome smile watches the girls make their approach. "Now, who do we have here?" he asks to no one in particular.

Petra returns his smile and Elsa tries her best to do the same.

"I'm Petra, and this is my friend Elsa," Petra replies excitedly as they put their drinks on the table and prepare to sit down.

"Well then, Fräulein, come join the party. I'm Dieter, and this is Max, George, and Gunther. The girls over there are Lotti and Erna."

After the introductions are finished, the boys ask the girls to dance. Elsa is very nervous since she has only ever danced with her brother, Peter, but she accepts a dance with Max. He is short, with blonde hair and grey eyes, and not nearly as handsome as Dieter, but Elsa is happy he asked her to dance. From his demeanor, she can tell that Max is just as shy and nervous as she is herself, and this helps to put her more at ease. While they dance, Elsa watches Petra dancing with Dieter and notices how well matched they look. She isn't sure whether she likes Dieter and hopes her initial impression of him is wrong, but something about him bothers her, and she puts up her guard.

When the band takes a break, Dieter asks everyone at the table if they want another drink, and after taking orders, he makes his way to the punch bowl. Elsa observes him secretly pour something from a bag into a glass and then quickly drink it down. She suspects Dieter is adding alcohol to his punch, and this makes her somewhat apprehensive.

Dieter brings a tray with the glasses of punch to the table, and he offers to pour some of the mysterious liquid into them. Everyone agrees to have some, but when he asks Elsa, she shakes her head.

"Nein, Danke," she says politely.

"Suit yourself!" Dieter shrugs and turns to Petra, pouring some into her glass. She drinks it down and giggles uncontrollably.

"Come on, Elsa, have some. Don' be such a baby!"

Elsa shakes her head and watches as the others slowly become intoxicated. She must be careful not to do anything that would go against her father's wishes because she knows the consequences, and to her, it's just not worth the risk.

As the evening continues, Petra stumbles her way to Elsa carrying a full glass of punch. Just as Petra is about to say something to her, someone passes and knocks the glass from her hand, spilling the contents over Elsa's new blouse.

"Idiot! Why don't you watch where you're going?" shouts Petra.

Elsa looks down at her new blouse as her eyes blur with tears and her face glows with embarrassment.

"I'm so sorry, Elsa," her inebriated friend whispers.

Elsa stands, grabbing her coat and purse. "I'm going home now. Are you coming with me?"

Petra looks at the boys who are watching them and turns back to her. "Nein, I'm staying! I'm having way too much fun!"

"Fine, I'll go home alone then."

Before she leaves, Elsa glances at Petra, her best friend since childhood, and notices that her back is turned. The hurt she feels burns inside her like a raging fire as her new blouse sticks to her skin, and the stink of alcohol permeates her nostrils. *I can't believe Petra did this to me! After all the years we've been friends, how could she treat me this way?* Elsa then focuses on going home and prays while walking quickly and cautiously through the streets that her father will be asleep when she arrives. If he is awake, he will be angry with her for coming home so late, and this is something she hopes to avoid.

OUTSIDE OF HER apartment, Elsa takes a deep breath as she puts her key into the lock and carefully opens the door.

"Do you know what time it is, girl? Where have you been?" her father yells as he snaps on the light.

She cringes when she sees the anger in his face and prepares herself for the worst. "I'm sorry, Vati. The meeting went much longer than we thought, and we walked rather slowly. I promise it won't ever happen again."

"Hang up your coat and go directly to bed."

"Ja, Vati," she says on her way to her room.

"Elsa! I said hang up your coat! *Now!*"

She stops, and with no other choice, she removes her coat and hangs it in the wardrobe by the front door.

As Elsa turns to go to her room, her father stands in front of her sniffing like a hound during an English fox hunt. "What is this now? You've been *drinking?* You stink like a drunkard! What's *wrong* with you, girl? Is this how you were *raised?*" he shouts furiously before slapping her face.

Elsa lets out a small whimper and holds her hand to her cheek while fighting the surge of tears that threaten to erupt at any moment. She is determined not to give her father the satisfaction of seeing her cry.

"Where did you get these clothes?"

Elsa ignores the question and makes another attempt to go to her room, but Heinrich blocks her way.

"Answer me!" he screams and once again raises his hand.

Just as Elsa braces herself for yet another blow, Frieda enters the room and is horrified by the scene unfolding before her. *"Enough*, Heinrich. Let Elsa go to bed."

"You be quiet, Frieda!"

Heinrich turns back to his daughter with a look of rage. "I asked you a question, girl, and I expect the *truth!*"

Elsa looks pleadingly at her mother, hoping she can rescue her from her father's fury.

"Come, Elsa, it's time for bed," Frieda says gently, cutting in front of her husband. She takes her daughter's hand and leads her to the safety of her room.

Perplexed, Heinrich stands there quietly and watches them leave. A moment later, he turns and stomps toward his bedroom, slamming the door behind him.

Frieda helps Elsa to undress and takes her blouse to soak it in the bathroom sink. After learning what transpired earlier that evening, she hugs her daughter.

"Don't worry, Liebling. I will talk to Vati tomorrow. Try to get some sleep now, ja?"

Chapter 7: A Bad Day Gets Worse

ELSA TOSSED AND turned all night, listening for any warning signs that her father may enter her room to continue his wrath, but thankfully, that didn't happen—this time.

In the morning, the family walks to church without speaking, and Elsa keeps her distance from her father just to be safe. She wishes she could have stayed home, but due to the preparations for her Confirmation, she must attend all the necessary classes.

After church, Elsa helps her mother prepare their lunch consisting of pork hock, sauerkraut and fried potatoes. Her nervousness toward her father makes the aroma of the cooking food almost impossible to endure. Her stomach churns and the thought of sitting down with her family to eat causes bile to rise into her throat.

When everything is ready, Frieda calls Elsa to the kitchen. "Sit down to eat while I get Vati, ja?"

Elsa listens to her mother but doubts she will be able to force down a single bite. She prays her nausea will pass so that she can get through this very stressful meal.

In the bedroom, Heinrich sits by the window, staring out, but not appearing to see anything. As Frieda gets closer to him, she notices a slight trembling in his extremities that typically occurs when he is overly agitated. "Lunch is ready, Heinrich," she tells him softly.

He doesn't respond. He is once again lost within himself, oblivious to the world around him.

Frieda goes over to him and gently places her hand on his shoulder. "Come, Liebling, you must eat."

Heinrich turns to look at his wife of thirty years with tears in his eyes. "What is to become of that girl? Does she purposely defy me? This is your fault—you baby her too much."

Frieda inhales deeply and takes a moment before speaking. "She is young, Heinrich, and must grow and learn just as we did."

He looks at her with anger and raises his voice as he replies. "She is nothing but trouble! She will never amount to anything! What man would want such a girl who does not obey? Has she not learned anything from the BDM meetings?"

Frieda stands in front of him, slowly losing her patience. "What do you want from her, Heinrich? She is sorry for what happened. Can you not just forgive and forget so that we may have a pleasant Sunday?"

He turns back to the window and ignores her, and feeling defeated, Frieda quietly leaves the room.

"Is he very angry with me, Mutti?" she asks when Frieda returns.

"Ach, you know how Vati can be! Just give him some time and all will be forgotten," her mother replies, trying her best to downplay her daughter's fears.

Elsa isn't so sure her mother is right. "Shall I go talk to him?"

"Forget about Vati now. Come, let's eat, ja?"

Elsa looks at her plate through tear-filled eyes and picks up her fork and slowly begins eating. Her stomach rebels against her actions and the food becomes impossible to swallow. She tries to get it down but finds herself gagging. Her mother gets up quickly to get her some water and a cloth, but before she realizes what is happening, Elsa runs to the kitchen sink and vomits.

"There, there, Liebling. Calm down now, ja?" She wipes her daughter's face and rubs her back.

"I'm sorry, Mutti. I'm *so* sorry!"

"It's okay, don't worry."

Elsa desperately wishes she were not so sensitive to her father's moods, but she knows she will never change or be free of her fear of him. Her mother had told her that her father was a very different man before the Great War, and Elsa often wonders if things would have been different had he not gone to serve his country.

Frieda helps Elsa to clean up and calm down, and afterward, they tidy up the kitchen. When they are finished, Elsa asks her mother for permission to visit Petra so they can talk about what happened the previous night. She is still very upset that Petra didn't leave with her, and it bothers her almost as much as the situation with her father.

"Go ahead, Liebling, you'll feel better to talk things over with your friend." Frieda watches Elsa get ready to leave the apartment and is relieved that she is going to settle things with Petra. The thought of the two of them no longer being friends breaks her heart since she knows Elsa has no other close friends with whom she can confide.

"I won't be long, Mutti."

"You take all the time that you need, Liebling. I will see you later."

ELSA GOES DOWN one flight of stairs to Petra's apartment and knocks on the door. After a few moments, Petra's mother answers and lets her inside.

"Guten Tag, Frau Braun. May I see Petra, please?"

Frowning, Frau Braun nods to Elsa and then yells to her daughter. "Petra! Elsa is here! Come now, Petra!"

Elsa has never heard Frau Braun raise her voice to anyone, and it disturbs her.

Finally, when Petra enters the living room, Elsa sees that her face is pale, and her eyes are red and puffy. She holds her head as though it would fall off her shoulders if she were to let go of it.

"Stop shouting at me, Mama."

"I will shout at you all I like, young lady. You only have yourself to blame for how you feel."

Frau Braun turns to Elsa with her hands on her hips. "So, *did you* drink last night?"

Before she can reply, Petra answers for her. "Nein, Mama, she was smart. She didn't have a drop because she respects her parents when I, apparently, do not. I'm sorry for what I did, Mama." She then turns to face her best friend. "I apologize to you, too, Elsa. I should never have let myself go like that. I should have come home with you," she says remorsefully.

Elsa is relieved that Petra has come to her senses and realizes now that had she not been drinking, she would never have treated her in such a way.

"Were your parents asleep when you came home?" Petra asks with concern.

Elsa shakes her head. "Vati was waiting for me."

"Did your papa hurt you?"

"It doesn't matter now. What's done is done," Elsa says, wanting to put an end to the entire episode.

The girls share a brief hug before sitting down on the sofa. "I feel terrible, Elsa. If it weren't for me, things would have turned out differently."

"Don't feel bad. How Vati reacted is not your fault."

Frau Braun softens once she hears the details of the previous evening. She knows about Heinrich's moods and is always sympathetic to Elsa's problems. "I hope you've learned your lesson, Petra. You must think about others before yourself, ja?"

Petra nods and immediately feels the throbbing in her head intensify.

"You stay here as long as you like, Elsa. I will get us some coffee now," Frau Braun says on her way to the kitchen.

WHILE ELSA VISITS Petra, there is a knock on Frieda's door. When she opens it, she is surprised to see her eldest daughter, Greta, and her children, Franz and Gerhard standing there. Greta and Arthur have twin boys who are now three years of age, and both are easy going and well behaved. Because Greta and her family live in Schwerin, they must travel the ninety–two–kilometre distance by train. They don't often make the trip, especially without Frieda's prior knowledge.

"Greta, what a lovely surprise it is to see you! Why didn't you tell me you were coming to visit today?" she says while searching the hallway for Greta's husband, Arthur. *"Arthur isn't with you?"*

Greta looks at her mother with concern lining her face and replies with a shake of her head.

"Come in, come in," Frieda says, and she moves to let them enter. She immediately senses that there is an underlying reason for this surprise visit, and judging from the tired and distracted look on her daughter's face, it isn't good.

Inside the apartment, Greta leads the boys to her sister's room to play. Once she has them settled, she closes the door so they won't overhear what she and her mother will discuss.

Greta returns to the living room and sits down. "Mama, I'm sorry to bother you, but I have nowhere else to turn."

Frieda's stomach suddenly tightens with fear. "What is it? *Arthur?* What's happened?"

"Arthur has lost his job at the hospital."

"Ach, well that's terrible," her mother says as relief washes over her, "but I know he will find another position soon. He is an excellent doctor."

"You don't understand, Mama, Arthur can no longer be a doctor." Greta inhales deeply and reaches for her mother's hand. "It was discovered that he has some Jewish blood. He is a *Mischling*—a crossbreed, and because of it, he is banned from practicing anywhere." Greta then pulls out her handkerchief to wipe away the tears that now flow freely down her cheeks.

The blood slowly drains from Frieda's face. "*What?* Did you *know* he was part Jewish?"

"Arthur didn't even know until his mother mentioned it a few months ago during a casual conversation. Apparently, it goes back more than two generations. His great-grandparents were Jewish but converted to the Lutheran faith just after their marriage. We have no idea how this was found out by the SS, but somehow they did. When the officers came to the hospital and confronted Arthur about his heritage, he tried to explain this to them, but they didn't care. They just told him his licence to practice was revoked. Since then, Arthur has been seeing patients in our home to earn some money. Someone must have reported it because two officers came to the apartment and took him away for questioning."

Frieda takes hold of Greta's hand as her fear intensifies. "When did this happen?"

Greta blows her nose and takes another deep breath to try to calm herself. "Last week, and I haven't seen Arthur since then. I'm *so* worried, Mama. I went to the local branch of the *Sicherheitsdienst* to ask about him, but no one would tell me anything. I don't know what to do!"

"Why didn't you come to me sooner, Greta?"

She looks lovingly at her mother. "I didn't want to upset you, and I thought he would be home by now. I tried to contact his parents but couldn't find them, and I'm afraid the SS may have taken them away as well. What if they come for the children next, Mama? *What will I do then?"*

Frieda gives her daughter a hug of reassurance. She is aware of the laws restricting Jewish rights, but because politics and the day-to-day struggle of the Jews are foreign to her, she had no idea just how terrible their plight could actually be. Frieda worries about her daughter and her grandchildren now more than ever. She takes a few moments to gather her thoughts and decides to get Heinrich's opinion. "We will speak with Papa. He will know what to do."

Frieda makes her way to the bedroom, but before she gets there, the door opens, and Heinrich steps out.

"Is this true, what you have told Mama?" he asks sternly after eavesdropping on the entire conversation.

"Ja, I'm afraid so, Papa. What shall we do?"

He scratches his beard and looks into his daughter's worried face. "There is nothing to do now except wait. You must go back to Schwerin with the children immediately. It will be best for everyone that you do."

His reply shocks Frieda. "But Heinrich, do you think it's safe for her and the children to go back to Schwerin? Wouldn't it be safer for them to stay here?"

"I will not have them here now. It won't be safe for us either."

Heinrich's past war experience has left him cynical. He distrusts Hitler and the Nazi regime and sees the restrictions placed on the Jews as a warning that all Germans should heed. *If the Führer deals with the Jews in this way, what is to say that he will not eventually turn on us?*

"You don't know that!" Frieda shrieks. "At least, let them stay here overnight, so they don't have to make the long journey back today."

"It's okay, Mama, I understand."

Greta glares at her father as she gets the children ready to leave.

"Why do we have to go? *We just got here!*" Gerhard says with disappointment.

"Do we *have to* leave now, Mutti?" whines Franz.

"Ja, we must go home to wait for Vati. He will be worried if we're not there when he returns. Now, be good boys and say goodbye to Opa and Oma."

Frieda follows Greta and her grandsons into the hallway, closing the door behind her. She reaches into her pocket and hands each boy a candy to occupy them briefly while she pulls Greta aside to speak to her quietly. "If Arthur hasn't returned home by next week, you come back to see us, ja?"

"Why, Mama? Papa doesn't want us here. *Nobody* wants us!"

"Don't say that! *I want you!* Don't pay attention to Papa. You listen to *me*. I will contact Tante Ida in Berlin to arrange for you and the boys to stay with her until we can figure out a way to get you out of the country—maybe to Switzerland. She has room and the means to keep you safe."

Greta bites her lip as she contemplates what Frieda is suggesting. "What about Arthur? *I can't just leave him!*" she anxiously whispers.

Frieda thinks for an instant and forms an idea. "Do you have a friend you can trust to watch for Arthur's return—someone who will let him know how to reach you?"

"Ja, Mutti, I'm sure my friend, Eva, will help."

"Okay, come back in one week, and we will talk then, ja?"

When they return to the children, Frieda hugs them and remains in the corridor, watching as the three of them make their way toward the staircase. She sighs, saying a quick prayer for her daughter and her family before heading back inside.

AFTER THEIR TALK, Elsa says goodbye to Petra and her mother and heads home. As she comes up the stairs and looks down the hall toward her apartment, she sees her sister and her nephews with her mother. She watches them share an embrace and Greta turns with the children, walking slowly in her direction.

Elsa waves to them excitedly. "Hello, Greta! Hello, boys!" She loves her sister and has an excellent relationship with her despite their sixteen-year age difference. "Where's Arthur? Aren't you staying to visit?" Elsa looks into Greta's face and can see that she has been crying.

"Hello, Elsa. We can't stay. I had to talk to Mama and Papa for a while, but we need to get back home now."

"That's a shame! But you're still coming to my Confirmation, *aren't you?*"

"Um—I'm not sure."

"But you *promised!*"

"We'll see, *okay?*" Greta snaps.

Her sister's sharp reply hurts Elsa, but she knows now that something is very wrong. The grim look on Greta's face confirms this, but she doesn't dare ask. Elsa just tries to overlook her injured feelings. "Okay—"

"I'm sorry, Elsa. We will try to make it, ja?"

They hug and say a quick farewell. As Greta turns and walks away, her eyes brim with tears yet again. She fights to control her emotions since she realizes that breaking down would serve no other purpose than to make things worse. With the boys in hand, they set off on their journey to the train station.

When Elsa enters the apartment, her mother is pacing back and forth, visibly upset by Greta's visit and a knot forms in her stomach.

"Mutti? Is everything okay?"

Frieda nods, giving her a half-smile. "It's nothing to concern yourself about, Liebling."

"Well, I'll be in my room if you need me."

Not learning the cause of her distress bothers Elsa, but she doesn't interfere. If there is anything that she needs to know, her mother will undoubtedly tell her.

Elsa dwells on the possible problem that could be causing so much stress for both her sister and mother. She allows her imagination to run wild with different scenarios, and the more she thinks, the more troubled she becomes. *Did Arthur and Greta have an argument? Is Arthur sick? Did he have an accident? Did he die?* Elsa's stomach tightens once again as these notions enter her mind, and she does her best to redirect them to try to dispel the fear washing over her.

AT THE STATION, Greta and the boys sit on a bench awaiting their train to Schwerin. The children lean against their mother, nodding off despite all the commotion, and the trauma of their situation plays havoc with Greta's thoughts.

"You must come with us, Frau Schweiger," the officer says.

Greta looks at the man in the SS uniform and a wave of fear crashes over her. "I don't understand. What do you want with me? I've done nothing wrong."

"Now, Frau Schweiger!"

"Nein! I will not go with you!"

"If you do not come with us now, we will shoot the children!"

The officer grabs the boys, and they let out deafening screams that seem endless.

Just as Greta is about to come to their defence, another officer grabs her arm and shakes her.

"Fräulein? Did you hear me?"

Suddenly, Greta's eyes snap open, and she looks fearfully at the man standing over her. "Nein! Nein!"

"I'm sorry to have startled you, Fräulein, but your train is here. I noticed you fell asleep and didn't want you to miss it," the station master says.

Once Greta recognizes the man, a surge of relief courses through her. "That's quite alright, Herr Stationsmeister. Dankeschön."

Chapter 8: Fear Reigns

EACH DAY OF the following week feels like an eternity to Greta, but she tries to remain hopeful of Arthur's return. By week's end, however, the harsh reality that this will not happen devastates her.

With no other recourse, Greta packs a bag for herself and the children. Since she can't carry much and still hold on to the boys as they travel, she is limited with what she can bring. Because the spring has been warmer than usual and with summer only weeks away, Greta decides to take lighter clothing. *We can get whatever else we need once we get to Switzerland.*

Once her suitcase is packed, she pushes the dresser away from the wall. From behind it, she retrieves an envelope filled with cash that Arthur had been saving. He feared for their future and placed any additional money in the packet and hid it away. At the time, Greta thought Arthur's actions were unnecessary, but after giving his reasons, she understood and believed it was the right thing to do. She is now grateful that he did since she and the children will need every Reichsmark they have to survive.

Following her mother's suggestion, Greta speaks to her friend, Eva. Fortunately, after carefully explaining the situation facing her, Eva agrees to watch for Arthur's return and give him the letter Greta has left for him.

"Don't worry, I will see that Arthur gets your message. I promise you that no one will know about this. Just take good care of yourself and the boys, and I will see you soon, ja?" her neighbour says reassuringly.

"Dankeschön, Eva. I really appreciate you doing this for me. You're a good friend."

They share an emotional farewell before Greta returns to her apartment to finish the preparations for their departure.

ON THE TRAIN, Greta is lost in her thoughts. She is worried sick about her husband and is apprehensive when she thinks of what lies ahead for her and the children. As fear threatens to overtake her, Greta looks out the window at the passing scenery. She bites her lip to try to calm herself. *I must be strong for the boys' sake. I can't let them sense my fear. They depend on me to keep them safe, and I can't let them down.*

When Greta and the children arrive at her parents' apartment, Frieda welcomes them with a smile. "Papa has gone for a walk in the park, so he won't return for a while."

"He isn't back, Mama."

Frieda nods and gives her daughter a long, comforting embrace. "I will go to Frau Schroder to use her telephone to contact Tante Ida and make the arrangements, ja?"

"Dankeschön, Mama."

Greta and the boys settle themselves in the living room after Frieda leaves, and Elsa comes out of her bedroom to join them. She has been anxiously waiting to learn about the problem that has gripped their family so fiercely, and she hopes that her sister will finally enlighten her.

"I thought I heard your voice, Greta. I'm happy you came for a visit. How long are you able to stay?"

"Only for a little while."

"Well, it's so good to see you!"

Greta nods and smiles tiredly. "It's good to see you too, Liebling. How are the preparations for your Confirmation going?"

"They're okay, but I'll be so glad once it's over."

Elsa looks at her nephews who are each holding a small toy horse and kneels down before them. "Well now, what is it that you boys have there? May I see?"

"Don't you *know*, Tante Elsa? It's a horse!" replies Gerhard as he shows the toy to his aunt.

"Well, of course, it is! How silly of me!" she says before grabbing both boys and tickling them until they laugh hysterically.

"Would you mind doing me a favour? Can you take the children out for a walk and maybe get some ice cream? I need some time to myself," Greta says once the boys settle down.

Elsa feels dejected yet again, but she doesn't want to pressure her sister. "Sure, I'll take them, Greta." She looks at her nephews and smiles. "Come on then, Franz and Gerhard, let's go for ice cream!"

Greta smiles and digs through her purse. "Here's some money, and be sure to buy yourself one as well."

"Dankeschön, Greta," Elsa replies and takes the boys by the hand, leaving her sister to wait for their mother's return.

Shortly after Elsa leaves, Frieda enters the apartment, looking much calmer than before, and she sits down next to her daughter. "Everything has been arranged, Liebling. Tante Ida will be at the station at one o'clock to meet you when you arrive tomorrow. She has already contacted her brother-in-law, and he has agreed to supply identification papers for you and the boys. They should be ready within a few weeks, and then you can make your way out of Germany to Switzerland."

"What will we do until tomorrow?"

"You and the boys will stay here tonight."

"But what about Papa? He won't want us here!"

"You let me worry about that," Frieda says reassuringly as she looks around the room. "Where are the boys?"

"They went with Elsa to get some ice cream."

When Elsa and the children return, the twins chatter excitedly on the way to their aunt's room to play.

"I saw Vati at the park. He's not himself again, Mutti."

"Okay, Liebling. We'll see how he is when he gets home, ja?"

Elsa looks at her sister and can feel the tension in the air. "You're staying here?"

"Just for tonight," her sister replies.

"Elsa, you will give your room to Greta and the children, ja? You sleep on the sofa," Frieda says.

"Certainly, Mutti." *I wish someone would just tell me what's going on. I hate it when they treat me like a child!*

LATER THAT AFTERNOON, when Heinrich returns from the park and sees Greta, he forms a frown, and his hands tremble slightly.

"Arthur isn't back?"

"Nein, Papa," Greta replies while wringing her hands.

"And you will stay here?"

"Only for tonight, *with your permission*, Papa. We are going to Berlin first thing tomorrow."

Heinrich looks at Frieda and then back to Greta. "Then the arrangements have been made, ja?"

"Ja, Papa, everything is in order. We will stay with Tante Ida until we get new identification papers and then we are off to Switzerland."

"Very well, Greta. You can stay here tonight, but when you leave tomorrow, you are never to return, *understood?* It's much too dangerous for us." Heinrich quickly looks away from his eldest daughter to avoid her pained expression. "We don't know you or the children. You are strangers to us. We are finished, ja?"

Greta doesn't reply because she knows that there is nothing left to say. She turns and goes to Elsa's room, quietly shutting the door behind her.

Elsa can't believe what she has just witnessed, but she knows it's not her place to voice an opinion, so she remains silent. She goes to the kitchen to give her parents some privacy but does her best to eavesdrop on their conversation.

Horrified by Heinrich's words, Frieda looks at him and takes a deep breath. "Is it really necessary to go to this extreme, Heinrich?"

Suddenly, his demeanor changes and he replies in a voice so soft that Frieda must strain to hear. "I have talked with some friends and have learned that it's getting worse for the Jews every day. Although I don't believe everything I hear, there are rumours that it could become dangerous to have connections with them. From now on, we must be cautious with whom we associate. There is just no way to know what tomorrow might bring."

"Surely things will not get *that* bad!"

"As long as the Führer is in power, things will get much worse before they get better," he tells her bluntly.

Frieda shakes her head unable to accept Heinrich's views. "Why must you always be so negative? The Führer is doing his best to ensure Germany's future."

He looks at his wife with a glint of anger in his eyes. "The Führer does what is best for the Führer. He only cares about power, not the German people!" Heinrich clenches his fists and turns toward their bedroom. He is once again haunted by the past—the trenches, the dirt, the blood and the sacrifice of so many brave men during the Great War.

Stunned by his words, Frieda quietly watches her husband leave the room. Heinrich has never before voiced his opinions about Hitler or the Nazi Party and it makes her wonder whether he could be correct in his beliefs. *If Heinrich is right, then God help us all!*

FRIEDA AND ELSA enter the kitchen where Greta and the children are having breakfast.

"Papa isn't coming to say goodbye is he, Mama?"

Frieda shakes her head and looks remorsefully at her daughter. "I'm so sorry, Greta, I tried to persuade him, but you know Papa, he can be stubborn."

Greta knows all too well how her father can be. All the Schumacher children have learned to be cautious where he is concerned. Frieda has always done her best to keep the peace in the family, and Greta wonders what her mother will do once Elsa marries and leaves home. *Will things be better then?*

"I don't understand, Greta. What's happening?" Elsa asks.

Greta snaps out of her thoughts and looks at her younger sister. She asks Frieda to take the boys to the living room, and once they are out of earshot, she explains to Elsa, in simple terms, what is happening. She tells her about the laws in place that revoke many privileges to the Jews, and since Arthur is part Jewish, those rules apply to them as well.

"That doesn't make any sense!"

"I know, but the law must be obeyed no matter how difficult or senseless it seems."

"Will you and the boys be alright?"

"Sure we will," Greta says emphatically, hoping her eyes won't betray her. She will never voice her concern for their uncertain future because to do so would make it real and only serve to intensify her fear. Greta knows if that should ever happen, she would never be able to cope rationally with the issues facing her. Greta embraces her younger sister and smiles bravely. "Don't worry about us, Elsa, everything will be okay. We'll see each other again soon, ja?"

WHEN GRETA AND the twins arrive at the train station in Berlin, Tante Ida and her driver, Carl, are there to greet them. After a welcoming embrace, they get into the car and settle themselves for the short trip to Ida's apartment.

As they drive through the city streets, Ida points out many landmarks to the children. Their excitement is contagious, and both Greta and her aunt chuckle at the boys' reactions to everything they see. It is the first time in many weeks that Greta has had any cause to laugh, and it feels so good, even if it is only temporary.

After freshening up from their journey, the four of them sit down to supper. Greta forces herself to eat despite her lack of appetite since she knows it is vital for her to keep up her strength. Once they finish their meal, she puts the boys to bed, and the two women sit in the living room with their coffee.

"My brother-in-law, Jakob, will come by tomorrow to take photographs for your new identification. It will take a while to get everything finished, but he does good work, and that takes time. He has forged identities for many Jews and can be trusted," Ida says and stops to take a sip of her coffee. "You and the boys will be safe here until the papers are ready."

"Dankeschön, Tante Ida. I'm sorry to cause you so much trouble."

"It's no trouble, Liebling. We are family and will work through this terrible time together, don't you worry."

Greta nods, and even though things seem to be going smoothly, an uneasy feeling overtakes her. *I guess I won't feel better until we are safely out of Germany.*

A WEEK AFTER Jakob's visit, Ida receives word that the SS have arrested him and taken all documents in his possession. With her niece's safety now at greater risk, Ida's thoughts wildly search for another possible plan of action.

"What am I to do now?" Greta asks her aunt in despair.

Ida strokes her hand reassuringly and looks into her eyes. "For your protection, I think it's best that you get an apartment of your own and live under an assumed name. Unfortunately, without proper identification, you will have to spend most of your time inside. I have a friend who will help and see to it that supplies are brought to you. I'm sure that with God's help, you and the children will stay safe."

"I guess I have no other option."

"Try not to worry, Liebling. I will contact my friend and have her search for a suitable apartment and make the necessary arrangements. Until then, you will remain here with me."

A few weeks later, Greta and the twins move to their own apartment. It is small but clean and in good repair.

"I'm sorry things didn't work out as planned, Liebling," Ida says as she prepares to leave her niece.

"It's not your fault, Tante Ida. You did everything you could for us, and I'm so grateful."

Ida hugs Greta and the children and leaves them to start their new life—alone.

Chapter 9: November 1938

IN THE WEE hours of November 10th, Elsa enters the bakery to start work for the day.

"Guten Morgen, Elsa. I trust you are doing well, ja?" Hans Mueller says as he wipes flour from his hands.

Elsa removes her coat and smiles at the baker. "Guten Morgen, Herr Mueller, I am very well—and you?"

"I am fine, but Frau Schmitt is home sick today, so you will need to do her chores."

"Certainly, Herr Mueller." Elsa knows most of the old woman's duties at the bakery so it is no problem for her to carry them out, and she is happy to help out in any way she can.

"You are a good worker, Elsa. You should be proud of what you have accomplished here in such a short time."

She blushes and thanks him, happy to hear that he is satisfied with her efforts. Elsa always works hard to please him, and in return, he is always nice to her and treats her well.

A SHORT TIME later, Elsa brings the first batch of freshly-baked cookies into the shop and arranges them in the display case. Suddenly the sound of shouting voices and shattering glass startles her, causing her to drop the last few cookies on the floor. She hurries to the window and looks out into the shadows of the pre-dawn light to see the soldiers of *Sturmabteilung* or SA marching down the street behind a group of civilians wielding sledgehammers and clubs. They smash shop windows and pull people, many of whom are still in night clothes, out of their apartments and into the street. The SA officers or "Brownshirts" as they are known, stand by and allow the attacks to continue. *Why are they letting this happen? Why don't they arrest these men for what they're doing?*

With the commotion intensifying, Herr Mueller rushes to Elsa's side. Together they observe the angry mob smashing, looting, and beating people onto the glass-covered road while it slowly advances toward the bakery.

"What's *happening?"* Elsa asks with a quiver in her voice.

"I don't know, but I want you to go into the kitchen and *do not* come out until I say."

Mueller's knuckles turn white as he nervously clutches the front doorknob and turns the lock. The old man realizes this is a futile attempt to protect his property, but he feels an undeniable urge to do something.

"But Herr Mueller—" Elsa begins while his back is turned.

"No buts, Elsa! Do as I say!"

Paralyzed with fear, she remains unmoving. Herr Mueller turns to her and barks, "Now, Elsa!"

She finally comes to her senses and does as he instructs without further question. In the kitchen, Elsa paces nervously, wringing her hands as her stomach clenches with fear. When the sound of breaking glass and shouting gets louder, she quickly hides within a cabinet below the baker's table and says a silent prayer that nothing bad will happen at the bakery.

Suddenly the front window smashes in, and Hans Mueller stands by helplessly while shards of glass fly at him. A moment later, three men carrying clubs enter and make their way to where the stunned baker stands—glass crunching beneath their feet as they make their approach.

"What is it you want?" Elsa hears her boss say nervously.

From her hiding spot, she peeks through a small opening, watching in silent horror as the three men raise their clubs and destroy the shop. When Herr Mueller tries to stop them, one man swings his weapon and strikes the old man in the head. Bloods spurts everywhere, and he immediately falls to the floor. Even with the dreadful scene unfolding before her, Elsa remains very still and quiet. *Dear God in heaven, how can you let this happen?*

The attackers enter the kitchen, and Elsa holds her breath while they walk around the baker's table and into the adjacent storage room. The men grab cookies from the cooling racks and eat them voraciously as they continue searching the kitchen. Once they are satisfied that no one else is in the bakery, they leave, but not before taking several loaves of bread.

The last man to go throws a liquid around the shop and all over Herr Mueller's lifeless body and then strikes a match. As the shop bursts into flames, terror freezes Elsa, and she is powerless to move. *What do I do now? How can this be happening? What did Herr Mueller do wrong?* Then, as though the hand of God himself reached down to shake her, Elsa snaps out of her stupor. She quickly gets out of the cabinet and rushes out the back door, still wearing her hair net and apron.

In the alleyway, she runs in a trance-like state as fast as her legs will carry her, taking care to avoid the main streets. The frigid November air attacks Elsa's lungs, causing sharp pain. She ignores her discomfort and continues to move quickly through the city. Finally, when her apartment building comes into view, an incredible surge of relief washes over her. She takes the front steps to the main entrance two at a time and races into the building.

Once Elsa reaches her apartment door, she suddenly realizes that in her haste, she has left her purse with her key behind at the bakery. Without any other choice, she anxiously hammers on the door and prays that her father is at home.

A LOUD BANGING startles Heinrich from his slumber. *Am I dreaming?* He waits for a moment and hears it again. A sudden fear sweeps over him. *Who could be at the door at this hour?* Another barrage of rapid pounding sets his heart racing. Heinrich gets up and slowly makes his way to the door. He grabs a knife from the kitchen on his way and grips it in his trembling hand.

"Who's there?"

Hearing no reply, Heinrich opens the door slightly and cautiously peers out, holding his weapon in front of him. What he sees alarms him. His youngest daughter stands there dressed only in her work uniform, covered with grime, and her dirty face streaked with tears. Heinrich places the knife down on the hall table before letting Elsa in.

"Come in, my girl. What has happened?"

Unable to catch her breath or control the tremors that attack her petite frame, Elsa finds herself powerless to move forward. It is as though her feet were cemented to the floor. She stares at her father and tries to speak, but words fail her.

Recognizing the symptoms of shock, Heinrich uncharacteristically puts his arm around her and leads her to the sofa. He covers Elsa with a blanket and goes to the kitchen for some water.

Heinrich holds the glass to her trembling lips and manages to get her to take a few sips. Noticing that this has done little to help, he rubs Elsa's arms to try to rouse her from her stupor. She blinks and her breathing slowly returns to normal. After a few minutes, Elsa recounts the horrible experience she went through.

"They *killed* him! They *killed* Herr Mueller!"

Heinrich's face pales, but he is quiet. He looks out the window toward the city centre and sees smoke billowing up into the cloudless morning sky.

"You must stay inside now. It isn't safe outdoors."

"*Why Vati? Why* did this happen? *Poor* Herr Mueller!"

Heinrich looks at his daughter, his hardened features softening ever so slightly. "You were right to hide in the kitchen, Elsa."

"Herr Mueller made me go. I wouldn't have gone into the kitchen otherwise, Vati."

Heinrich nods and with his voice almost a whisper he says, "Herr Mueller was a brave man and a good friend. I will miss him."

Elsa sobs uncontrollably as she realizes that the kind man who gave her first job to her and treated her so well lost his life, even though he managed to save hers.

"Come now, Elsa, enough with the tears! Wash up and change your clothes, then go to the kitchen to prepare lunch, ja?"

She stares at her father incredulously. *How can he think about food at a time like this? Can't he see how upset I am? How can he be so heartless?* Elsa knows she has little choice, and she does her best to control her emotions.

"Ja, Vati, I will," Heinrich's ever-obedient daughter says in defeat before going to her room.

A FEW DAYS after the attacks known as *Kristallnacht*, Elsa sits with her father at the kitchen table while he reads the morning newspaper.

"Was Herr Mueller Jewish like Arthur, Vati?"

"He was."

"I didn't know that."

They sit quietly for a few minutes before Elsa once again breaks the silence. "Is it safe to go outside now?"

"Ja, we have nothing to fear. We are not Jewish."

"What's *wrong* with being Jewish?" Elsa asks innocently. She remembers how good Herr Mueller was to her and didn't think there was anything wrong with him.

"That, my girl, is something only the Führer knows," Heinrich says without communicating his views on the situation.

Elsa recalls when she had the privilege of meeting and shaking the Führer's hand when he came to visit her school. At the time, the children learned how he was helping Germany to secure its future, and he seemed like a nice man to her. *How is it possible that he can allow these terrible things to happen?*

"Elsa, you must look for other work."

She snaps out of her memories and looks at her father. "Mutti says they need help at the factory so I'll try there first."

"Very good. You know we're counting on you for the additional income so don't disappoint us, ja?"

LATER THAT AFTERNOON, Elsa walks cautiously to the factory. Although her father said it was safe for her to go outside, she feels nervous.

As she rounds a corner a few blocks from her home, Elsa bumps directly into an SA officer who is with two other men. Her heart drums against her ribs as she recognizes the man. All at once, she is transported back into the cabinet under the baker's table, watching this man attack Herr Mueller with a club.

"I... I'm very sorry, mein Herr. Please excuse me," Elsa says quickly.

The officer looks at her and smiles. "Don't be sorry, Fräulein. The pleasure was all mine!"

Elsa manages a weak smile while attempting to fight her nausea. She is about to continue on her way when the man blocks her path.

"What's your hurry?"

"I... I..."

Revelling in his ability to frighten this young girl, he laughs, and the other men join in.

"Have I left you speechless, Fräulein? Why don't you come with me, and I'll help you to find your voice, ja?" The officer winks and reaches for Elsa's hand.

Paralyzed with fear her thoughts race. *Dear God! What should I do? Run! But what will happen if I do?*

The touch of his hand has an immediate effect. Elsa turns away quickly and retches as acid burns her throat.

The officer jumps away to avoid her mess, and the others laugh hysterically.

"You're quite the ladies' man, Wilhelm! That's some impact you have!"

Anger etches the man's face, and he storms off across the street with his friends following close behind.

Elsa wipes her mouth and takes a few deep breaths. Once she feels better, she continues on her way to the factory.

DESPITE HER TERRIFYING encounter, Elsa completes her application and hands it to the secretary. While she waits for her interview, she slowly calms down.

After speaking to the hiring manager, she receives a job offer to work in the same area as her mother. Much to her delight, her new job will pay her more money than she earned at the bakery. *Perhaps Vati will allow me to keep some of the money I make now*, Elsa thinks on her way home.

Chapter 10: September 1939

THE DOOR TO the apartment slams shut after Heinrich enters. "Well, here we go again. The Führer has refused to pull our troops from Poland, and now Britain and France have declared war! That devil is never satisfied!"

"Shhh—keep your voice down, Heinrich. You must be careful with what you say," Frieda says as the blood drains from her face.

"He is playing with fire! Power has gone to his head, and the German people *will* suffer because of it! Mark my words!"

"Well, what can we do?"

"We can only hope for a quick end to this madness."

"I just pray our Peter will stay safe and return to us unharmed. This is all so unbelievable, first all the troubles for the Jews, and now war," Frieda says with a shake of her head. "Perhaps you are right, Liebling, and the thought of it frightens me to death."

Heinrich goes to his wife and embraces her. This unexpected show of affection surprises Frieda, making her realize exactly how serious things are, and fear grips her like a vise.

When Elsa arrives home after being out with Petra, she finds her parents in the kitchen. Their dire expressions immediately cause a wave of panic to wash over her. *I pray that nothing has happened to Greta and the boys!*

"Mutti? Vati? What's wrong?"

Frieda looks bravely at her youngest daughter and explains that Germany is now at war.

"What does *that* mean? *Must we leave?*"

Frieda tries her best to calm Elsa's fears. "Nein, nein—we're not going anywhere. We go on the way we always do, Liebling."

Elsa studies her mother's face and senses that there is more to it than what she has said, so she turns to her father. "Then everything is okay, Vati?"

"Ja, for now, everything is fine. We will see what time brings."

Elsa shifts her eyes from her mother to her father, trying to determine what they are keeping from her.

Frieda notices her uneasiness and smiles reassuringly. "Don't worry, Elsa, we are safe here. Go and clean up now, supper is almost ready."

As she washes her face, Elsa's mind floods with a multitude of thoughts. *I knew that something was going on. There are more soldiers on the streets, and I've heard many whispers at the factory. I don't understand what it means to be at war, but I trust Mutti and Vati. If they say everything will be okay, then I'm sure it will be.*

AS AUTUMN SHIFTS towards winter, the main differences to their lives are the nightly use of blackout curtains and regular air raid drills. The family tries to go on as they have always done, and Frieda and Elsa continue to work at the factory as usual.

There are more ships, mostly military, and even submarines in Hamburg harbour now. Soldiers from those ships fill the streets, and the sight of them reminds Elsa of poor Herr Mueller and the events of Kristallnacht. In the months since the attacks, she has done her best to forget the horror she witnessed, but vivid nightmares still regularly invade her sleep. She is careful to avoid going anywhere near the burned-out bakery because the sight of it is much too painful for her.

With the reducing supplies of items such as coffee, sugar, butter, milk and eggs, the German people must now use ration cards or *Marken.* These Marken are required to purchase those restricted items and only in the quantity specified on the cards.

Support for the war effort increases as the months pass. Many employees at the factory believe that the Führer is looking out for the German peoples' best interest, but Elsa knows that belief isn't one shared by her parents. They have made it clear that views on the war and politics are private and not to be disclosed to anyone. Elsa has no concrete opinions on either of those topics since she is uncertain about what she hears, but she respects her parents' wishes and remains silent. The only thing she knows for sure is that she is fearful of what the future might hold.

The family worries about Peter, especially after he was sent to Poland in September. Since that time, they have heard little from him, and they hope he stays safe. Heinrich hates the thought of his son in combat. He wishes there was some way to have prevented him from having to fight, but under the circumstances, there was no other choice. Heinrich trusts that Peter will survive his duty in the *Wehrmacht* and that the war will be over quickly. *Come home intact in both mind and body my son,* he prays.

Chapter 11: November 1939

PETRA AND ELSA walk back to their apartment after their BDM meeting. Along the way, Petra talks eagerly about some neighbourhood boys who are now in the Wehrmacht. When Elsa fails to share her enthusiasm, Petra uses another tactic to try to change her friend's sombre mood.

"Aren't you getting excited for your birthday? It's not every day you turn sixteen!" says Petra.

"I suppose so," Elsa reluctantly responds.

"Come on now. We need to do something special to celebrate. I know! Let's go to the carnival! We haven't been there in ages."

"I don't know. I don't really feel like celebrating."

Petra looks at her and smiles mischievously. "Maybe we can meet some handsome soldiers, ja?"

"Ach, Petra, they're just so young and immature. All they do is show off for the girls, and it's really pathetic."

"Well, I'm sure there will be older ones there, too. Come on! Say yes—*please!*" Petra pleads, folding her hands together as though she were about to pray.

Elsa looks at her friend and can't help but laugh at her ridiculous display. "I'll think about it," she says as she approaches the staircase inside their apartment building. She is always amazed by Petra's positive attitude and ability to make her laugh.

"Well, be sure to let me know tomorrow, ja?"

Elsa waves her hand in surrender. "Okay, Petra, I will. Auf Wiedersehen."

I wish I could be more excited about my birthday, but I keep seeing poor Herr Mueller with his blood spraying everywhere. I just can't seem to get it out of my mind. Mutti says that as time goes on, my memories will become less painful. I sure hope she's right.

WHEN THE DOOR opens, Frieda looks up from her knitting to see Elsa, and she smiles. "Hello, Liebling. Did you and Petra have a good meeting tonight?"

"It was okay, I guess."

Frieda studies Elsa's face, and can see that something is bothering her. "What's wrong, Elsa?"

"Nothing."

"Are you sure? You say there is nothing wrong, but your face says otherwise. Why don't you come sit and talk to me? I'm sure you'll feel better if you do."

Elsa frowns and thinks for a minute before sitting down beside her mother. "Petra wants to go to the carnival to celebrate my birthday."

"And this is a problem, Liebling?"

"Well, I don't know. It just doesn't feel right to celebrate with all the bad things happening," Elsa replies with tears flooding her eyes. She is angry with herself for showing so much emotion, but she can't seem to control it.

Frieda opens her arms, and Elsa clings to her. "Shhh—it's alright. Just let it all come out now. Sometimes it's helpful to have a good cry."

After a few minutes, Elsa blows her nose, and her mother continues her advice with patience and understanding. "I know you feel sad about what has happened, but these things are beyond your control. You must be strong because you're growing up in difficult times, and the future is uncertain," she says while gently stroking Elsa's hair. "It isn't easy, but the first step is to put the bad times behind you and focus on living the best way you can."

"But Mutti, everything is so different now. How can we just continue like nothing has changed?"

"You just take each day as it comes. There is no sense in worrying about what you can't change. You must live today, ja? You're only young once, so you need to have fun when you can, Elsa. I'm sure Herr Mueller would want you to enjoy your birthday."

Could Mutti be right? Maybe going out to have some fun might help to take my mind off things for a while.

"Why don't you think about it before you make a decision, ja?"

Elsa wipes her face and nods. *How is it that Mutti always knows when something is bothering me and always knows just the right things to say?*

"Do you feel a little better now?"

"Ja, I'm sorry for being silly."

"There's no reason for you to be sorry. It's never silly when something is troubling you. Now, go and wash your face so Vati doesn't see you like this, ja?"

While Elsa cleans the last traces of tears from her face, she concludes that her mother is right. *Herr Mueller would want me to celebrate my birthday with a trip to the carnival.* As she thinks about it, a tiny spark of excitement ignites within her, sending a smile to her face. Although guilty for having set aside her sadness of past events, Elsa feels a small sense of joy to finally have something special to look forward to in the future. While this battle rages within her, Elsa can feel her joy overtake her feelings of guilt, but regardless, she knows she will never forget all that she has experienced.

HEINRICH ENTERS THE living room and looks at his wife. "So, what's wrong with the girl *now?*"

"Ach, everything is fine, Liebling. Elsa is still upset about Kristallnacht. It will take time for her to come to terms with it."

Heinrich dismisses his wife's comments with a wave of his hand. "You coddle her too much, Frieda. It's time for her to grow up. Kristallnacht was almost a year ago."

"Come now, Heinrich, she is still young."

"Almost sixteen years old! She should be out searching for a husband, not sitting around here crying like a baby!"

Frieda shakes her head. *Through all our years together and dealing with your unpredictable moods, there are times when I feel like I barely know you anymore.* To continue their conversation when Heinrich is in such an unreasonable state would only cause more conflict, so she keeps her opinions to herself once more.

When Elsa approaches the living room, she overhears her parents' discussion and suddenly feels her happiness wane.

Heinrich senses her presence and turns to see her there. "So, are you finished being a baby and ready to be an adult?"

She looks at him and using all her strength, she manages to control her tears. "Ja, Vati! I will be an adult and no more crying—*that I can promise you!*" Elsa says in a slightly defiant tone as she turns toward her room. Once the words have left her lips, she immediately regrets how she spoke to her father. Elsa turns cautiously to look at him, fully expecting a verbal assault, but thankfully he had either not noticed her tone or he was ignoring it. Whatever the reason, Elsa is relieved not to have caused any additional friction between them. She lives in constant fear of her father's mood swings and always tries to behave in a way that limits any hostility he could have toward her.

ON THE AFTERNOON of Elsa's birthday, Petra and Elsa talk excitedly on their way to the carnival. They stop to peer in a shop window, and as they are looking, Petra turns to her friend and hands her a small package wrapped in brown paper held together with a piece of twine. "Happy Birthday, Elsa!"

"Dankeschön, Petra," Elsa says cheerfully before removing the twine and paper. Inside she finds a colourful knitted scarf. "It's so beautiful!"

Shrugging, Petra replies, "It's nothing fancy. I made it with some leftover wool Mama had."

"Well, it's special to me!" She puts on the scarf and Petra adjusts it. "Dankeschön, Mutti!" Elsa jokes.

It is cold for the beginning of November, but the girls don't seem to mind. When they arrive at the carnival, they buy tickets for the amusement rides and enjoy a few sweets while watching the antics of various buskers.

The number of soldiers at the festival makes Elsa uncomfortable, but she paints on a smile, attempting to quell her anxiety.

"Let's go on the Ferris wheel!" Petra shouts excitedly and grabs Elsa's hand, pulling her into the queue to wait for their turn.

A while later, someone behind them shouts, "Petra! Hey, Petra!"

Petra turns quickly to see who called her and notices her cousin, Rudolf, dressed in his uniform, standing further down from them. "Rudi! I didn't even recognize you!" Like a salmon swimming upstream she goes to him, and pulls him up the line to where Elsa waits.

After Petra introduces Rudi to Elsa, she turns to him and asks, "Are you here alone?"

"Alas, my comrades have deserted me," he says in mock sadness with his hand over his heart.

The girls giggle at Rudi's performance. "Well, you *must* stay with us then, ja?" his cousin says enthusiastically.

"Sure—*why not?*" After a few awkward minutes, Rudi has an idea. "Hey, do you want to go to a party later?"

Petra looks at Elsa pleadingly, and she quickly nods back. "We would love to come! It's Elsa's sixteenth birthday today!"

Elsa is both nervous and excited at the same time, but she reasons that it should be okay to attend this party since Petra's cousin will be there, so she relaxes slightly.

Rudi's eyes light up when he smiles. "Well, Happy Birthday, Elsa. We will have to celebrate, ja?"

Elsa smiles shyly and nods to him. As they wander around the carnival, they play amusement games, go on rides, and make jokes until it comes time for them to leave.

A while later, the three of them walk together arm in arm on their way to the party, enjoying each other's company. Elsa can't remember ever feeling this happy. *I'm so glad I listened to Mutti.*

MUSIC ECHOES FROM an open second-floor window of the old building on Friedrichstrasse.

"Here we are. I'm sure you'll like my friends and have a good time, ja?" Rudi says joyfully.

They enter a small apartment that is crowded with a half dozen soldiers and their girlfriends. Over in a corner, beside the Victrola, a man in his late twenties holds a cigarette and sings an old song that Elsa recognizes. He is tall and blonde with beautiful blue eyes, and she wonders why this man is not in uniform like the rest.

After a few introductions, Rudi leaves the girls to get them a drink. In his absence, Elsa looks around the stuffy apartment and then at the man singing in the corner. His voice isn't bad, and he can keep a tune. He entertains the group by acting out the song about springtime and a girl named Veronika, and Elsa finds herself tapping her foot along with the melody and laughing.

When he finishes the song, everyone claps. The man puts another record on the Victrola and gets a bottle of beer from the icebox before sitting down beside Petra and Elsa. He flashes a charming smile. "So, you like my singing, ja?" They return his smile and nod shyly back at him.

Rudi comes over and puts his hand on the man's shoulder. "Erich, this is my cousin, Petra Braun, and her friend Elsa Schumacher. Petra and Elsa, this is my friend Erich Kaufmann."

"Pleased to meet you, Fräulein," he says with a slight nod.

"Nice to meet you, too," the girls reply in unison.

"Today is Elsa's birthday, so we need to celebrate!" Rudi yells loudly over the music thumping from the Victrola. The guests call out "Happy Birthday" and various cheers and Rudi proposes a toast to Elsa. Although embarrassed by the attention, Elsa manages to set aside her anxiety and socialize. Petra and Elsa spend the rest of the night dancing, singing and enjoying their newfound friends.

Some time later, Elsa looks at her watch. "Petra, we better go. It's almost curfew, and we have a long walk ahead of us."

"Is it that late *already?* I wish we didn't have to go yet!"

"Come on," Elsa says firmly, although she silently shares her friend's sentiments. *I wish we could stay, too.*

Petra gets up reluctantly and follows Elsa to the corridor. Once they have their coats on, Petra hugs Rudi and the girls say their goodbyes.

"Dankeschön, Rudi, for making my birthday extra special," Elsa says timidly.

"Wait!" yells Erich.

Surprised, Elsa and Petra both turn to look at him.

"I'll escort you home. You know the streets aren't safe, especially at this time of night."

"Are you sure?" Rudi asks his friend. "It's a bit out of your way, you know?"

"Ach, that's no problem! Come along, Fräulein. You are safe with me!" Elsa and Petra laugh, and he offers them each an arm before leading them out of the apartment.

THE FRIGID NIGHT air assaults the three new friends as they begin their trek down Friedrichstrasse.

"So, where do you live?" Erich asks.

"On Lillienstrasse," Petra replies while holding the collar of her coat against a sudden gust of wind. "Do you know where that is?"

"Ja, I have a friend who lives there."

The trio talks about their work and friends, and they are surprised to discover that they know some of the same people. Petra later monopolizes the conversation by telling funny stories about her cousin, Rudi, which make Erich and Elsa both laugh.

When they finally arrive at their apartment building, Elsa and Petra thank their escort and bid him goodnight before heading up the front steps to the entrance.

As Elsa checks the door to make sure it latched behind her, she looks through its small window to see Erich still there. He smiles when he notices her and tips his hat. She returns his smile before heading upstairs to see Petra and feels a sudden warmth spread across her cheeks. *What an odd sensation.*

"Dankeschön for today, Petra. I had so much fun."

"I'm glad! I knew you would!"

Elsa hugs her best friend and makes her way home.

After entering the apartment, Elsa realizes that her parents have gone to bed, and she breathes a sigh of relief as she tip-toes to her room.

That night, Elsa dreams of dancing and singing. It's the first night in almost a year where she is able to sleep without having nightmares, and in the morning, she wakes up feeling rested and happy.

Chapter 12: Life Continues

FOR THE NEXT few weeks, life goes on in a way considered normal for wartime. Frieda receives a vague letter from her sister, Ida, in Berlin telling her that things with Greta and the boys didn't go as originally planned but failed to provide any details. With all correspondence now read and censored by the Reich, she knows Ida must be cautious with what she writes. Frieda's fear for the safety of her family once again overtakes her, causing her many sleepless nights.

Elsa and her mother continue to work at the factory. They now sew uniforms for the soldiers and work shifts to keep up with the demand. While the days go on as usual for the women of the Schumacher household, Heinrich becomes more withdrawn, spending much of his time alone in his own world. Frieda blames the war for the change in her husband's behaviour. His mannerisms are much like they were after returning from the Great War, and she prays for the additional patience to deal with him.

HE SEES HER approaching with her shopping bags of rations and smiles. Erich steps away from the brick wall of the apartment building and walks toward Elsa.

"Guten Tag, Fräulein. How are you?"

Elsa is surprised to see him and smiles shyly, feeling her cheeks heat up despite the cold. "I'm well, Dankeschön, and you, Erich?"

"I'm much better for having seen you," he says with a wink. "I was wondering if you would like to go for coffee."

"That would be nice," she replies nervously, feeling her heartbeat accelerate. "Just give me a few minutes to bring the rations to Mutti and then we can go, ja?"

Erich rushes up beside her, attempting to grab the bags from her hands. "Here, let me take those up for you."

"It's fine, Erich. I can manage. You really mustn't trouble yourself."

"It's no trouble, Elsa."

She hates to refuse his offer of assistance, but the thought of him meeting her father terrifies her. "Please—just wait here for me, *okay?*"

Erich looks at her briefly and noticing her agitation, he agrees to stay outside and wait for her return. He lights a cigarette and watches her enter the building. *Is she ashamed to be seen with me?*

"YOU'RE BACK ALREADY, Elsa?" Frieda asks when she enters the kitchen.

"Ja, Mutti," she says, placing the milk in the icebox. "There weren't that many people in line when I arrived."

"Well, why don't you take off your coat?"

Elsa shakes her head. "I'm going out for coffee."

"With Petra?"

"Nein, I'm going with the boy I met the night of my birthday."

"I see, and what is his name?"

Elsa smiles and feels her cheeks go warm once again. "His name is Erich."

"Well, why don't you invite him to come in for a moment? I would like to meet him."

Elsa's expression grows serious. "I'm afraid of how Vati might react. Next time, okay, Mutti?" she whispers.

Frieda understands her daughter's apprehension, but it makes her feel terrible. "Very well, Liebling, have a good time, ja?"

Elsa kisses her mother's cheek and heads to the door. "Until later, Mutti."

ERICH LEANS AGAINST the building, rubbing his hands together trying to warm them. He sees Elsa exiting the building and heads in her direction.

"Are you ready to go?"

Elsa nods and they carefully walk down the icy street. Their conversation is awkward as they both try to think of things to say.

At the café, they get a table in the corner. The place is small, but quaint, with the sweet aroma of freshly baked cakes. Unfortunately, due to rationing, the shop only carries a substitute coffee and a very limited supply of desserts. They each order the pretend coffee and a piece of torte and are fortunate to get the last two pieces the café had.

Erich takes a sip of the hot liquid and enjoys the warmth spreading in his stomach. "So, Elsa, what have you been up to?"

"I've been working mostly, and what about you? What have you been doing?"

"I've been working too." Erich talks about his job as a bricklayer and the enjoyment he gets from his work. Because it is winter, he is fortunate to have a job at a hotel refurbishing its old fireplaces.

Elsa listens intently to him, and when he stops talking, they nibble at their torte, savouring every bite since it is becoming increasingly difficult to get.

"So tell me about you," Erich says, wiping his mouth with a napkin.

"Where should I begin?"

"Why not start with where you went to school."

She tells Erich about school and about her family. "Vati is very strict, and his moods are unpredictable. He fought in the last war, and Mutti says it changed him." Elsa realizes that she has never told anyone about her father before now and wonders why she would tell Erich this since he is practically a stranger to her. She continues to talk about her siblings but is careful not to mention anything about her part Jewish brother-in-law. Elsa opens up and speaks in a way she has never done with anyone before. It is like someone opened a tap, allowing the stories to come flowing out. Finally, after taking another bite of her torte, Elsa's face reddens. *"I talk too much,"* she admits.

"It's okay, I enjoy listening to you," he says with a smile.

Elsa smiles back awkwardly. "Well, you must tell me more about yourself now."

Erich talks about his childhood, including how his younger brother died at the age of two from tuberculosis and that he, too, contracted the terrible disease but was fortunate to survive. This is the reason that Erich was rejected by the army. "The Reich is very strict about the health of its soldiers," he explains.

He goes on to tell her that he was mostly raised by his grandmother because his mother couldn't accept the fact that he was male. "She only wanted a girl, so when I was born, she told the nurse she didn't want me and to take me away."

"That's *awful!*" Elsa says, reaching out and touching Erich's arm compassionately.

"Ja, well, she is a strange woman, but she *is* my mother. I do have lots of aunts, uncles, and cousins who I spend time with. My mother is the second youngest of 11 children."

Erich tells Elsa that his father joined the French Foreign Legion in 1915, and when he later wrote to his mother to have her and the boys join him in Alsace-Lorraine, she refused. "She wrote to my father and told him that we wouldn't be joining him because she didn't want to leave Hamburg, so we stayed here, and I never saw my father again."

"That's *so* sad! Do you know where he is now?"

He shakes his head and replies without emotion. "He's probably dead, but who knows?"

Erich explains how his mother filed for divorce on the grounds of abandonment. "She later married a wealthy man, who I didn't like much. He caught me smoking a cigarette on the street one day, and he came over, knocked it out of my hand, and gave me a cigar. He told me if I was going to smoke, I should smoke something good. He was quite a character, but he made my mother happy for a few years until his death."

"Do you live with her now?" Elsa asks, hoping Erich won't think the question too forward.

"Nein, I share an apartment with some friends on Finkenstrasse."

They continue talking and getting to know one another, and Elsa can't believe how stimulated and comfortable she feels with Erich.

As the sun sets in the winter sky, they realize the time is getting late. Erich pays the bill, and the two of them slowly walk back to Elsa's apartment.

"Dankeschön, Erich, for the lovely afternoon," she says, wishing that the day would never end.

"You're most welcome, Elsa. May I call on you again?"

She turns to him and smiles shyly. "I would like that very much."

"May I call on you next Saturday, for supper, perhaps?"

"That would be lovely," she says nervously and touches Erich's hand.

Responding to this sign of affection, he reaches down and kisses her cheek. "Until then," he says with a bow.

Elsa watches from the door as he leaves, joy filling her very soul. *I've never felt like this before! I'm so happy!*

OVER THE NEXT few weeks, the couple sees each other every Saturday, and they become very close. Elsa counts down the days until they can be together and wonders if Erich feels the same way.

On one of their Saturday night dates, they enjoy a walk in the park after their supper. They sit down on a bench across from the water fountain, and Erich turns to Elsa with a serious look.

"I know you're fearful of your father, but don't you think it's time I met your parents? I really don't like the idea of us seeing each other without having met them."

"I don't know, Erich. Maybe we should still wait a while." Elsa isn't only fearful of her father's reaction to her relationship with Erich, but she is also afraid of what he will think should her father respond negatively. The possibility that she could lose Erich is at the forefront of her mind, increasing her anxiety.

"Okay, Elsa, I understand. I don't mean to pressure you, but we will have to meet at some point." He has dated many girls, but none of them ever made him feel the way she does. *I wish you would just let me meet your parents. I can handle whatever your father says or thinks about me. They need to get to know me before I can ask for your hand in marriage.*

Frieda is aware that Elsa and Erich see each other regularly, but she keeps this from Heinrich at Elsa's request. Realizing that their fondness for each other is growing, Frieda finally concludes that regardless of her wishes, the next time Elsa goes downstairs to meet her young man, she will follow her and invite him for supper during the Christmas holidays.

Chapter 13: December 1939

WITH CHRISTMAS FAST approaching, Elsa must help her mother with the preparations. Frieda has always loved this time of year and has taught Elsa the importance of this holiday and their age-old traditions. This year will be difficult with the rationing and the family split up, but Frieda assures her daughter that they will celebrate the holiday the best way they can.

"The war can take many things away from us, Liebling, but we cannot allow it to take our spirit."

Elsa admires her mother's strength and wishes she could be more like her.

ON DECEMBER 22ND, Elsa and Frieda work the evening shift at the factory. The night starts out as usual with the women doing various tasks to produce uniforms at their sewing stations on the second floor.

Around 8 p.m., the air raid siren suddenly blares, and the lights in the building immediately turn off. The factory prohibits the use of flashlights since any light source could potentially provide the enemy a target. Emergency lighting in the stairwell is the only source of illumination to guide the workers to safety, and many push and shove to be the first ones out of the building.

When Elsa reaches the dimly-lit staircase, she looks around for her mother but can hardly see anything. She stands on her toes, trying to get a better view, but it doesn't help, and Elsa nearly loses her balance when the group forces her down the steps.

Outside, the women break into a nervous run, in the direction of the bomb shelter across the street, and Elsa reluctantly joins them.

"Have you seen Frieda, Ingeborg?" Elsa asks her mother's co-worker when they enter the shelter.

"Nein, not since before the sirens went off. I think she went to the washroom, so she probably isn't out yet."

Elsa searches through the sea of women, but her mother is nowhere to be found. *Where could Mutti be?*

After the doors close, Elsa becomes frantic and suddenly feels the room shrink around her. She can't catch her breath and is overcome with an urgent need to escape. Before Elsa realizes it, she is climbing over people and rushing toward the exit.

"You cannot leave," the warden says firmly. "We must wait for the all-clear signal. Now go back to your spot!"

Elsa turns and sits back down, trying desperately to calm herself. The small shelter is cramped, stuffy and stinks of body odour. *How long will we be here? I have to find Mutti,* she thinks while waiting impatiently for her freedom.

Finally, after an agonizing hour, the siren goes off again, giving the all-clear notice, and the warden opens the doors. People move out of the shelter as quickly as they can and head back to the factory to resume their duties.

ELSA SEARCHES EVERYWHERE for her mother, and when she doesn't find her, she visits her supervisor, Herr Lubeck, to tell him that she is missing.

"When did you last see her?"

"We saw each other at break time."

"She was not at the shelter?"

"Nein, Herr Lubeck, and I'm afraid that something may have happened to her."

A feeling of uneasiness sweeps over him, and he gives her a weak smile of reassurance. "Don't fret, Elsa. Go back to work now. I will have the factory searched and let you know once we have found her.

Your mother probably got turned around in the dark and went into the basement when she couldn't make it to the shelter in time."

Elsa goes back to her station but can't concentrate on her work. She is much too upset and finds herself staring off into space.

"Elsa! Elsa!" Herr Lubeck shouts over the factory noise.

The sound of his voice calling her name breaks Elsa's trance-like state, and she quickly stands, looking in his direction.

"Come into my office, please."

Moving forward, Elsa's heart races and each step feels exaggerated—like trudging through deep snow. When she finally enters the room, Herr Lubeck tells her to sit down and gestures to the chair across from his desk.

"My dear, I have news of your mother."

"Where is she? Is she *alright?*"

"There has been an accident, Elsa."

"*What?* What happened?" She tries to listen to her supervisor's explanation, but she can barely hear him over the roaring sound of blood as it pulses in her ears.

"It appears that when the air raid siren went off, she was accidentally pushed into the laundry chute. She is injured but alive, and an ambulance is on its way to take her to the hospital."

Elsa stares at her boss and appears to have forgotten how to speak.

"Did you hear what I said, Elsa? We must go to tell your father."

Elsa blinks and her speech finally returns. "I... I want to see her. I want to stay with her until the ambulance arrives."

THE PUNGENT SMELL of wet fabric immediately assaults Elsa when she enters the laundry area. She sees three women gathered together in front of the laundry chute, and as Elsa makes her way to them, they notice her and separate. On the floor before her, her mother lies with her eyes closed and her white hair and face covered in blood.

"Mutti! Mutti!" Elsa yells and her vision suddenly blurs with tears. She runs over and gently takes hold of her mother's hand. One of the women touches Elsa's shoulder sympathetically, but she doesn't seem to notice, she is lost in the trauma of what she sees.

Elsa sits quietly on the floor beside the woman who gave her life, still holding her hand and allows her tears to pour down like a heavy rain. *I must be having a nightmare! This can't be happening!*

A short time later, two men enter the basement laundry with a stretcher. They gently transfer Frieda's broken body to it and prepare to take her to the hospital.

"Fräulein, you have to let go now," the medic says.

When Elsa doesn't respond, the man tries once again.

"I'm sorry, Fräulein, but you really must let us take her to the hospital. The doctor is waiting for her."

Elsa reluctantly releases her hand and stares down at her own, now stained with her mother's blood. When she stands, she is immediately attacked by dizziness.

"Take it easy now, Elsa," the woman beside her says as she puts an arm around her and silently guides her up the stairs.

Herr Lubeck holds the door open for the ambulance attendants as they carry Frieda outside. Once they have exited the building, he sees Elsa and rushes over to her, taking her by the arm. His heart is breaking for this poor girl, knowing how difficult it will be for her and her family to deal with this senseless tragedy, especially at Christmas time.

"Come, Elsa, I'll take you home."

HERR LUBECK HELPS Elsa out of the car and up to her apartment. With the unpleasant task of notifying Frieda's husband of her accident ahead of him, the man takes a deep breath to prepare himself.

"Do you have your key, Elsa?"

She stares at the door and replies in a monotone voice. "It's in Mutti's purse."

Herr Lubeck knocks, waiting for Elsa's father to let them in.

Alarmed by the late-night intrusion, Heinrich stands behind the closed door. "Who's there?" he asks cautiously.

"Johann Lubeck from the factory with your daughter, Elsa."

Heinrich opens the door, and Elsa runs to him, hugging him tightly. He pulls her away, and the sight of her pale, anguished expression causes fear to seep into his veins. "What is it? What has happened?" Unable to form a reply, Elsa remains at the entrance, her eyes brimming with tears.

Herr Lubeck informs Heinrich about the accident and tells him that Frieda is at the hospital. He then offers to drive them there since taxi and streetcar services don't resume until 6 a.m.

HEINRICH AND ELSA enter the hospital after thanking Herr Lubeck for his kindness. Before enquiring about Frieda, Heinrich tells his daughter to sit in the waiting area. She reluctantly complies and anxiously awaits news of her mother's condition.

"Dr. Burger will be out to see you shortly. Please, take a seat," the nurse tells Heinrich compassionately.

He thanks her and joins Elsa in the waiting room. As they sit, Heinrich notices her staring down at her hands. He follows her gaze and observes the dried blood on them. He feels his heart beating like a drum, and his body trembles uncontrollably—like it had a mind of its own.

"What is it, Vati?" Elsa asks with concern as Heinrich's shaking intensifies. When her father doesn't reply, she goes to the nurse's station to ask about her mother.

"The doctor will be out to see you soon."

Elsa turns to go back to the waiting area when a door to one of the examination rooms suddenly opens, and a doctor comes out and walks toward her.

"Fräulein Schumacher?" the doctor asks, and Elsa nods her reply. "I'm Dr. Burger. Is your father here?"

"He's in the waiting room," she says anxiously.

Together, they make their way to Heinrich, and Elsa sits down beside him, gently touching his arm. "Dr. Burger is here, Vati."

Heinrich's tremors worsen as he continues to stare at the wall.

"Herr Schumacher? *Are you alright?*"

"My father suffers from shell shock, Herr Doctor."

"I see," the physician says with a look of empathy.

"How is Mutti? Can we see her now?"

"Fräulein, I'm very sorry, but your mother's injuries were too severe—she has died. Thankfully she never regained consciousness, so she went peacefully. There was nothing we could do for her. She was in God's hands."

Elsa wears a blank expression and takes hold of her father's hand. "Dankeschön, Herr Doctor," she says in a tone devoid of emotion.

"Come, Vati, we must go home now and make arrangements."

Heinrich gets up from his seat while still staring off into the distance, and Elsa guides him toward the exit.

Outside, the early morning sun shines just like it would on any other day, unaffected by the terrible tragedy that took place only short hours before.

Elsa hails a taxi to take them home, and as they drive silently through the city, she stares out without any awareness of where they are or how much further they must travel.

When they finally arrive at their apartment, Elsa helps Heinrich to bed before going to the kitchen. She is numb—unable to feel anything. It is as though she is outside of herself, watching her world turn upside down and being utterly powerless to stop it.

In a dream state, Elsa makes herself some tea and sits down. After taking a sip of it, she folds her hands. "What will we do now?" she says aloud, as tears once again flow down her cheeks. "Please help me find a way to deal with this, dear Father, *please.*" She puts her head down on the table in despair and weeps until exhaustion finally claims her.

Chapter 14: A Spirit Shattered

SEVERAL HOURS LATER, Elsa wakes to the sound of Christmas carols coming from the next apartment. She stretches and looks at the clock. It is much later than she thought and as the reality of what she must face today enters her mind, she prays for the strength to get through it.

Once Elsa cleans up and puts on fresh clothes, she goes to her father's door. When he gives her permission to enter, she sees he is dressed and sitting in his chair by the window.

"Can I make you some breakfast, Vati?"

"Nein, we have to make preparations for Mama," he says while staring at the wedding photograph of him and Frieda on the dresser.

"But you need to eat first."

"First, we make arrangements—then we eat," he replies while still gazing at the photograph.

Elsa nods, knowing it is pointless to argue. She leaves her father and heads back to the kitchen to wait until he is ready to go.

When the door clicks shut, Heinrich's eyes fill with tears. He blinks them away and takes the picture from the dresser and holds it in his trembling hands. *How will I ever manage without Frieda and her income from the factory? Can Elsa take over the responsibilities of cooking and cleaning in addition to her job the way Frieda did?* He shakes his head in frustration, returning the photo and reluctantly prepares himself for the coming day.

AT THE FUNERAL parlour, they discuss the arrangements with the director, and they learn that the funeral will have to wait until after the holidays. This news disappoints Elsa. She had hoped to have the funeral earlier so they could put it behind them, allowing the long and painful process of healing their broken hearts to begin.

Despite the delay, they plan as much as they can, and the director tells them the cost. The added expense of the funeral is something they neglected to consider, and it leaves Elsa wondering how they will afford it.

"Do we have any money saved, Vati?" Elsa asks while waiting for the streetcar.

"That's none of your business!"

"I'm only asking, so I know how much extra we'll need to cover the cost of Mutti's funeral."

"The money I have is not to be touched. We need it to live."

Realizing that the responsibility of paying for her mother's burial now rests with her, Elsa's mind frantically searches for a way to obtain the money. *I won't let Mutti be buried in a pauper's grave.*

ELSA GOES TO Frau Schroder's apartment to inform her of Frieda's death and to ask if she may use the phone to call her Tante Ida in Berlin.

Once Ida hears the tragic news of her twin's death, she is in shock, and it takes a few moments before she is able to speak.

"I'm so sorry, Liebling. I know how hard this must be for you and Papa. What can I do to help you?"

Elsa finally breaks down and tells her aunt that they don't have the funds to pay for the funeral.

"Don't worry, I will send you the money you need."

Elsa is relieved that her aunt has offered her assistance since she could think of no other way to cover the unexpected cost.

"Dankeschön, Tante Ida. Please don't tell Vati. I will pay you back, okay?"

Ida knows that Heinrich is a proud man and would never accept charity from her, but it warms her heart that Elsa has asked for her help and plans to repay her. She has no intention of letting Elsa reimburse her for the funeral, but right now, Ida will go along with her niece's wishes because, like her father, she also has a sense of pride. "Okay, Elsa, we will work things out later, ja? Telephone me once all the arrangements have been finalized," the older woman says with emotion choking her words.

"I will contact you as soon as they are in place. Will you bring Greta and the boys with you to the funeral?"

There is a short pause before Ida replies. "I will let you know the next time we speak, until then, take care of yourself and Papa."

With calls now monitored, Elsa's aunt is cautious of what she says over the phone. She fears that if she told Elsa that Greta and the children wouldn't attend due to the danger involved, it could somehow alert the SS and possibly lead to their arrest.

After thanking Frau Schroder for the use of her phone, Elsa returns home. As she walks up the stairs, she wonders how to contact her brother Peter. *Sending a letter will be difficult since I don't know where he is right now. I guess the only thing to do is to visit the Wehrmacht Office. I will ask Vati to notify them this afternoon.*

Elsa hopes that the delay with the funeral will give her brother the time necessary to receive the news of their mother's passing and allow him to attend.

STILL NUMB FROM the previous day's horror, Elsa gathers the food her mother had acquired for the Christmas Eve meal. She knows how important the holiday was to her and how much she would have wanted them to keep with tradition.

While she is busy with the preparations, there is a knock on the door, and Elsa opens it to find Petra there.

"Fröhliche Weihnachten, my friend!" she says, holding a small gift out to Elsa. Petra immediately senses that something is wrong. "What's the matter? *Has something happened?*"

Elsa immediately breaks into tears, and Petra enters the apartment, leading her distraught friend to the sofa. When she is finally able to speak, Elsa recounts the horrible ordeal she has faced, and Petra embraces her.

As the two young women sit together, Petra tries to think of what to say. It is the first time in her young life that she finds herself at a loss for words. The only way she can think of to comfort Elsa is by holding her hand. After an awkward half hour, Petra informs her that she needs to return home to help her mother with their holiday plans.

"I'm so sorry, Elsa. If you need anything, please let me know."

"Dankeschön, Petra," she replies, hugging her friend.

Elsa resumes preparations for their traditional Christmas Eve meal. Trying to concentrate on the work before her is impossible—her mind is lost. She performs her tasks instinctively, without feeling and as though in slow motion.

A while later, Heinrich enters the kitchen and looks indignantly at his daughter. "Just what do you think you are doing?"

"I'm making the Christmas Eve supper. Mutti would want that, don't you think?"

Heinrich stands there staring at her without uttering a word.

"Will you go to get the Christmas tree, Vati?"

He still doesn't reply, he just turns and walks away.

Elsa wants to make this Christmas a tribute to her mother, and right now, she can't think of any other way to keep her mind off her grief.

Ignoring her father's behaviour, Elsa resolves to get the tree herself. On the way, she will also visit the office of the Wehrmacht to have them notify Peter of their mother's death. Elsa hopes the sad news will reach him before too long.

I wish I could see Erich. I could really use his support right now, but there just isn't enough time with everything I have to do. Maybe I can visit him tomorrow.

When most of her work is complete, Elsa once again tries to speak to her father. "I'm going out for a while, Vati. Do you need anything?" She waits patiently outside his bedroom door, and when he doesn't respond, she leaves him alone with his tortured thoughts.

ELSA'S VISITS THE army office to request that they notify her brother of their mother's passing. Once the paperwork is filled out, the next thing on her to-do list is getting a Christmas tree.

When she arrives at the lot, she wanders around searching for the perfect tree. After finding one, she pays for it and slowly drags it down the snow-covered street. The tree is cumbersome, and Elsa struggles with it the best she can, stopping every so often to catch her breath.

"Do you need help, Fräulein?" a man's voice from behind her asks.

Elsa stops and turns to see a soldier standing there. "That would be..." she pauses briefly to take a closer look at the man in uniform, *"Rudi?"* she says with surprise.

He looks at her with his eyes widening. "Elsa! Fröhliche Weihnachten. It's so wonderful to see you!" Rudi takes the stump of the tree from her grasp, pulling it with ease.

While they walk, Elsa tells Rudi of her mother's death, and he is visibly upset by the news.

"I'm so very sorry, Elsa. You shouldn't be doing this by *yourself."* Rudi listens as she tells him of her Christmas plans. He admires the strength of this young woman. "Have you told Petra?"

Elsa nods, "I saw her earlier this morning."

They continue walking in silence until they reach her apartment building. Rudi carries the tree up the stairs, and once Elsa unlocks the door, he brings it into the living room and sets it in place.

"Dankeschön, Rudi. I don't think I could have carried the tree up the stairs by myself. Can I make you some tea?"

"Nein, Danke. I really must be going. If you need anything, let Petra know, and I will come if I can." Rudi hugs her briefly before leaving.

After closing the door, Elsa retrieves the decorations from a small storage cabinet in the living room, carefully positioning candles on the branches just as her mother had taught her.

"You must always be careful to place the candles so they are not near another branch or decoration, Elsa," Frieda had told her.

Elsa can hear her mother's voice as though she were right there directing her, and it gives her comfort. She has heard it all day, with each step of the Christmas preparations. Elsa knows this is a crazy notion, yet she can't help feeling better because of it.

"Life goes on, Elsa," she remembers her mother saying, *"no matter how difficult."* She sniffles a little and grabs her handkerchief. "Ja, Mutti, I know," Elsa says aloud.

LATER THAT EVENING, when everything is ready, Elsa once again approaches Heinrich's room. "Supper is ready, Vati," she says and waits for his reply. Receiving no response, she tries again. "Vati?"

Elsa opens the door to see Heinrich lying on the bed in the fetal position. She goes to him and gently shakes him awake. "You must eat some supper."

Without saying a word, Heinrich looks at his daughter and slowly gets up. He moves toward the door and stops when he sees the living room with the beautifully decorated tree.

"Come now, ja? Let's go to the kitchen." Elsa takes her father's hand and leads him past the living room. She seats him at the table and serves his supper, but Heinrich remains silent, staring off into space. Unsure of what to do, Elsa tries to think of how her mother would handle this situation. Then suddenly, like earlier in the day, she hears her voice. *"Talk to him, Elsa, even if he doesn't respond, just talk to him."*

Following this unearthly advice, she tells her father about her trip to get the tree and her meeting Rudi. Heinrich finally looks down at his plate and picks up his fork and knife. Elsa does the same, and together they eat in silence, barely tasting their meal.

When they finish, Elsa clears the table and takes her father into the living room to sit in his favourite armchair. She goes over to the tree and removes a small package, which she hands to him. "Fröhliche Weihnachten, Vati," Elsa says while attempting a smile.

Staring at the parcel, Heinrich notices his wife's handwriting on the paper, and it immediately causes him to tremble.

"Here, let me help," Elsa says, taking the gift from her father. After opening it, she hands it back to him. Inside is a small framed photograph of her mother, together with a card signed *"To my dearest husband, with all my love, Frieda."*

Heinrich glares at the photo and his tremors intensify. Tears well in his eyes, and a few seconds later, he stands and throws Frieda's picture into the corner, breaking the frame and shattering the glass. Then in a fit of rage, he stomps over to the Christmas tree, knocking it over, sending decorations and lit candles scattering over the rug.

"*What are you doing, Vati?*" Elsa screams with alarm as she runs over to stamp out the candles before they cause a fire.

Heinrich ignores her and makes his way to his room, leaving Elsa to deal with the consequences of his actions.

A few tense minutes later, she manages to extinguish all the candles before collapsing on the floor beside the remains of the tree and the broken decorations. "I'm sorry, Mutti! I tried so hard! *I'm so sorry!*" she says aloud, burying her head in her hands and sobbing. She has never felt *so* alone.

"Come now, Elsa! Get up and wash your face and clean up the mess, ja?" her mother tells her. Bewildered, Elsa lifts up her head and looks around the room. *I am going crazy*, she thinks, but after a moment, she stands up and does exactly what she knows her mother would want.

Chapter 15: Christmas Day

ELSA SLEEPS FITFULLY as vivid dreams invade her unconscious mind, causing her to toss and turn all night. In many of the dreams, she sees herself in the darkness of the factory desperately searching for her mother but never finding her. Others have Elsa screaming soundlessly while rapidly sailing down a never-ending laundry chute. Some torment her further when her mother's bloody face suddenly comes to life. Flaming eyes stare at Elsa as the expression contorts with sinister laughter. Following each nightmare, she wakes in a cold sweat and has difficulty catching her breath, but despite this, Elsa finds herself drawn back into her dreams.

When the sun finally rises, she gets up to make herself some tea, and while the kettle heats, she tries to approach her father. After Heinrich once again fails to respond, Elsa feels it best to leave him alone.

As she does the breakfast dishes, a sudden knock startles her, nearly causing her to drop the plate she is washing. Elsa quickly dries her hands before going to the door. When she opens it, Erich stands before her wearing a look of concern. She is immensely relieved to see him and hugs him fiercely.

"Rudi told me about your mother, Elsa. I'm very sorry."

She looks at him and nods, feeling her emotions choking her. "Can we go for a walk? I think I need some air."

"Sure, anything you want."

Elsa turns to get her coat and Erich steps into the apartment. He looks around and notices the burn marks on the rug and the ruined tree. "Is everything alright?"

"Everything is fine. It was an accident. I guess I didn't set the tree up correctly, and it tipped over," she says, not knowing why she is covering up for her father.

Erich somehow doubts this was an accident, but he remains quiet and waits for Elsa to get ready.

When they leave the apartment, Erich takes hold of Elsa's hand, giving it a supportive squeeze. She smiles back at him appreciatively.

"I'm so glad you're here."

THE AIR IS cold, and the snow crunches beneath their feet as they walk. They watch as families make their way to church. The children run and laugh, so innocent and unassuming. *How can the world continue to go on normally, while my life has been completely shattered?* Elsa yearns for her childhood years and feels very sad knowing they are gone forever. *What will the future hold for those children? What will it hold for anyone?*

They continue walking in silence until they arrive at the park where they sit on their favourite bench in front of the snow-covered fountain.

"What will you do now?"

"Take each day as it comes. What *else* can I do?"

"What about your father?"

Elsa looks at him as though the question were absurd. "I will take care of him."

"He should be taking care of *you*, Elsa!"

"Well, he *can't*, so I must take care of *him*, just as my mother did. *She would want me to!*" she shouts as hot tears spill down her cold cheeks.

Erich reaches into his pocket, giving her a handkerchief. "I'm sorry, Elsa. I spoke out of turn. It's not for me to tell you how to live your life."

She nods and thanks him, and they sit in silence, watching the snow float around them like feathers from a broken pillow. Elsa stares at the handkerchief, noticing the monogram. "This is *your* handkerchief?"

Puzzled by her question, he answers, "Well, sure it is, silly. Who else's handkerchief would I have?"

Elsa shakes her head and opens her purse, pulling out another handkerchief, which she unfolds and hands to Erich.

Confused by this, he takes it and looks at the monogram. He is shocked to discover that it is one of his own handkerchiefs. "I don't understand. *Did I give this to you?* I don't remember giving it to you."

"*You don't?* Well, I guess you wouldn't remember. It was a long time ago."

Erich looks questioningly at her, and she smiles.

"You stopped to help a family stranded on the road many years ago, do you remember? A wagon stuck in the mud?"

He thinks for a few minutes when his expression suddenly changes. "I *do* remember! I gave my handkerchief to a little girl."

"That's right—that little girl was *me!*" Elsa says with her smile widening. This is the first time she has felt any sense of happiness since her mother's accident.

Erich looks deep into Elsa's eyes, and something about them is suddenly more familiar to him. "Wow, this is *incredible!* Can you *believe* this?"

"I guess we were destined to meet again. Mutti always says..." She then stops for a moment, realizing her mistake. "Mutti always *said* that everything happens for a reason," Elsa corrects as her thoughts trail off.

They sit quietly for some time until Elsa finally tells Erich that she needs to go back and check in on her father.

Standing outside her apartment building, Erich reaches into his pocket and pulls out a beautifully wrapped box, which he hands to Elsa. "I know this is a difficult time for you, but Fröhliche Weihnachten, my Elsa."

She looks down at the gift in her hand and tears well in her eyes. "I haven't anything to give *you*, Erich!"

"It's okay."

Elsa carefully unwraps the package and opens the box. It contains a silver brooch with blue stones forming the shape of a flower. "It's beautiful, Erich, but it's *too* much!"

"Nothing is too much for you, *mein Schatz,*" he says with affection, gently lifting her chin and gazing into her eyes.

Elsa feels her cheeks radiate with heat. After they share a long embrace, she kisses him tenderly, to which Erich responds in kind. "Vielen Dank, Erich. You have made my Christmas better than it could have ever been." She turns slowly and reluctantly walks up to the entrance as tears fall down her cheeks once again, only this time, they are tears of joy.

Chapter 16: An Aunt's Love

AFTER THE HOLIDAYS, Tante Ida comes from Berlin to attend Frieda's funeral. She plans to stay with Elsa and Heinrich for a few days to help them in any way she can, and Elsa is grateful, even if it means having to give up her bedroom.

When she looks at her aunt, she sees her mother, and although they were not identical twins, the resemblance is strangely comforting to her.

Unfortunately, Greta and the boys didn't make the trip, and although this disappoints Elsa, once her aunt explains the situation and the inherent danger to them, she understands. Their well-being means more to her than having them attend the funeral, and she prays for their continued safety.

Peter is also absent, and Elsa isn't sure whether he has yet received word of their mother's death. She knows her brother will feel guilty for not attending the funeral and being there for the family, but this is just another hardship of war.

Heinrich is there but remains quiet and withdrawn. He has not spoken since Christmas Eve, and Elsa doesn't force him. She is hopeful that he will eventually come out of his silence.

Erich is there to support her, and for that, she is very thankful. He has spent countless hours listening to her, holding her and when necessary, drying her tears.

With the ground frozen solid, Frieda's body, like others in Hamburg, remains in a crypt until the ground has thawed enough to make burial possible. The funeral is nothing more than a church service, but it still gives Elsa a sense of peace.

"I really appreciate you being here," Elsa tells Erich as they stand outside the church.

Erich gently touches her cheek and looks into her eyes. "You know I wouldn't let you face this day without me."

ONCE ELSA INTRODUCES Erich to Tante Ida and her father, Heinrich stares at him as though he could see right through him, but he says nothing. Finally, after a few awkward moments, he retreats to his bedroom and shuts the door.

Erich and Ida sit in the living room and talk quietly while Elsa goes into the kitchen to make some tea. They talk about the effects the war is having on Berlin and speculate what the future may hold for the country.

When Elsa returns with the tea and cookies she has made, Ida looks at her and smiles. "You must come to Berlin to visit me, Elsa. It will do you good to be away for a while. Perhaps we can also arrange for you to visit with Greta and the boys."

"Maybe," she answers, being very non-committal.

"We will make arrangements before I leave, ja?"

"Can we discuss this tomorrow, Tante Ida?"

"Of course, Liebling, that would be fine."

Friends stop by throughout the afternoon to give their condolences. Finally, as evening approaches, the visits come to an end.

While Elsa cleans the kitchen, Erich enters and gently embraces her. "I have to leave now," he says regretfully. "I promised my mother I would join her for supper tonight. Will you be alright?"

"Don't worry, Erich, I'll be okay. Tante Ida is staying for a few days so I won't be alone."

After Erich says goodbye to Ida and wishes her a safe trip back to Berlin, Elsa follows him into the hallway, closing the door behind them. She thanks him for coming to support her through this stressful day and kisses him before heading back inside.

ELSA CONSIDERS HER aunt's offer all night, and the next morning she agrees to visit her in Berlin. They discuss arrangements for her to come and stay for two weeks in April. Elsa will ask Herr Lubeck for time off from work to make the trip, and she is almost certain he will allow it.

Ida is glad that her niece plans to visit her because she knows how difficult it will be for her now that she has lost her mother.

Since Ida and her husband couldn't have children, she has always been very close to Frieda's and thought of them as though they were her own. Her motherly instinct has taken over, and she wants nothing more than to give Elsa the love and support she needs during this difficult time in her life. If it were up to her, she would have Elsa move to Berlin to live with her permanently, but Ida knows her niece would never agree because she feels a great responsibility for her father.

"I like that boy Erich. He is very nice, you know, Elsa," Ida says.

"I think so too."

"Did Mama ever meet him?"

"Only once, a long time ago," Elsa says and proceeds to tell her aunt of their roadside meeting so many years before.

Astounded by the story, Ida forms a slight smile and reaches over, gently placing Elsa's hair behind her ear. "I'm sure Mama liked him as much as I do and would be happy that the two of you have found each other again. You know that all things happen for a reason, Liebling."

OVER THE NEXT few days, Ida helps her niece pack up her mother's personal items to give to charity. It is a difficult exercise for Elsa, but she is glad her aunt is there to help her sort through everything.

Heinrich remains silent, despite Ida's many attempts to bring him out of his grief, and Elsa worries that he may never speak again.

"Don't give up on Papa. You must keep trying to get him to talk. I know he will, once he has gotten over the shock of losing Mama. It has only been two weeks, so you must be patient and give him time."

"I will do my best to try to get him back, but I'm afraid that I have lost him to himself."

Ida holds Elsa's face in her hands and looks into her eyes. "You must be strong, my child, and have the patience to deal with him. Life isn't easy, especially now, but without strength, none of us can get through it. You know that we never face anything in life that we are not able to handle. Every obstacle we encounter only makes us tougher."

"But what if I don't know how to deal with things that happen? What then?"

"You do what you think is best. If it doesn't work out, then you keep trying until it does. You must always keep your faith."

Elsa knows her aunt is right, and she embraces her. "I miss Mutti," she whispers into Ida's ear, and tears form in her eyes.

"We all do," Ida says as she, too, is overcome with emotion.

Elsa is extremely grateful that her aunt is with her and slowly realizes how alike both her mother and her twin sister were. She hopes that she can be just as kind and understanding to her own children someday.

As Ida prepares to leave for her home in Berlin, Elsa enters the bedroom with a look of sadness on her tired face.

"I wish you didn't have to go, Tante. I will miss you terribly."

"I will miss you, too. Although the circumstances of my visit are not the best, I have become accustomed to being with you and your papa." Ida embraces Elsa and looks into her eyes. "I will see you in a few months, ja? We will have a lovely visit when you come to Berlin."

Ida reaches into her pocket and takes out an envelope, handing it to her. "Here, Liebling, you take this and use it however you see fit."

Elsa takes the envelope and opens it to find it filled with Reichsmarks. "I can't accept this, it's too much. Besides, you know Vati—he is much too proud to take charity—even from you."

"I don't want you to tell him. This is for you, and you alone. Your life will be much harder without Mama and even though this will not replace all that you have lost, it will, at least, make your life a little bit easier, ja?"

Elsa looks at her with appreciation and nods. "Dankeschön, Tante Ida. It will definitely do that."

Chapter 17: Berlin

IN THE MONTHS that follow, Elsa continues to work at the factory and care for her father the best she can. Heinrich still refuses to speak, and he wanders around the apartment in a trance-like state. Elsa talks to him regularly in the hope that she will eventually break through the barrier of silence he has erected.

She and Erich continue to see one another and their feelings for each other grow with each passing day. He is an immense comfort to her in her time of mourning, and Elsa finds herself thinking about him constantly. When they are together, she feels a sense of joy and contentment. She has never felt this way before but assumes that this must be what it is like to be in love.

Herr Lubeck agrees to give Elsa a two-week leave of absence from the factory, and as she prepares for her trip to Berlin, she becomes more excited. She has not visited there for many years, and she is hopeful that Tante Ida can arrange a visit with Greta and the boys.

Elsa can't imagine how difficult the situation must be for her only sister, especially with having to care for the children on her own. She hopes that if she can see Greta, it will bring some happiness into both their shattered lives and perhaps she can help her find a way to deal with her unfortunate situation.

Leaving her father for two weeks is a huge concern for Elsa, but Petra has agreed to check in on him. *I wish I could just leave him to care for himself, but since he has always been so dependent on others, he would never be able to do things on his own.*

"Don't worry, I'll take good care of your papa. Just go and have a nice time in Berlin."

Elsa is thankful for having such a good friend, and knowing that Petra will assume the responsibility of caring for her father in her absence reduces the stress of leaving.

AFTER THE FOUR-HOUR trip, Elsa gets off the train in Berlin and searches for her aunt. When she isn't able to find her, she sees a young man holding a sign with her name on it, so she approaches him.

"I'm Elsa Schumacher."

The man tips his hat and smiles. "I am Carl, Frau Traupt's driver. She has asked me to pick you up and take you to her apartment."

Elsa is surprised that Tante Ida wasn't at the station to meet her as arranged but assumes that she was probably too busy planning for her visit to make the trip.

When Elsa arrives at her aunt's apartment, she sees her standing in the hallway. Overjoyed, she rushes to greet her. "Guten Tag, Tante Ida!"

"My dear girl," Ida says, and tears suddenly stream down her wrinkled cheeks.

Fear immediately grips Elsa, and she feels her heart hammering against her ribs. "What is it? What's *wrong?*"

Ida wipes her eyes and leads her into the apartment. "Put down your things and come sit with me."

Elsa complies and patiently waits for her aunt to speak.

"It's Greta and the children... They've been taken away," she says, trying to catch her breath.

"*What?* What do you mean '*taken away?*'"

Ida explains that she received the news from her most trusted friend, Lisbeth, who has been caring for Greta and the children.

"Apparently, two SS officers came to Greta's apartment and took her and the boys away. Lisbeth believes that they may have been identified from the confiscated documents my brother-in-law had in his possession when he was arrested. I know Greta has always been cautious on the rare occasions she went out, but it's possible that she could have been recognized by someone and reported."

Elsa sits there speechless while her brain tries to comprehend what she has heard. *How can this be happening?*

"This is *my* fault! I should have kept them here with me, but I thought it would be safer for everyone if they lived on their own under assumed names. I should have *never* done it!" The older woman trembles as an insurmountable feeling of guilt attacks her.

Elsa takes Ida's hand and strokes it gently, trying to console her. "Nein, Tante, it's *not* your fault. You could have done nothing to change the outcome. You did everything you could for them. Even if they were here with you, they would have found her and the children eventually, and they may have taken you as well."

Ida knows Elsa speaks wisely. She has heard rumours of people disappearing or taken for no apparent reason, and the thought of what lies ahead for Greta and the twins causes her emotions to come crashing together like ocean waves during a violent storm.

"Lisbeth tried to learn where they were taken. She went to the Reich Main Security Office pretending to be Greta's landlord and told the officer that she owed her money for the rent. All she found out was that they are at a work camp and will be released in time."

Elsa has heard of these camps. They are for prisoners of the Reich, and it is rumoured to be horrible for those held captive there. She has heard many stories about people starving and dying from disease in these places, but she tries to block those disturbing thoughts.

Ida does her best to make Elsa's visit a pleasant one despite the dire situation that has befallen their family. They do some sightseeing, but even this isn't as nice as it once was. Many museums are now closed, and the presence of soldiers everywhere provides a constant reminder that theirs is a country at war.

"I'm so sorry, Liebling. This was supposed to be a relaxing visit to help you get over Mama and give you a break from Papa, and now all of this is put upon you!" Ida says as they wait on the platform for the train that will transport her niece back to Hamburg.

"There's nothing to be sorry about. Despite everything, you managed to make my stay a pleasant one. I know you feel responsible for what happened, but we have to have faith that things will be better soon," Elsa says, even though she has her doubts.

"I know, Liebling, you are right. Have a safe trip home, and I will see you next time, ja?"

She hugs Ida one last time and boards the train. Once Elsa finds a seat, she loses herself in her thoughts. *Dear God, how much more can one family take? Please, help me to cope and keep me strong.*

Chapter 18: Parental Dilemmas

ERICH IS AT the train station to meet Elsa when she arrives in Hamburg. They remain locked in an embrace for a few minutes as the rest of the world moves around them. He reaches for her suitcase and takes her hand. "I missed you, Liebling. Let's go now, ja?"

Elsa nods and they make their way through the crowd. She is quiet on the way home because if she were to speak, it would most likely cause her to cry. Erich assumes her silence is due to her tiredness from the journey, so he doesn't encourage any conversation between them.

After Elsa puts her suitcase in her room, she and Erich sit on the sofa in silence. She wrestles with her emotions and finally tells Erich about Greta and her family. Elsa trusts him and realizes that she doesn't want to keep things from him.

Once she reveals her secret, Erich sits quietly staring at the wall while he considers the seriousness of what Elsa has told him. A few seconds later, he turns and takes her in his arms. Although Erich has always supported her through difficult times, it is an immense relief knowing that this information has done nothing to change that, and she is glad to have finally told him.

"I'm really sorry, Elsa. I know this is hard for you, especially so soon after losing your mother. It just doesn't seem right that this should happen." Erich shakes his head and tries to make sense of it. "Please let me know what I can do to help."

"Dankeschön, but I highly doubt there's anything anyone can do. I just have to take each day as it comes and pray that Greta and the children will be safe."

Erich nods, not knowing what else to say. They sit in silence, wrapped lovingly in each other's arms, and it isn't long before Elsa calms down and eventually drifts off to sleep.

LATER THAT AFTERNOON, the apartment door opens and Heinrich stomps in. He sneers at Erich and looks to Elsa with contempt.

"Hello, Vati, how are you?"

"How do you *think* I am? So, you *finally* came back, ja?"

Her father's comments confuse her. *I don't understand why he's so upset. He knew when I was coming back.* She ignores his words since responding would only make things worse, but Elsa is relieved that he has finally spoken.

"Have you eaten, Vati?"

"Of course, I have! I'm not an *invalid!*"

The sting of her father's reply upsets her, but she keeps calm, using a comforting tone when speaking to him. "I know you're not. I just wondered if you wanted me to make you something."

"I don't want anything from you!"

Erich watches silently as Elsa and her father converse. It takes every ounce of control he has not to intervene and come to her defence. He wonders how she can put up with him. *If only I could say something! That man should be put in his place!*

"I have news about Greta and the children," Elsa says carefully.

"I told that girl she was no longer my daughter, so whatever happens to her and those children is not *my* concern! *She* is the one responsible for the mess she finds herself in!" Heinrich fumes and heads to his bedroom, slamming the door.

STARING OUT THE window of his room, Heinrich once again thinks about his eldest daughter and his grandchildren. Anger over their situation causes him to tremble. *This is her fault! She should have never married that Jew!* Heinrich's thoughts and feelings run wild, and he shakes his head in an attempt to clear it. *How can I put the sole blame on Greta? I was the one who gave my blessing to their union.* Suddenly, the consequences of his past actions dawn on him, and he is consumed by guilt for having cut ties with Greta and the boys. *God forgive me, but I thought I was doing the right thing.*

AFTER HEINRICH'S EXPLOSIVE outburst, Elsa is humiliated by his heartlessness.

Erich approaches to console her, but she moves away. "I'm sorry, Liebling, but you'd better go now."

"I won't leave you this way."

"*Please*, Erich? I'm exhausted from my journey. We'll see each other tomorrow, ja?"

He hates the thought of going but respects Elsa's wishes and heads toward the door. She follows him there and holds him close.

"Don't worry about me, I'll be okay."

Erich bends down and kisses Elsa tenderly. "I worry about you because I love you. Please try to get some rest. I'll see you tomorrow."

Elsa makes her way to the kitchen after Erich leaves. Sitting at the table, she replays the incident with her father. *Could I have handled things differently? What would Mutti have done? Perhaps I shouldn't have gone to Berlin to visit with Tante Ida. Maybe if I had stayed home, things would have been different. Well, I guess it doesn't matter since I can't change what happened. I just have to try to put this behind me and live each day the best way I can.*

THE NEXT DAY, when Erich and Elsa are together, they don't speak about what happened. They spend the afternoon making small talk and enjoying each other's company.

Erich is very concerned about the emotional abuse Elsa endures. *I wish you would just stand up for yourself, Elsa.* He understands the difficulty of dealing with someone who is unreasonable. He encounters this with his own mother and feels he has learned how to handle these situations. *Maybe if she sees how I deal with Mama, it may help her.*

"I wonder if you might come to meet my mother, Elsa. I have told her about you, and she would like me to introduce you."

Elsa is surprised that he has mentioned her to his mother because she knows they don't get along well. "If you want me to, then, of course, I will meet her."

"Wunderbar! I will make the arrangements, ja?"

THE FOLLOWING SATURDAY, Erich calls on Elsa, and they go to his mother's apartment for lunch.

"I'm very nervous," Elsa confesses as they walk.

"Ach, don't be! It's no big deal!" Erich assures her with a wink.

When they arrive at the apartment, Erich makes the introductions. "Mama, I would like you to meet Elsa Schumacher. Elsa, this is my mother, Anna Wahlberg."

"I'm pleased to meet you, Frau Wahlberg." Trembling, Elsa hands her a small bouquet of flowers she bought from a passing street vendor they encountered on their way there.

Anna thanks her, giving them to her son to put into a vase.

"So, Erich tells me you work at the uniform factory."

"That's right."

The two women continue making small talk until Erich returns. Anna then goes into the kitchen to finish with preparations for lunch and Elsa follows her, offering her assistance. Anna asks her to set the table, which she is more than happy to do.

When they finish eating, Elsa helps clear the table, and the three of them sit in the living room.

"So, when will the two of you get married?" Anna asks.

Stunned by her forwardness, the young couple looks at one another, and Elsa's face turns red.

"We haven't talked about that *yet*, Mama."

"You haven't? Well, I thought that was the reason you wanted me to meet Elsa. You aren't getting any *younger*, Erich. You're almost 30, and people are talking about you!"

"So let them talk! Why does it matter to you or them what I do with my life? It's no one's business but my own!" Erich feels his anger increasing by the minute and tries to control it.

"Ja, *your* life! You do not care about your *poor mother!* I probably will not live to see Christmas!"

Erich shakes his head in disgust. "Ach, here we go again—always with the talk of dying! You'll probably outlive us all!"

"How dare you speak to me that way! Have you no respect for the woman who gave you life?"

Erich quickly gets up from his chair, knocking it over, and he takes Elsa by the hand. "You give me no reason to respect you! Oma was more of a mother to me than you have ever been! Come, Elsa, we are leaving now."

Anna remains seated with a scowl on her face. "Fine, go then!"

What Elsa has witnessed shocks her, but she now realizes that she and Erich have something in common. They both have a difficult parent to deal with—and they both deal with them in different ways. *Was Erich right to yell at his mother?* Elsa knows that it is not her place to judge since she is unaware of what has transpired in their past, but she hopes never to see Erich that angry again because it frightened her.

Chapter 19: The War Hits Home

AS THE SUMMER of 1940 continues, Heinrich scarcely leaves his bedroom. Elsa does her best to make a life for them but finds herself spending more time with Erich when she isn't working then she spends at home, and Heinrich seems oblivious to her actions.

One afternoon while Elsa is at work, her father receives a telegram indicating that Peter lies wounded in a field hospital in Belgium. The news sends Heinrich deeper within himself, and Elsa, although upset, tries to cope with yet another tragic episode in their lives.

A TRANSFER A month later brings Peter to the army hospital in Hamburg, and Elsa takes Heinrich to visit him. They are unaware of the severity of his injuries, and Elsa speaks to the doctor before they go in to see him.

"He will never walk again. Shrapnel has severed his spinal cord, and he will require much care," explains the doctor.

Elsa is heartbroken by the news, but her father shows no emotion. When they go in to see Peter, he is asleep. They haven't seen him in over a year, and Elsa is stunned by his appearance. *He looks so thin and pale!* She reaches down and touches his hand, and after a few moments, he opens his eyes and smiles at her.

"I knew you'd come," he whispers. "You look so grown up, Elsa."

"Vati is here, too," she tells him, wiping a tear from her eye.

Peter looks over to see his father staring back at him from the corner of the small hospital room. "Hello, Papa."

Heinrich blinks and does his best to reply, but his words come out no more than a whisper. "How do you feel, son?"

"I feel nothing right now. They gave me something for the pain so all is good."

A while later, a nurse enters the room and tells them they must let Peter rest. They say their goodbyes, promising to come back to visit the next day, and Elsa and Heinrich leave.

PETER'S INTENSIVE TREATMENT lasts almost a year and along with it, the added strain on Elsa to provide for the small family and keep it together. Erich has been by her side through it all, and she is grateful for his unwavering support.

Arrangements for Peter's release from the hospital and his ongoing care are finalized in April 1941, and he finally comes home. Elsa gives up her bedroom so that he can have a quiet place to convalesce, and she sleeps on the sofa.

The hospital sends a nurse to the apartment to care for Peter during the day while Elsa is at work, but since Peter requires around-the-clock care, it leaves Elsa with the dilemma of how to care for him at night. Seeing no other alternative, she speaks to Herr Lubeck at the factory to ask his permission to work the day shift only. This would allow her to tend to her brother at night once the nurse has gone home. Her supervisor agrees because he feels the company owes a tremendous debt to Elsa and her family after the tragic accident that claimed her mother's life.

Elsa is run ragged with everything she must now do. She barely has time for herself, and she and Erich see each other rarely. *"You can manage things, Liebling. Just remember, you must take one day at a time,"* she hears her mother say.

AFTER WEEKS OF caring for her brother, Elsa suffers from extreme exhaustion, causing her to lose weight, and sickness eventually claims her. Her illness is so severe that she isn't able to work or care for her brother and father.

Petra comes in to nurse Elsa when she can, and Erich takes time off from work to help her.

"This is too much for you, Elsa," Erich tells her once she is healthy enough to get up. "You can't continue this way."

"I know, but what *choice* do I have?"

He kneels down and takes her hand. "I love you and want to make you my wife, Elsa. Will you marry me and allow me to take you away from all this?"

Elsa's cheeks flush and tears blur her vision. "I would like nothing better, but who will care for my father and brother? And how will they live without my income from the factory?"

"Don't worry, Liebling, I have spoken to your father, and he has given us his blessing to marry."

This shocks Elsa and renders her speechless.

"Arrangements have been made for an evening nurse to care for Peter, and we will check on your father regularly. I promise you we will help them both as much as we are able. Well, Elsa? What do you say? Will you marry me?"

Tears flow down Elsa's face, and she is finally able to answer. "Ja, Erich, of course, I will!"

DURING THE SUMMER of 1941, Erich and Elsa begin the lengthy process to obtain a marriage licence. With the Nazi relocation of Jews to the labour camps, it is much harder to get than before the war. They must provide documented proof to ensure that they are not Jewish, and even after supplying the evidence required, it is still delayed.

Weeks turn into months, and the couple gets discouraged. Erich has lost track of the number of times he has gone to City Hall trying to have the licence issued, only to learn that the application has yet to be processed. He goes back once again, hoping things might be different this time. When he arrives there, he goes to the front desk, and the clerk recognizes Erich and sympathizes with him.

"I'm sorry, but the request for your marriage licence is still under investigation, Herr Kaufmann."

"Is there any way that you know of to help speed up this process?" Erich asks the man at the desk.

The clerk looks around and whispers, "*Well,*" he says, stopping briefly to look around again, "if your fiancée were pregnant, the paperwork would be rushed—but you didn't learn this from me."

Erich nods, thanking the man, and he leaves the office with a tiny spark of hope. On his way to see Elsa, he thinks about how she will react to the clerk's suggestion. *Will she even agree to this?*

WHEN ERICH FINALLY gets up the nerve to inform Elsa of the possible solution to their problem, she is quiet for a few minutes before agreeing to it.

"Are you sure you want to do it this way?"

"We love each other, and we've tried everything else. If this will speed up the process, then this is what we *must* do."

Erich is relieved that she has agreed to this plan of action, but he has some reservations. "What about your father? Won't he be angry?"

Elsa knows this goes against her strict upbringing, but she loves Erich so much, she couldn't bear the thought of them not being together. "I'm sure he won't be happy about it, but he has rarely been happy about *anything*, so what difference will it make?"

"I hope you're right, Elsa. *I sure hope you're right.*" He kisses her tenderly and smiles. *My desire for you grows every time your lips touch mine. I can hardly wait for the opportunity for us to express our love for each other!*

IN EARLY FEBRUARY 1942, Elsa is happy to discover she is pregnant. Erich takes the doctor's note indicating her condition to City Hall, but it isn't until the end of May that they finally receive the licence and can arrange for the wedding to take place at the beginning of June.

Although Heinrich had given his blessing to their marriage, now that it is a certainty, Elsa must tell him. Erich insists that they inform her father together, and she is relieved to have his support since the thought of approaching him frightens her.

"Should we tell him about the baby?" Erich asks.

Elsa quickly shakes her head and her face pales. "I don't think that's a good idea."

"Well, I'm sure that once the baby comes, he will be able to figure out that you were already pregnant before our marriage, and it may be worse than if we told him now. I think we should just get it over with, it will be easier for us."

Elsa considers Erich's suggestion for a few minutes and takes a deep breath. "Okay, Liebling, I guess you might be right."

"YOU JUST COULDN'T wait, *could you?* Ach, you young people have no patience!" Heinrich says after Elsa and Erich tell him their news.

"We really had no other choice, Herr Schumacher. Marriage licences are tough to get. Our application was held up for months due to the backlog since each one must be thoroughly investigated to prove the heritage of the couple," Erich says patiently. "This was the only way to speed things up."

Heinrich shakes his head in frustration, but even in his tortured mind, he realizes that there is nothing he can do.

"Now that Elsa must quit work, you must take full responsibility for her. *I will not* care for her any longer," he tells his future son-in-law.

Erich is about to reply, but Heinrich doesn't allow him the opportunity and immediately turns his attention to Elsa, pointing his finger at her. "You are now on your own!"

Elsa stares at him in disbelief. *He's delusional! I've been on my own ever since losing Mutti, and I've been taking care of him! Does he really think he has taken care of me my whole life?* She pushes those thoughts to the back of her mind and swallows her anger. "We know that Vati, and we don't expect anything from you."

Chapter 20: A New Beginning

THE DAY OF the civil ceremony, Elsa and Heinrich are the first to arrive at City Hall. As they wait for Erich and his mother, Heinrich sits beside his daughter on the wooden bench outside the marriage office.

"You are now going to be Erich's wife and his responsibility, but just remember, if there are any problems between the two of you, they are entirely *your* fault. Do you understand?"

Elsa looks at him too stunned to speak, but she manages a nod. She turns away and stares at the wall, trying to make sense of what he has said. *Any problems between us are my fault?* Elsa tries not to let him upset her on this special day, but despite her best efforts, his words still haunt her.

When Erich and Anna finally arrive, he smiles warmly at his bride-to-be. Immediately sensing Elsa's distress, he whispers, "What's wrong, Liebling? You haven't changed your mind, *have you?*"

"Of course not. I guess I'm just nervous."

"*Nervous?* There's nothing to be nervous about. You and I both know we're meant to be together. Otherwise, we would have never found each other again."

"I realize that. Don't worry, Erich, I will feel better once the ceremony is over and we can start our life together. This whole process has taken far too long, and I'm just tired."

He places a kiss on Elsa's cheek and grabs hold of her hand. She instantly feels her stress diminish. As she looks at him, he winks back, and she manages a smile. *I know now that everything will work out fine.*

After a celebratory lunch at his mother's home, Erich and his bride head off to their apartment to begin the next chapter in their lives.

ONE DAY, ON his way home from work, Erich unexpectedly meets Petra's cousin, Rudi, on the street. On leave from the army, Erich invites him to come to the apartment for a visit. He knows Elsa will be thrilled to see him. Although Rudi seems hesitant, he finally accepts the invitation.

"Look who I found, Elsa!" Erich says when he and Rudi enter the apartment.

She turns quickly to see the two men standing there. "*Rudi!* I'm so glad to see you!" Elsa rushes over to him and embraces him.

"You look lovely, Elsa! Congratulations on your marriage and the little one on the way."

She blushes slightly and thanks him. *I feel like I'm as big as a house! How can I possibly look lovely?*

Elsa sets the table for supper, and the three of them sit down to eat and catch up. Erich and Rudi have some schnapps, and this seems to brighten Rudi's mood. They sing songs and make Elsa laugh—it's so good to be together again—almost like old times. It gets very late, and both Erich and Rudi have had too much to drink.

"Stay here tonight Rudi. You're in no condition to head back home," Elsa tells him.

Rudi graciously accepts the offer, and Elsa instructs Erich to set up the cot beside the stove while she retrieves a pillow and blanket from the bedroom. Once the makeshift bed is ready, Elsa kisses Erich and wishes both men a good night.

After she goes to bed, Rudi becomes very sombre. He stares at the wall in a dream-like state.

"What is it, my old friend?" Erich asks.

"It's all this fighting! It's *too* much! I must go to the Eastern front after my leave. I... I just don't think I can do it anymore," Rudi admits with despair while running his hands through his hair.

Erich has never seen his friend fall apart like this, and he isn't sure how to help him. He pauses briefly and says the only thing he can think of to try to lift his spirits. "I'm sure it's terrible, but we need good men like you to fight for our country."

Rudi looks back at him with tears in his eyes. "Terrible doesn't even come close to describing the senseless brutality of this God-forsaken war. We're going to lose our country, Erich. This will all be for *nothing*. The Führer has signed our death warrants."

Rudi's comments shock Erich. *Lose Germany?* This thought has never entered his mind. *Could Rudi be right?* "All I can say is that your sacrifice is appreciated by all of us, but you have to be careful with what you say. You can get yourself into a lot of trouble."

"I know, you're right. Ach, give me another drink and then go to bed with your lovely wife, ja? You are a very lucky man, Erich," Rudi says with a wink.

"Are you sure? I hate to leave you when you're like this."

Rudi places his arm around Erich's shoulders. "Go to bed, my friend. *I'll be okay*. I'll just finish my schnapps and go to sleep. I have to be up early to catch the train."

Reluctantly, Erich says goodnight to his friend and enters the bedroom. Elsa is already asleep, so he undresses quietly and lies down beside her. *Poor Rudi, I can't imagine what he's had to endure. I wish I could do something for him. I just don't understand how things could possibly be this bad when all the reports say we are winning the war and that it will be over soon. Is what we are being told a lie?* Even with these thoughts flooding his mind, the alcohol helps him to fall asleep soon after his head hits the pillow.

HOURS LATER, A loud noise rouses Erich and Elsa from a deep sleep, causing them both to jump.

"*What was that?* Elsa asks with alarm.

"I'm not sure, but I want you to stay here, okay?"

"Okay, but *please be careful.*"

Erich opens the door slightly and listens for a moment before he says, "*Rudi?* Is everything alright?" When his friend doesn't respond, he reaches for the light switch and snaps it on. What he sees both shocks and nauseates him. Rudi has taken his service revolver and shot himself in the head, splattering brain matter and blood all around the small kitchen. *Dear God in heaven!*

"What is it, Erich?" Elsa asks with fear.

"Stay there! Do not come in the kitchen!" he says as he closes the door behind him. Even though Erich knows his friend is dead, he goes to him and checks his wrist for a pulse. *Ach, Rudi! How could you do such a thing?* He shakes his head, trying to come to terms with it. *I should have never left him alone!*

After a few minutes, Erich comes back into the bedroom and sits on the bed shaking.

"Tell me, Erich. *What's happened?"*

Erich takes her hand and swallows hard before speaking. "Rudi broke down and told me that he couldn't face going back to the fighting and without seeing any other option open to him, he... *took his own life."*

Elsa shakes her head and tears form in her eyes. *"Nein! Not Rudi!* He would never do that—*never!"*

Erich holds her and rocks her until she eventually cries herself back to sleep. Afterward, he goes back to the kitchen with a bucket and rags to clean up the mess that was once his friend. *Elsa cannot see this, especially in her condition,* Erich thinks as he takes a sheet and covers Rudi's body.

He contemplates what he needs to do while filling the bucket with water. *I must report this to the Wehrmacht, and I really ought to do so before touching anything else.* Erich leaves the pail in the sink and returns to the bedroom. Although the thought of making the report scares him, he realizes he has no other choice. He will bring Elsa along with him so she won't be alone in the apartment.

When Elsa finally wakes, Erich informs her that they must go to report Rudi's death. The two of them dress in silence and get ready to leave.

"Are you set to go, Liebling?"

Elsa responds with a subtle nod while her stomach churns at the thought of what lies beyond their bedroom door.

"Just remember to keep your eyes closed. I will guide you through the kitchen and out of the apartment, okay?"

Elsa manages another nod and prepares herself for the difficult task ahead.

Erich takes a deep breath before opening the door. "Okay, Liebling, close your eyes now."

Elsa does what her husband says, and she feels him take hold of her arm as he guides her toward the horrific scene that awaits them.

Once outside of the apartment, Elsa opens her eyes and notices the pale look on Erich's face.

"Are you alright?" she asks with concern.

"I'll be okay once I get some fresh air."

ERICH AND ELSA hold hands as they quietly walk to the trolley stop. Along the way, they pass a group of Jews wearing the yellow *Jude* stars, waiting to be loaded on trucks headed for the train station. Although this has become a familiar sight, it is one that always sends shivers down Elsa's spine. It reminds her of her sister, Greta, and her family and the fear she has for their safety. She says a silent prayer, not only for her sister but also for these unfortunate people persecuted for their beliefs. *What will become of them? Why can we not all just live together in peace?*

"You there, halt! Papers please!" says one of the soldiers guarding the group.

Erich and Elsa stop immediately. Elsa feels her stomach knot with fear, and noticing her anxiety, Erich squeezes her hand reassuringly before turning to face their interrogator. They give their identification to the man with the rifle and standby waiting patiently as he reviews the documents.

"Where are you going?"

"To the Wehrmacht office, mein Herr," Erich replies calmly.

"And what business do you have there, Herr... Kaufmann?" the soldier asks while looking at Erich's identification.

Erich's mind races for an answer that will satisfy the officer without divulging the reason for their visit. "I am reporting for duty today, mein Herr," he says convincingly.

"Wunderbar! There is nothing better than fighting for the fatherland, ja?"

Erich nods, and after checking their documents and being satisfied that they are legitimate, the soldier hands them back.

"Everything is in order. *Heil Hitler,"* the man in uniform says enthusiastically as he clicks his heels and gives the Nazi salute.

"Heil Hitler," Elsa and Erich reply in unison. They quickly take their leave and continue in the direction of the trolley stop without looking back.

"I hate it when we get stopped like that. It always makes me feel like I'm guilty of something," Elsa whispers.

"I sometimes think it's a game to them. Seeing how far they can push us before our fear makes us say or do something that will get us into trouble. It's disgraceful how far some of these soldiers will go to purposely make someone's life a living hell."

LATER THAT DAY, after having reported Rudi's death, two officers come to the apartment to investigate. They are unmoved by what they see and it isn't long before they are satisfied that Rudi has taken his own life. The officers fill out some forms and remove his lifeless body, leaving Erich to clean the mess that remains.

The newlyweds never speak about the terrible incident that occurred in their kitchen. They try their best to forget.

Chapter 21: The New Addition

IN THE EARLY hours of October 8, 1942, Elsa wakes from a restless sleep as the twinges of her first few contractions grip her. She lies in bed patiently waiting for the waves of pain to increase. Once they become more intense, she places her hand on Erich's arm and gently shakes him. "Erich—wake up."

"Hmmm—what is it?"

"The baby's coming, we need to go to the hospital."

"That's nice," he replies groggily, turning over and snoring loudly.

Elsa shakes him again. "*Hey,* wake up! I said the *baby's coming!*"

Suddenly, the implication of what his wife tells him registers within his sleepy brain and he jolts upright. "*The baby?* It's coming *now?*"

"That's what I've been trying to tell you, *silly fool,*" she replies with a laugh.

"*Ach, ja?* Well, come on then—*let's go!*"

It isn't long after they arrive at the hospital that Elsa gives birth to a healthy six-pound baby girl.

When Erich is allowed to visit Elsa, he stands at the entrance of the room, shyly peeking in.

She looks at him and smiles. "Well, aren't you coming in, Vati?"

He walks over and looks at his wife holding their new daughter. "Did it... um... *did it hurt?*"

Laughing at the absurdity of the question, Elsa replies, "Ja, just a *little* bit."

She hands the baby to Erich, and he holds her nervously. He looks down into her tiny face and immediately falls in love with her. "She's beautiful, just like her Mutti. What should we call her?"

"If it's okay with you, I want to name her Frieda."

"I think it's a perfect name. She looks like a Frieda."

ERICH AND ELSA are very happy and content now, and life goes on as one day turns into the next.

Elsa visits with her father and brother twice a week to cook for them and do any necessary chores. She brings Frieda with her, and that always seems to brighten everyone's mood.

Many rumours quietly surface about the atrocities faced by Jews all over Europe and about the approaching Russian army. The Nazi government downplays these stories, calling them propaganda and continually make reports about the success of their war efforts, claiming that victory will be theirs very shortly.

As conflicting as the news has become, Elsa feels like what she hears isn't real. Perhaps this is a way for her brain to cope with these terrible stories. Even though she still worries about her sister, right now, her world seems far removed from everything happening around them, giving her a false sense of security.

ELSA'S BROTHER, PETER, suffers a severe infection due to his injury, and in the spring of 1943, he returns to the hospital. The doctors aren't able to cure him, and in mid-May, he passes away.

Elsa is very upset to lose her only brother and with this, the harsh reality of war once again shakes her to the core. Thankfully, with Erich's support, she is able to deal with yet another tragic loss.

Her father is once again distant and scarcely speaks to anyone. Elsa expected he would react in this way, and she does her best to cheer him by bringing baby Frieda to visit. Frieda seems to have a knack for getting her Opa to smile, even if it is only for an instant, and this gives Elsa hope that he will once again overcome his grief.

Chapter 22: July 28, 1943

THE SOUND OF an air raid siren whirring in the distance wakes Erich and Elsa yet again. Sadly, it is a sound that has become all too familiar with the people of Hamburg. They have experienced many bomb attacks over the past three days and have spent more time in the shelters than out of them. During every attack, they pray that their home will withstand the bombs, and so far, they have been fortunate.

While Erich quickly grabs their few meagre belongings and once again throws them into a suitcase, Elsa gets Frieda and wraps her in a blanket. The baby shows her displeasure at being taken from her crib by wailing loudly, and Elsa does her best to console her.

During the time it takes them to get to the street, they hear the unmistakable whistling of the bombs as they make their earthbound descent.

"Come on, Elsa, we must hurry. The bombs are getting really close this time."

They scurry out of the building and watch the crowds of people, many of whom carry possessions they cannot bear to leave behind, rush to the safety of nearby shelters.

Erich and Elsa quickly join the anxious horde, and perspiration from the intense summer heat causes their clothes to immediately stick to their bodies.

Elsa's fear escalates with every bomb that drops. She holds Frieda protectively against her body and tries to calm her frazzled nerves. Suddenly, the ground shakes beneath their feet, and in the distance, the night sky flickers as enormous arms of flame give a mesmerizing, almost dance-like performance toward the heavens. Looking for solace, Elsa turns to her faith and says a quick prayer for their safety.

THE DIMLY-LIT shelter is unbearably hot, and the humid air is thick with dust, making breathing difficult.

After some time, the frightened occupants feel a distinct blast of pressure that tells them the bombs are closer than before. When this happens, a man loses control and fights his way out of the shelter. Others try to stop him from leaving, but they are unsuccessful. They watch in horror as a blast of hot wind catches him mid-step, sucking him up into the air like a cyclone. The screaming man becomes a human torch carried into the oncoming flames.

The sight of this causes a surge of panic. People scream and push their way to the rear of the shelter, away from the entrance.

An older man with an air of authority takes control of the situation. "Everyone, please calm down and listen! We have to leave the shelter at once and make our way to the river."

"The river? You're *crazy!* I'm *not* taking my family from the safety of the shelter! Didn't you see what happened to that poor man when he tried to leave?" a man shouts frantically.

"If we don't leave now, the fire will eat up the remaining oxygen, and we'll suffocate in here. Our only hope *is* the river. It's only about 30 metres behind us, so we should be able to make a run for it."

The man looks around the shelter and his eyes settle upon Erich. "You there—bring that fire axe over here and smash the bricks of this back wall as fast as you can, we don't have much time."

Erich complies with the man's instructions and is immediately drenched in sweat. Perspiration stings his eyes, but he ignores it and concentrates on his task. "Come on, you *damned* wall—*break!*"

Elsa holds Frieda tightly, watching while her husband desperately smashes away at the bricks. Strangled by fear, she puts her faith in his efforts to save them all. *God in heaven, please help us.*

After what seems like an eternity, the wall finally gives way.

"Help me clear the opening," Erich says impatiently.

Both men and women anxiously pull the loose bricks away by hand, creating a gap large enough through which they can make their escape.

Standing at the newly created exit, Erich and the man in charge can immediately feel the scorching heat, and they cautiously peek out to see whether they can safely make it to the river. The fires burn brightly, illuminating the area, and the arid wind blows the flames wildly around them.

Erich hears screaming and looks over to the road. He watches in horror as the melting asphalt engulfs a family, swallowing them within its sticky, burning goo. The man beside him notices the look of shock on Erich's face and grabs his arm to get his attention.

"Look over here," the leader says, pointing to the right.

Erich turns, and they notice that the way is relatively safe, other than the severe heat emanating from the smoldering ground.

"We have no other choice," the leader whispers to Erich. "Come along everyone, *let's move!* Go to the right and run to the river. When you reach it, get into the water as far out as possible."

Erich assists the terrified men and women out of the shelter. "Run, but be very careful not to fall."

When it is Elsa's turn, Erich kisses her. "Go now, Liebling! I will join you soon, ja?"

Elsa looks at him and shakes her head indignantly. "*I won't go without you!*"

Upon seeing the exchange between them, the leader tells Erich to go with his wife and child. "I will stay to finish here, the three of you go now!"

They thank him and wish him good luck before racing toward the river. Along the way, the soles of their shoes soften beneath their feet, and the air becomes so hot that their lungs burn with each attempted breath. *We are in hell!* Elsa thinks while they continue their journey in silence, watching in horror as the city around them becomes an inferno.

WHEN THEY FINALLY reach the river, they cautiously wade into its murky depths. At first, the water feels cold against their hot skin, but after only a few seconds, it becomes warm as bath water. They go out further until the water surrounds them almost up to their necks. Taking their wet handkerchiefs, they cover their faces. Erich takes baby Frieda and holds her against him, carefully keeping her tiny head above the water, and she doesn't make a sound. They stand together quietly with several other dazed people as the shock of the experience hits them. No one speaks, but they all share the same feelings.

Erich isn't sure how long they have been in the water, but he knows it has been quite some time judging by how their skin has wrinkled and by the shivers that now attack their bodies. He fears that they will suffer from hypothermia, but he keeps this thought to himself. *We need to get out of the water.*

A while later, the air becomes slightly cooler and easier to breathe. The bombs have finally stopped falling, and although many fires still burn, they have decreased in severity.

People with faces blistered from the intense heat, slowly make their way out of the water, looking like zombies as they climb up and stand on the smouldering riverbank.

Erich, with Frieda in his arms, and Elsa by his side, join the dazed group on the shore. They sit down on the scorched ground, shivering uncontrollably while the heat from the earth warms them slightly, and they wait for the sun to rise.

Even with the onset of daybreak, thick black smoke makes it difficult to distinguish day from night. It takes some time before the sky clears, and the devastation around them becomes apparent. Upon viewing the extent of the damage, Erich knows now that their apartment building, like so many others, lays in ruin. Elsa has come to the same conclusion, and it causes her to weep.

"What are we to do now, Erich? There's nothing left! *Nothing!*"

He goes to her and places his arm around her damp shoulders. "Shhh—I know, but we're alive, and that's all that matters. We can find another place to live and the things we need—those are replaceable—our lives are not."

Elsa nods, knowing that he is right, but it doesn't make it any easier to accept. Then another fear enters her mind. "We must find Vati and your mother!"

"Come, Elsa," he says, offering her his hand. "Let's go and search for them."

THEY BEGIN THEIR journey through the once great city toward the location of Heinrich's apartment. As they make their way from the river, the sight of the destruction shocks them, and the odour of burning flesh immediately attacks their nostrils. Many fires still burn and smoke stings their eyes. Erich helps Elsa to climb through piles of bricks and mortar that block their path. The gruesome sight of charred bodies that look more like tailor's dummies than the remains of real people traumatizes them as they plod their way through the rubble.

After two hours, they reach the neighbourhood where Elsa grew up. Many buildings are in ruins, but some managed to survive the bombings with only minor damage. They are surprised to see that Heinrich's building is one of the fortunate few, although the exterior shows scorch marks and the roof will require extensive repair.

They enter cautiously, and once they get to the apartment, Elsa bangs on the door and shouts to her father. A few seconds later, he appears at the threshold. Relief washes over her, and she rushes to embrace him. "Thank God you're alright, Vati!"

Heinrich pushes Elsa away, and he looks at the three of them, dirty from their ordeal and shakes his head. "Have you been in the trenches?"

Erich and Elsa exchange a knowing glance. They realize that the raids have put Heinrich's mind back into the past, so they play along with him, hoping to avoid any unpleasantness.

"Ja, Vati, we just came from there. It was horrible!"

As they try to get settled, Elsa goes into the bathroom to wash up, but the taps fail to turn on. The extensive efforts to fight the fires that rage throughout the destroyed city have used up the water supply, so she does her best to clean Frieda and herself using a cloth dampened with the water remaining in the kettle.

Once they are somewhat clean, Elsa looks inside the wardrobe in her old bedroom for any clothes they could use. Thankfully, a few of her things are still there. After changing, she finds a cotton undershirt in the drawer and fashions it into a diaper. Elsa then dresses Frieda in one of her old blouses. *It isn't the best, but at least, she's clean and dry.*

Elsa takes the baby into the living room where Erich and her father sit in silence.

"Elsa, you and Frieda stay here. I'm going to search for Mama, and once I find her, I will return," Erich tells her.

Although she wants to protest, she knows he is right. "Okay, Liebling, but *please* be careful."

AS ERICH APPROACHES the area where his mother lives, he notices a makeshift shelter and a line of people waiting for blankets, food, and water. He joins the queue and patiently waits his turn. When he is finally inside the tent, he must give his name and home address to the attendant. The clerk informs him this is necessary so that there will be a record of the survivors from the area. Erich nods, giving the information, and he receives a bag with food, a container of water and one wool blanket.

"Can you check the list of survivors for my relatives?" he asks the clerk hopefully.

"There's a list up on the board over there. You can check it yourself—just don't hold up the line."

Erich thanks him and waits for his turn to view the list. After a few minutes of scanning, he sees his mother's name, and he is flooded with relief. *Thank God she survived.*

He exits the tent and searches through the endless crowd of stunned people. A while later, he finally sees her and rushes over to where she sits on the ground. "Mama! Mama!"

Anna looks at him with surprise and struggles to get up. Erich helps her to her feet and hugs her briefly. She informs him that her apartment is gone, and she has nothing but the clothes she is wearing. He nods, telling her they are in the same predicament.

"Come, Mama, let's go to Heinrich's apartment."

Knowing she has no other alternative, Anna reluctantly agrees.

THE RAGGED FAMILY sits in the living room silently pondering their circumstances.

"We must leave Hamburg," Erich finally tells them. "The city is a target for enemy attacks for many reasons, but mainly because of its industry, large port, and shipyards. These bombings will continue until there is nothing left."

"And where would we go, Erich?" Elsa asks with despair.

"I have heard that things are much better in Neubrandenburg. The five of us could go there and make a fresh start."

"How do you know it will be any different there?"

"Neubrandenburg doesn't have the industry like here in Hamburg, so it isn't a threat to the Tommies."

Noticing that this has done nothing to alleviate Elsa's distress, Erich takes her hand and looks into her worried eyes. "Liebling, I know how afraid you are, I am too, but if we stay, we may lose more than our belongings. It just isn't safe here any longer. We must leave now while we still can and have faith that life will be better for us there."

"We have no other option, Erich?" his mother asks.

"I'm afraid not."

"Very well, if you honestly believe that, then we *must* go."

Hugging herself for comfort, Elsa finally speaks. "Okay then, I suppose we're off to Neubrandenburg."

Heinrich suddenly comes out of his stupor, and a wild expression paints his face. He stomps his foot on the floor with anger. "I *will not* leave Hamburg! You can go, but I will *stay!*"

"But Vati, it isn't safe to stay here."

"*Nein!* I'm not going!" he says, heading toward his bedroom and slamming the door behind him.

"What are we to do, Erich? We can't just leave him here."

"I don't think we have a choice. If he's adamant about staying, how can we make him come with us? Let's prepare to leave. Pack up whatever rations Heinrich can spare and maybe by the time we're ready to go, he will have changed his mind."

Once they are ready, Erich and Elsa approach Heinrich. He sits in his armchair staring into space. After repeated attempts to communicate with him, Elsa sadly realizes that they must leave her father behind.

THEY MEET PETRA by chance as they walk down the hall toward the exit, and Elsa is relieved to find her unharmed. She hugs her and tells her of their plan to leave Hamburg.

Although Petra is upset that her best friend is leaving, she understands. *I wish Papa would agree to go too.*

"You have a family to worry about now, Elsa. You're making the right decision. You really have no other choice."

"I know that, but Vati refuses to come with us. I'm so worried about him, but we just can't stay. Are you and your family going to leave, too?"

"Papa believes the worst is over, so we're going to stay," Petra says with a slight quiver in her voice. "Please don't worry about your papa, Elsa. I'll look in on him and make sure he's okay."

Elsa hugs her again. "Dankeschön, Petra. Stay safe, and we'll see you soon."

Chapter 23: Casualties of War

AS THEY MAKE their way to the train station, they learn that of the eighteen rail stations in the city, only three are left in operation. Thankfully, the central station, Hamburg Hauptbahnhof, survived the bombings with only one of its clock towers having been destroyed.

At the station, the number of people waiting to leave astounds them. Several in the crowd fight for a spot on one of the trains. Some people trample over others or push them aside. *How barbaric! These people have lost their minds!* Elsa thinks while watching the commotion.

After many uncomfortable hours of waiting, an announcement from the loudspeakers informs the horde of people that no further trains will be leaving the Hamburg station that day.

"Well, I guess we'll have to head back and stay with Heinrich tonight," Erich says as he picks up their belongings.

THEY FIND THE apartment door unlocked and enter carefully.

"Are you here, Vati?"

Elsa approaches her father's room and stands at the threshold. "Vati? Are you in there?" Hearing no reply, she opens the door and immediately lets out a scream. Her knees buckle beneath her, and Erich rushes to her side, grabbing her before she hits the floor.

He peers into the room and sees that Heinrich has taken a rope and hanged himself from the ceiling beam—his sad face blue and contorted.

"Come, Elsa, let's go to Mama, ja?" He shuts the door and leads her into the living room where Anna and Frieda wait. Elsa says nothing, as the trauma of what she has seen takes hold of her.

"Mama, take Elsa to the sofa."

Erich goes into the kitchen and pours a small glass of water from the rations they received, and he takes it to Elsa.

"This is my fault! If I hadn't agreed to leave Hamburg, he wouldn't have done this," she laments.

"Nein, Liebling, this is *not* your fault. Your father was a sick man. This has been building for many years, *you know that."*

Elsa straightens her body and wipes her face with her hands and nods. She knows Erich is right, but she wishes there was something she could have done to prevent her father's drastic actions.

When Erich sees that Elsa has settled down slightly, he leaves the women in the living room and returns to his father-in-law's bedroom with a knife to cut him down from the rafters. After cutting through the rope, Erich gently places Heinrich's body on the bed and covers him with a blanket. He then goes to see Petra to tell her the news of Heinrich's death.

Over the next few hours, the trauma gradually wears off, and Elsa ruminates about her losses. She has lost her mother, her sister, her nephews, her brother, and now her father, all in just over three years. *This war has taken its toll on my family, but I won't let it defeat me. We will survive and live to see a better life, so help me God!*

Elsa looks at Erich with determination. "We will stay here tonight, and tomorrow we will leave for Neubrandenburg!"

The change in Elsa's usually passive behaviour surprises both Erich and Anna, but they know that trauma has a way of changing people.

EARLY THE NEXT day, after arranging to have Heinrich's body taken away, they once again head to the station in hopes of getting on a train to Neubrandenburg.

Fortunately, the tracks going eastward are still intact, making travel there possible—for now. The biggest issue facing them is getting on one of the trains.

During the wait, the distant whistling sounds of bombs cause people to instinctively duck for cover and several run into the station for shelter. Luckily, the attacks remain far enough away, allowing the exodus to continue.

It takes nearly eight hours before finally securing a spot that can accommodate the entire Kaufmann clan. They, like so many others, are crammed into boxcars. Without seats, they must stand on the dirty, straw-covered floor.

As the train chugs along, Elsa thinks about her aunt and wishes there was some way to contact her to let her know they survived the bombings and have left Hamburg. Although she realizes this is impossible, she prays Tante Ida will be safe and that they will one day be reunited.

After travelling close to 300 kilometres, the train finally pulls into Neubrandenburg. The discomfort of spending many hours standing in the heat of the crowded, stinking box car has taken its toll on its passengers, but their long journey is far from over. They now must deal with mayhem as thousands of people make their way along the platform and into the overcrowded train station.

THE DISPLACED FAMILY wades through the sea of anxious people, walking without knowing their final destination.

When Frieda cries, Elsa rocks her gently to console her. "We have to stop so I can feed the baby."

Erich finds a shady spot under some trees not far from the road. They sit on the hard ground and enjoy a slight reprieve from their arduous journey.

"Where are we going to go, Erich?" Elsa asks once she finishes feeding Frieda.

Preoccupied with his racing thoughts, he fails to respond.

"Erich? Answer me! Where are we going?" she asks impatiently.

He turns to his wife and gives her a smile of reassurance. "Don't worry, Elsa. We'll find a place soon, I promise you."

She wants to believe him, but until they have actually found refuge, she can't stop her overwhelming feelings of dread and despair. *I sure hope Erich is right. We can't go on this way for much longer.*

Erich enters each building they pass in hopes of securing shelter for his family, but they are all filled to capacity. Left without any other choice, they must continue their trek.

Hours later, they find themselves in the country. With nightfall upon them, they are desperate to find sanctuary. They finally see a farmhouse in the distance and make their way to it. Erich goes to the door and speaks to the farmer while the rest of the family patiently waits.

Erich secures two small rooms in the house by striking a deal with the farmer, named Max Schnell. They will receive room and board as payment for repairs Erich will make around the farm. It isn't ideal, but considering the circumstances, it is the best he can do.

The repairs are completed a few weeks later, and during that time, the two families become good friends. Max allows them to stay, with the proviso that Erich pays him what he can, and Erich happily takes on odd bricklaying and carpentry jobs around the area to repay the farmer for his kindness and generosity.

THE FAMILY HAS a quiet Christmas that year, and they celebrate the New Year of 1944 with as much hope and enthusiasm as possible.

By the end of February, Elsa discovers she is pregnant once again, and on October 25th, she delivers a baby boy in Anna's bed, with the assistance of Max's wife, Liesel. The little family is growing, and they are happy despite the circumstances they are forced to endure. They name the boy Rudolf, after the friend they lost. *Little Rudi will grow up to know a better world,* Elsa thinks as she looks into his tiny face. *By the grace of God, may you never know the hardships of war.*

WITH RATIONS NOW in short supply, life is becoming increasingly more difficult. Thankfully, living on the farm provides them with a variety of vegetables, but not much else. Although illegal, they depend on the Black Market for other items, and that takes a great deal of money. Unfortunately, cash is scarce, and payment for the majority of the work Erich does for people is made using the barter system or with ration cards.

The family, like others in the area, suffers the consequences of the diminishing supplies. Baby Rudi is incredibly thin since Elsa's milk doesn't adequately nourish him. She must improvise to supplement his diet, and resorts to putting potato soup broth into a bottle to feed him. Elsa worries that he will get sick without proper nutrition and blames herself for this. Her own weight is down to less than forty-five kilos, and she has been without her monthly flow since becoming pregnant.

Concerned about the health of her children, Elsa takes them into town to see the doctor.

Upon seeing Elsa, the doctor insists on examining her first. "Well, Frau Kaufmann, you needn't worry about your monthly courses. Once you gain some weight, they will return."

After examining Rudi, the doctor informs her that he suffers from malnutrition, the effects of which are already visible by the slight distension of his tiny stomach.

"What am I to do, Herr Doctor? I can't feed him properly without milk," she says tearfully.

"You must feed him three tablespoons of butter daily, one at each meal to alleviate the symptoms little Rudi suffers."

Elsa nods and watches him examine Frieda. *How will we ever get the butter Rudi needs?*

A few minutes later, the doctor reports, "Frieda is somewhat thin, but due to her age, she stands a better chance of survival than Rudi."

Elsa thanks the doctor and readies the children for the journey back home. On the way, she tries desperately to figure out a means to obtain a supply of butter to help her baby. Without the hard currency or items of value to barter to get it from the Black Market, her only hope is that Erich will have some idea of what to do.

AFTER LEARNING ABOUT their visit to the doctor, Erich feels responsible for not adequately providing for his family, and it makes him more determined than ever to improve things for them. *This is all my doing! I brought us here, so I must find a way to make things better.*

Erich hears of possible work in Schwerin and decides to go there to try to secure a steady job that will pay him the money they so desperately need.

Elsa hates the thought of him leaving, but she knows that she can't travel with the children just in the hope that he might find work.

"You know I have no other option, Elsa. I can't make money here. Mama will help you with the children, and once I have found work I will come for you."

"I'm sorry you have to do this. I feel it's my fault that things have turned out this way."

Erich holds his wife in his arms and assures her that she isn't to blame. "Be strong, Elsa. I promise things will get better soon."

"Are you sure it's safe in Schwerin? It's not that far from Hamburg."

"It's still almost one hundred kilometres away from there, and from what I've heard, it hasn't experienced the same devastation. Please try not to worry. I have to do this for all of us."

Elsa nods reluctantly, fighting back her tears. "Please be careful, Liebling. I don't know what I would do if I lost you."

Erich speaks to his mother and asks her to help Elsa with the children while he is away. She isn't happy with this turn of events, but she agrees to make the best of the situation.

"I will do what I can, my son. Take care, be safe, but remember we need you, so don't let us down, ja?"

Erich shakes his head. "I won't, Mama, don't worry. I'm *not* my father. Just help Elsa with the children until I return."

While Erich is away in Schwerin, Anna honours her promise and cares for the children while Elsa helps with chores around the farm.

Although Erich has left them enough provisions to last until his return, Elsa is fearful that they may run out. She does sewing for people in the town in exchange for things they need, and this gives her a sense of pride knowing that she can contribute something to care for her family in Erich's absence.

MAX AND LIESEL are called away to visit a sick relative in the next town, leaving Elsa and Anna in charge of the farm until their return.

One afternoon, while the children are down for their naps, the door bursts open and two Russian soldiers storm into the house.

The intrusion startles the women, but they try not to show it.

"What do you want?" Elsa asks them gruffly, hoping her tone won't convey the fear that threatens to swallow her.

The men can't communicate what they want with words, but their actions soon become apparent. They push Anna aside and unbutton their trousers as they make their way toward Elsa. Realizing the inherent danger, Elsa's mind frantically searches for a way to protect her family. Instinctively, her feelings erupt, and she contorts her face until it turns red before falling to the floor convulsing and gasping for air.

Confused by what they have seen, the soldiers turn to Anna.

Not knowing what else to do, she yells at them and pounds her fist on her chest and coughs. "TB! TB!"

The soldiers look at one another and seem to comprehend what the old woman is trying to tell them, and they quickly do their pants up and rush out of the house.

Once they are gone, Anna breathes a sigh of relief and rushes to her daughter-in-law's side. "Elsa! Elsa! Are you *alright?*"

Elsa stops moving and cautiously opens one eye and whispers, "Did they leave?"

Bewildered, Anna looks down at her. "I... I don't understand. You were *acting?*"

"Well, of course, I was!"

Anna helps Elsa to her feet, and the two women laugh and hug each other. They both realize that this action hasn't only saved their lives, but those of the children as well, and this gives them a newfound respect for one another.

Chapter 24: Schwerin

ERICH SENDS WORD that he has found work and a place to stay in Schwerin before returning to Neubrandenburg to prepare for their move.

After a long, exhausting journey, Erich finally arrives at the farm. Elsa is overcome by a sense of relief when she sees him, and the two of them hold each other.

"I missed you, Liebling," Erich whispers. He looks around their room and sees that Elsa has already packed up their meagre belongings, most of which fit into Rudi's pram.

"The trip to Schwerin won't be an easy one. The train can't take us the entire way there, so we'll be forced to travel a considerable distance on foot."

"Why is that?"

"Many of the tracks have been destroyed by the bombs, leaving us no other choice."

"How far will we have to walk?"

"About forty kilometres."

"Dear God! How are we supposed to travel that distance with the children? Where will we sleep?"

"Don't worry, we'll find a place. We've been lucky this far, and there's no reason to believe that our luck will change. If all goes well, we should be able to make the journey in four to five days."

"I don't know about this, the trip seems insuperable. Remember, we have to carry the children."

"We'll manage, I promise you, Liebling. Have I ever let you down?"

"Nein, but…"

"Don't you trust me?"

"Certainly I do." Elsa realizes that this move is for the benefit of their family. While the prospect of travelling that distance on foot terrifies her, she finally concedes. "I guess we really have no other option."

He smiles and kisses her tenderly. "It will be fine, you'll see."

Anna shakes her head and regards her son with resentment when he tells her about their upcoming journey. "You can't expect *me* to walk all that way!"

"It's either walk the distance or stay here on your own—the choice is yours, Mama."

"And what am I to do without you? How will I live?"

"Well, I guess you've made your decision then, *haven't you?* We leave in three days."

Anna stands there flabbergasted. *How can he treat me like this? He's just like his father!*

ALTHOUGH TRAVEL WESTWARD should be safe, Elsa says a silent prayer after they leave the farmhouse in Neubrandenburg. She hopes they are doing the right thing, but her faith, coupled together with her trust in her husband helps to keep her fear at bay. *"Take each day as it comes, Elsa. Remember, everything happens for a reason,"* she hears her mother say, and Elsa smiles and feels more at ease with their decision.

The first segment of their trip by train brings them more than three-quarters of the way to Schwerin, but the most difficult part of the journey now confronts them. Erich places the pram with all of their belongings on the road and pushes it along while Anna and Elsa walk behind with the children in their arms. They face the path ahead with courage as they commence the long walk toward the city that gives them hope of a new and better life.

As evening approaches, they find safe shelter in an abandoned shed. Although it isn't in the best condition, it provides some protection from the elements. The next day they continue their travels, and by afternoon, they stop to rest in a farmer's field.

The farmer sees the exhausted family there, and he and his wife invite them in for supper. During the meal, the farmer tells Erich that he is going to the next town in the morning and offers to take them along in his truck. This kind action will take several kilometres from their journey by foot, and Erich thanks the man once again as he shows them to the barn where they will spend the night.

"I know it isn't much, but it's warm and dry," the man says.

The next day they are one town closer to Schwerin, thanks to the kindness of this stranger. Erich figures that if they are fortunate, they should reach their new home within the next two days.

"See, Elsa, I told you that our luck would continue."

"Ja, it seems you were right. Perhaps you have horseshoes in your blood," she says with a giggle. *I just pray that our good fortune lasts.*

THEY CONTINUE THEIR journey cross country when a group of three Russian soldiers suddenly stop them on the road. After their previous encounter, the sight of these men terrifies Elsa and Anna. Erich stands protectively in front of them but remains silent.

The soldiers look ragged and hungry, and they search the pram while the family stands by watching helplessly. Within minutes, they find a large stockpot, which they take, along with some small household items before getting back into their vehicle and driving off.

Relieved that the men left without harming them, Elsa laughs.

"What's so funny?" Erich asks.

"They took the pot!" she chuckles.

"Ja, *so?"*

"Won't those soldiers have a fit when they open it and find dirty diapers instead of soup?"

Elsa laughs harder, and Erich and Anna look at each other and laugh too. Before long, tears are streaming down their faces, and Elsa suddenly stops, with her expression turning serious. She now realizes that she has no diapers for Rudi, except for the one he is wearing.

"What will we do with only one diaper?" Elsa laments.

Anna turns her back to them, and they hear a ripping sound. She then hands Elsa a piece of her cotton slip. "Here, the young one has diapers now."

Elsa takes the fabric. *It will have to do.* She hopes they will arrive in Schwerin soon so that she can get the proper cotton cloth to make diapers for her baby.

THE NEXT DAY, the exhausted family finally reaches their new home, and Erich gets them settled. Their place is small and slightly rundown, but Elsa already feels at ease there. *Life will be much better now that we are here!* Her sense of optimism surprises her, but she has faith that, for the first time in a long while, things will finally improve.

Erich is now able to provide many of the basic necessities for his family. They get a small supply of restricted foods from the Black Market, and after a couple of weeks of supplementing Rudi's diet with butter, he looks somewhat healthier, which is a relief to them all.

Elsa and Anna work tirelessly to make a life for the family while the children grow and provide them with reasons to smile and laugh. *The children are what make this life livable,* Elsa thinks, and she is thankful for them and for the new opportunity they have been given.

Chapter 25: The End of Tyranny

ON THE AFTERNOON of May 1, 1945, Elsa and Anna take the children out for some fresh air. When they return home, they stop to say hello to a neighbour, and she invites them in for a visit. As the women sit talking, the *Reichssender Hamburg* radio station plays in the background.

Suddenly the broadcaster interrupts the music. *"The German wireless broadcasts serious news for the people of Germany."* Three drum rolls play. *"We have a report direct from the Führer's headquarters that our beloved Führer, Adolf Hitler, continued the fight against Bolshevism to his final breath and fell for Germany at his operational headquarters within the Reich Chancellery."*

"Before his death on April 30th, the Führer appointed Grand Admiral Dönitz as his successor. Today, the grand admiral—successor of the Führer speaks to the citizens of our great nation."

They continue to listen as the new leader promises to save Germany from destruction by continuing militant action against their enemies. He calls on the German public to maintain order and discipline by allowing the soldiers to do their duty for the Reich.

"Well, that was certainly unexpected," Elsa's neighbour says.

"That's for sure. I wonder what will happen now that the Führer is dead, and the grand admiral has taken over," Elsa replies.

Anna waves her hand casually. "Admiral Dönitz will continue to fight—you heard what he said."

"Ach, I don't know about that. The Führer had absolute control over people. It may be difficult for him to take over," the neighbour states.

Elsa nods adding, "I just hope he has enough sense to end this terrible war and let everyone get back living a normal life—if there is still such a thing."

"Well, I guess we will have to wait and see what happens," the neighbour says as she pours them each another cup of tea.

ON MAY 8, 1945, Erich arrives home early from work and enters their apartment excitedly. "Elsa! Mama! Come quickly!"

The women bring the children with them into the kitchen and place them down on the floor with their toys.

"What is it? *What's happened?*" Elsa asks fearfully. Erich's smile is unlike any she has ever seen him wear, and the sight of it makes her excited, but cautiously optimistic.

"It's over! It's *finally* over!"

"I don't understand, Erich, *what's over?*"

"The war! *The war is over!* Germany has surrendered to the Allies!"

The three of them hug each other and wipe tears of joy from their eyes. After Hitler's death, they hoped the war would end, and now that it has, they can hardly believe it.

The family, like so many others, attend a church service to celebrate the end of the war. People, visibly relieved, cry tears of joy as well as tears of sorrow for all they have lost. With cities laying in ruin, and the arrival of the Allied troops, the German people can't help but speculate what their future will be like. *Will it be better than before the war? How will we rebuild our lives? Will Germany pay the price for Hitler's wrath?*

AS THE REALITY of peacetime sinks in, Elsa is determined to learn the fate of her dear Tante Ida, and of her sister and nephews. Since leaving Hamburg, communication to Berlin was almost impossible, and she is now anxious to make contact with them.

Once Elsa is finally able to have use of a phone, she gives the operator her aunt's number and patiently waits for an answer. After some time, Elsa hears a man's voice at the other end of the line.

"Forgive me, I must have been put through to the wrong number," she says with disappointment.

"Who are you looking to speak with?" the man asks.

"I'm hoping to talk to my aunt, Ida Traupt. Would you happen to know her?" she asks hopefully.

"Is that you, Elsa?"

"That's right. How did you know?"

"It's Carl, your aunt's driver—you remember me, ja?"

"Of course, Carl. It's good to hear your voice. May I speak to Tante Ida, please?"

He pauses before answering. "I'm so sorry to be the one to tell you, but she died in May of 1941. The doctor said she had a heart attack and died peacefully in her sleep."

Elsa grips the receiver tightly, trying desperately to comprehend Carl's words. Her brain seems to refuse what her ears have heard, and she fights to control her emotions. *It's not true—it can't be!*

"Are you still there, Elsa?"

"Ja, Carl. Dankeschön for telling me, I'm sorry for bothering you."

"It's no bother. Please accept my belated condolences."

Elsa thanks him again and hangs up the phone. She remains there momentarily staring at the wall as the reality of Tante Ida's death slowly registers. The news devastates her and sweeps away any feelings of joy she previously had. It will take time, but once Elsa can come to terms with the loss of another loved one, she and her young family can begin the difficult process of healing and adjusting to post-war life.

WITH THE WAR now over, the first noticeable changes in the city of Schwerin are the influx of Allied soldiers and the removal of Nazi symbolism. The country, like others in Europe, suffers from inflation, making daily life extremely difficult. The hardships of war scarcely improve during peacetime. The only real benefit is the elimination of violence and bloodshed.

Now that the clean up of rubble and debris has slowly begun, so too has the process of rebuilding. Erich's work as a bricklayer keeps him very busy, although the pay is insufficient to meet the needs of his family.

"I don't know what we expected when we prayed for war to end," Erich says with despair. "Life is just as hard—maybe even worse in some ways—now that Germany is paying retribution for Hitler's actions."

"Don't lose hope, Liebling. We had almost six years of war. It will take a while before the country bounces back to its former glory," Elsa tells him.

"I know that, and I'm trying to be patient, but I guess I'm just tired and frustrated with everything."

ELSA AND HER family make their way back to Hamburg in 1947 to try to pick up the pieces of the life they once had there. With the city now under British occupation, travel there is regulated by special permit. Part of the application process includes filling out a questionnaire to prove they have no affiliations to the Nazis. After receiving the necessary permission, the Kaufmann family enters the remnants of their once vibrant hometown.

Even though it has been two years since the war ended, the devastation remains. They are surprised to discover many people living in tents, or in the basements of destroyed buildings due to the lack of adequate housing. Those fortunate enough to have a proper place to live must protect their homes. If a dwelling is found to be unoccupied for a period of time, there is a good chance that it will be seized and given to someone else.

With the Allies now in control of the food supply, rations are not much better than they were during the war. The relationship between the British and Germans is an uneasy one. Ordered to be cold, curt and aloof in their dealings, the Allies are torn between wanting to punish the people of Germany and wanting to help reform them to make certain that they can never again lead the country into another war.

Upon their return, the Kaufmanns are forced to stay at one of the many camps within the battered city while Erich desperately searches for a place to live. One day as he continues his hunt, Erich runs into his cousin, Hans.

"Is Tante Anna with you?"

"Ja, and my wife, Elsa, and the two children."

"Where are you living?"

"Right now we are at one of the refugee camps. I have been searching for a proper place for us, but it seems an impossible feat," Erich says with despair.

"Well, you're welcome to come and live with my family and me. It will be very cramped, but at least, it will be better than the camp."

"Are you sure, Hans? I hate to impose, and what will Trudi say?

"Don't worry, Erich, we are family, and right now we all have to pull together to survive any way we can."

Although the apartment is small and overcrowded, they consider themselves very fortunate to have a roof over their heads.

NOW THAT THEY are settled, Elsa is anxious to find her friend Petra. Without knowing how to conduct her search, she takes a chance and returns to her old neighbourhood. To her surprise, the building where she grew up is still standing. With her spirits lifted, Elsa quickly enters the complex and within minutes finds herself standing in front of Petra's apartment. She knocks but gets no response and resorts to calling her friend's name. After several attempts, Elsa finally gives up.

Crestfallen, she goes to each of the neighbours hoping to learn Petra's fate. Elsa finds many people are either not at home or are too afraid to open their doors, and those who do, tell her that they are unaware of what has happened to Petra and her family. She eventually finds herself standing before Frau Schroder's apartment, and a small glimmer of hope surges through her. When the door finally opens, Elsa is relieved to see her old neighbour.

"What do you want?" the elderly woman says gruffly.

"Guten Tag, Frau Schroder, how are you?"

She looks at Elsa, trying to place her face. "Do I know you?"

"I'm Elsa Schumacher, my mama was Frieda—you remember—don't you?"

The woman thinks for a moment. "Ja, of course! Come in, Liebling. Let me make you some tea."

"That would be lovely, Dankeschön."

Once she has poured the tea, her old neighbour sits down. "So, tell me, what happened to you after you left here?"

Elsa gives her a synopsis of her time since leaving Hamburg and Frau Schroder shares her experiences.

"Do you know what became of my friend Petra Braun?"

"Petra Braun? I don't think I know her."

"Well, sure you do. She and I were best friends. We used to visit you, and you baked us cookies, remember?"

Frau Schroder waves her hand carelessly. "Ach, she and her family probably moved away like everyone else. Not many of us stayed after the bombings, you know."

Elsa nods, feeling discouraged by her lack of progress in finding her friend. When she finishes her tea, she thanks Frau Schroder and leaves the apartment building.

As she walks back home, Elsa's disappointment grows. *I miss you terribly, Petra. I was so sure you would be here when I came back.*

BY 1949, ELSA once again feels an overwhelming need to find some connection to her pre-war life. She is determined to search for her sister, Greta, and her family, but doing so would require travelling to Berlin to make the necessary inquiries. Elsa knows that making this trip is impossible because of the needs of her young family, and this adds to the sense of loss she feels.

"Why don't you try writing to Berlin? Maybe they can search whatever records they have and notify you of their findings by mail," Erich suggests.

"I guess I could try that, even though I doubt it will work," she says with hopelessness in her voice. "But if nothing else, I will feel like I'm making an attempt to find them."

Elsa takes Erich's advice and writes several letters to the Red Cross in different towns in and around Berlin. She knows it will be tough to find information—if at all—due to the Allied occupation and the restructuring of the country. Germany is now a divided nation, consisting of The Federal Republic of Germany to the West, occupied by the US, Great Britain, and France, and the German Democrat Republic to the East, held by the Soviet Union. Berlin itself is split between the US and Soviet Allies, and this adds to Elsa's skepticism that she will ever learn the fate of her sister and her family.

Months go by, and Elsa's inquiries remain unanswered. She had hoped she would receive some reply, even if it were just to tell her that there was no information. Elsa can't hide her disappointment, and Erich does his best to cheer her. He brings her flowers and makes her small gifts in hopes of bringing her out of her despair, but his actions only provide her temporary happiness. In her sorrow, she once again hears her mother, calming her by reinforcing her past advice. *"You must be strong and continue to live one day at a time."* Elsa follows this suggestion by focusing all her thoughts and energies on her children and the needs of her family.

THE POST-WAR economy is slow to recover, and even though there are jobs for skilled trades, it is hard to make a comfortable living due to the many shortages of food and other items.

By 1950, things still don't improve much for the people of Germany, and Erich contemplates the idea of moving to another country to provide a better life for his family.

"I have applied for immigration to Canada," Erich tells his wife.

"Canada? Why Canada?"

"It's a very prosperous country, and they're looking for skilled trades so I stand a good chance of getting a job there."

"You're actually serious about leaving Germany?"

Erich nods. "Things are just too slow to recover here. I work hard, and still haven't much to show for my efforts. Not only that, food and other items are still scarce. As long as the Allies remain in control, who knows if it will ever get better?"

"I agree that things aren't the best, but are you sure it will be better in Canada? It's a risk leaving your native country to go off to one where you don't speak the language and the outcome is uncertain."

"I know you're scared, Elsa, but I really feel that this is the best solution for our family. You've always trusted me—don't stop now, Liebling. When my application has been approved, I'll go there to work, and once I make enough money, I'll send for you and the children. Everything will work out fine, and we'll be happy there."

Although Elsa realizes he is probably right, the idea causes her chest to tighten. "Alright, Erich. I know you have our family's best interest at heart, and I trust you to do what is necessary for our future."

Erich receives approval of his application to immigrate in May of 1951. He obtains a sponsor in Canada who arranges a job and a place for him to live, giving him the long-awaited opportunity for an improved standard of living.

WHEN THE DAY comes for Erich to leave, he and his family say a tearful goodbye. Elsa hugs him and gives him a parting gift—a brand new white shirt. "You must have a new shirt for our new country," she says bravely while trying to control her emotions.

"Dankeschön, Liebling. I promise to send for you and the children as soon as I can."

Erich leaves his family and boards the *SS Homeland*—the ship that will take him on his journey to a new life and a new adventure.

While onboard, he sells the shirt Elsa gave him to another man for fifty cents. When Erich lands in Halifax, Nova Scotia in June, he arrives with only the money from selling his shirt in his pocket and a load of determination.

He eventually makes his way by train to Hamilton, Ontario where his Ukrainian sponsor, Viktor, meets him. Thankfully, Viktor speaks German, and they become good friends. He helps Erich settle into a rental house, and prepares him for his job at the steel plant. Erich works on a labour gang fixing the blast furnaces. The job is strenuous and hot, but he is happy with his new home and knows that Elsa and the children will be too.

IN OCTOBER OF 1951, after saving enough money for their passage, Erich sends for his family to join him in Canada. They are fortunate to get tickets for the last sailing of the season, and they land in Halifax at the end of November. Rough seas made the voyage difficult, but they arrive unharmed.

After travelling 6,300 kilometres from Hamburg, they finally reach Hamilton by train. Exhausted but happy, their reunion is a joyful one, and Elsa and the children are anxious to start their new life together.

Part Two: Canada—A Better Life

Chapter 26: New Beginnings

THE FAMILY SETTLES into their little home in East Hamilton, not far from Viktor and his wife, Hanna. After a week in Canada, Hanna helps Elsa to enroll the children, now aged seven and nine, in school. Because they don't speak English, they are held back a grade to learn the language and get the fundamentals required for the Canadian education system. Frieda and Rudi are unhappy to be in classes with children younger than they are, but they have no other choice.

Although life is much different from what they are accustomed to, the family adjusts the best they can. Their house is cozy with only four rooms, but it is much better than the accommodations they left behind in Germany. Elsa works hard to make their new home comfortable by sewing curtains and adding other personal touches. She is excited to have her first refrigerator, electric stove, and washing machine. *Life is so much easier here.* It isn't long before Elsa wonders how she ever did without these luxuries.

The abundance of fresh fruit and other foods available in Canada astound Elsa and the children. They take photographs of fruit to send back to Anna in Hamburg to show her how much better life is for them now. Elsa writes her that they never again have to worry about dealing with ration cards, food shortages or buying food that isn't fresh. With food now readily available to them, their appetites grow, and for the first time, the children reach a healthy weight. Although Elsa was hesitant about moving to Canada, she is now thankful that they were given the opportunity. She knows that had they remained in Germany, they would probably never live as well as they do now.

ERICH'S WORK AT the steel plant is physically demanding, and after the day is done, he goes to the tavern with his coworkers to drink and unwind. Elsa isn't at all happy about his new habit because most nights he comes home drunk. She never knows when to expect him, and she keeps his supper warm in the oven awaiting his arrival.

One evening, Erich comes home late from the pub with his face swollen and his mouth bloody.

"What happened?" Elsa asks with concern.

As he opens his mouth to speak, she notices that his front teeth are broken.

"Were you in a fight?"

"No, it was nothing. Joe made a bet that he could hammer a four-inch nail into a two-by-four with his fist, which he did. I wanted to show him up, so I made a bet that I could pull it out—with my teeth. They broke off when I did, but *I won* the bet!" he says proudly, exposing the jagged remnants.

Elsa just shakes her head. *What a fool he has become! What's happened to the man I married? What could be the cause of this change in his behaviour?* This isn't what she expected with their new life, but she tries not to let it dominate her thoughts. *We've been through too much together to let this be an issue. After all, he's the man of the house and the one who puts food on the table and a roof over our heads.* She knows she can't complain since it is her job to take care of the needs of her family and look after of the house.

AS THE MONTHS pass, Elsa tires of Erich's daily routine of working and going to the bar. She notices that the money isn't lasting as it should, and they are living paycheque to paycheque.

When Erich returns home from the tavern one night, Elsa puts his supper on the table.

"Erich, we need to talk. The landlord came to the door today asking for the rent money. I told him you paid it, but he said you hadn't. Did you forget?"

He shakes his head as a look of annoyance crosses his inebriated face. "I *didn't* forget! There just wasn't enough money to pay it right now. I'll pay the rent on Friday when I get paid."

"Okay, but maybe you should make a budget. Pay the rent first and then other things in order when they are due to prevent this from happening again."

"You just let me worry about that! I'll see that everything gets paid. Don't *ever* tell me what *I* should do!" he says, slurring his words. He then gets up from his chair, leaving his uneaten supper on the kitchen table.

Erich's outburst stuns Elsa, rendering her speechless, and she blinks away tears while she cleans the kitchen. *What's happening here? Why is he acting this way? I don't understand this, we've always been able to discuss our problems.* As her thoughts continue spiralling out of control, she is brought back to her senses by the sudden shouts of the children from their bedroom. Elsa quickly pulls herself together before going to tell them to get ready for bed.

Elsa can't sleep that night, so she gets up and heads to the living room where she sits quietly, waiting for exhaustion to finally claim her. Suddenly her father's words resurface from the depths of her brain, as clear as they were all those years ago. *"Just remember this—if there are any problems between the two of you, they are entirely your fault. Do you understand?"* The memory of her father's statement on her wedding day shocks her. She had completely forgotten it, and it hits her like a blow to the gut. *No Vati, I don't understand! How can this be my fault? I didn't cause the change in Erich's behaviour, he did! He doesn't even realize the harm he's doing. I can't stand by and let him ruin the new life we have here. But how can I go against him? He's the one who earns the money and keeps a roof over our heads. What am I thinking? A wife is never supposed to question her husband. He made the sacrifice to come to this country to give us a better life. I'm sure the stress of that decision isn't easy for him. If it weren't for the children and me, he would have never had to leave Germany. No, I can't hold Erich responsible. Vati was right, this is my fault. I have to see that I make things better between us. I will have to learn to keep my thoughts to myself and watch what I say, no matter how difficult it will be for me. I have to have faith that things will work themselves out.*

THE NEXT MORNING, Elsa is in the kitchen making breakfast when Erich enters. He doesn't say a word but sits at the table waiting for his food.

"Good morning, Liebling," she says as she puts a plate of eggs, bacon and toast in front of him.

"Morning," he coldly replies.

"I... I want to apologize for the way I acted yesterday. I had no right to question your actions. Please forgive me—I just don't know what came over me."

"You are forgiven. Just don't let it happen again, ja?"

"I promise you, Erich, I won't ever speak to you that way again."

"Alright then. Can I have some more coffee?"

Elsa nods and obediently pours him another cup. She is relieved to have made peace with Erich, but deep inside a battle rages within her.

WITH THE CHILDREN out of school for the summer, Elsa must try to keep them entertained all day. She loves taking them to visit museums and parks in the city and having picnic lunches when they can. Although money is tight, she does her best to save some from the allowance Erich gives her for the food.

On Friday evenings, when the weather permits, Elsa packs their supper, and they meet Erich at the beachfront on Lake Ontario to eat and enjoy the refreshing breezes off the lake. The beach strip has an amusement park that reminds Elsa of the carnival back home in Hamburg. She smiles when she remembers this and is happy that they can share this with the children.

Frieda and Rudi teach English to their mother, and Elsa now feels somewhat confident in her abilities to communicate with others when she goes out. Although she is nervous about making a mistake, she knows this is the only way she can ever hope to become fluent. Most shopkeepers are very patient and understanding, helping her practice her new language and treating her with respect.

One day, Elsa visits a newly opened butcher shop. She walks in and peruses the aisles and the sizeable meat counter. She has never seen such a large selection of meats in her life.

A large man with a crisp white apron stands behind the display case. "Can I help you, Madam?"

Elsa slowly attempts to translate the German words forming in her brain into English. *"Ich mochte...* I'm sorry... I mean I would like... ah... ah..."

"What is it you *want?* I don't understand you—speak English *why don't you?"*

"I... I'm sorry. I want... ah... ah... *Schweinefleish,"* Elsa says nervously, pointing to the pork chops in front of her.

"What? Is that *German* you're speaking?"

"Ja, I am sorry, but my English is not yet so good."

"Well, we don't serve *Krauts.* Now, get out of my store!"

Unsure of what the butcher has said to her, she remains standing there. When she doesn't move, the man comes from behind the counter and takes her by the arm, leading her toward the door.

"No Nazis here! You get me, you *Deutsche Kraut?"*

Trembling, Elsa exits the shop. The word "Nazis" was enough for her to understand that even in a country like Canada, hatred against Germans exists. *What an ignorant man! If he doesn't want my business, I will take it elsewhere! Ah well, it isn't the first time I've come across such narrow-mindedness. I'm sure things will get better once we're permitted to become Canadian citizens.*

ELSA'S DAILY ROUTINE returns to normal in September when the children go back to school. She misses their company but busies herself with household chores that were neglected through the summer.

Erich continues his routine as well, but Elsa is careful not to say anything to annoy him. They still have issues paying bills, and she realizes that their financial problems are due to Erich's inability to handle money properly. *I wish I could just tell him my thoughts, but I refuse to be the cause of another disagreement. Ah well, I'm sure that he'll eventually figure things out. I just have to be patient.*

AFTER MORE THAN a year of struggling to get by, and receiving two eviction notices for late payment of the rent, Erich feels that he has failed his family—and himself. Disheartened, he turns to the bottle as a way of dealing with his problems.

Each day is a challenge in the Kaufmann household. Elsa wrestles with her feelings about Erich's behaviour and their worsening financial situation. *"You must talk with him, Elsa! Don't let this continue!"* she hears her mother warn. To this day, she still can hear her mother's voice, advising her and helping her through tough times. With the way things are going, she knows it is time for her to act. She must swallow her fear of confrontation and speak to him. *I will approach him on Saturday morning once the children go outside to play with their friends.*

When Saturday arrives, and the children are outdoors, Elsa finishes the breakfast dishes and turns to pour Erich another cup of coffee. As she does, the cup accidentally slips from her fingers and drops to the floor with a crash, sending coffee and broken shards of ceramic everywhere.

"I'm sorry, Erich. I'll get you another cup," Elsa says nervously.

"That's okay, I think I'm finished with coffee for today," he replies as he moves his dirty plate to an empty spot on the table to make room for his newspaper. He notices that Elsa is shaking.

"What's wrong?"

She sits down at the table and takes a deep breath. "I'm worried, Erich."

"Worried? Worried about *what?"*

"I'm concerned about us. We seem to be drifting apart," she says carefully. "This trouble with the money and you going to the tavern is becoming a problem for us. You see this, *don't you?"*

Looking down at the newspaper, he replies, *"Yes*, the money is a problem. *Maybe* it's time that you look for work, Elsa. We can't seem to survive on the money *I* make."

Elsa stares at him in amazement. "Well, *maybe* if you stopped going to the tavern every night, we would have more money!" She immediately places her hand over her mouth, realizing that she should never have blurted out what she was thinking. She is angry with herself for having let her frustration get the better of her, and icy fear seeps into her veins.

Erich's face goes red, and his expression turns severe. "I work hard and *deserve* to have a good time! Who are *you* to begrudge me a little happiness?"

Elsa fights to control her emotions and calm Erich before he loses control. "I'm not saying you can't go to the tavern. I just think if you cut down the number of times you go, we could save a bit of money, *that's all.*"

Erich remains silent and just stares at her. A few minutes later, he gets up and makes his way to the living room. As he passes her, he stops and issues her an order. "You *must* look for work, Elsa!"

The shock of his words causes her to tremble once again. *What can I do? I have no choice but to obey him.* She feels that she has only herself to blame for the outcome of their discussion. *My father was right! If only I had kept quiet and not questioned Erich's actions. This is entirely my fault! Why do I do this?*

OVER THE NEXT few weeks, Elsa searches for employment and is fortunate to find work at the local cotton mill. It is hard working, raising the children and looking after the house, but she manages and doesn't complain. Elsa vows not to be the cause of any more conflict between her and Erich. She realizes that no matter how difficult it is for her, she must hold her negative feelings inside. Gradually, their relationship becomes slightly better with the improvement of their financial situation.

With the upturn in their circumstances, Erich joins the German Heritage Club, and they now have several German-speaking friends. They often host parties at their home where alcohol is in abundance, and although Elsa isn't a drinker, she plays the gracious hostess, always wearing a smile to hide her displeasure over their drunken display. She has become close friends with a woman named Margrit, and the two of them get together when they can. Elsa is happy to have a good friend to talk to—someone who shares the same background and understands her.

AFTER A FEW months, Elsa feels that her job is affecting her ability to properly care for the children, and with summer fast approaching, she must now deal with the issue of finding adequate supervision for them. She and Erich discuss this and decide to send for Erich's mother, Anna, to come live with them and tend to the children while Elsa is at work. Erich makes the arrangements and in the spring of 1954, Anna arrives in Hamilton.

Frieda and Rudi are very excited that their Oma has come to live with them, and she dotes on them. Elsa is grateful for her mother-in-law's help and is now able to focus on her work without having to worry about the children's welfare.

It isn't long before Elsa notices a change in Frieda and Rudi's behaviour. Whenever she asks them to do something, they ignore her. If they hurt themselves, they run to Oma to have her kiss away their tears. Elsa assumes this is most likely because she is away at work and Anna is always there for them, but it still hurts her. She can't seem to shake the uneasy feeling that she is losing her relationship with her children. When she confronts them about this, they both assure her that everything is okay, but Elsa feels that Anna could be turning them away from her. *This is silly! Why would Anna turn them against me? It doesn't make sense!* As hard as Elsa tries, she still can't seem to get over this feeling, so she decides to speak to Erich about it.

"Oh, you know Mama. She spoils them too much—*that's all!*"

"Maybe you could speak to her?" Elsa suggests.

"I can try, but I'm not sure what good it will do," he says, wishing she would just drop the matter.

"Couldn't you just try, *please?"* She hates begging him to do this, but it bothers her so much that it overtakes her thoughts, making her unable to concentrate on little else.

"Okay, I'll talk to her, Elsa."

Elsa is relieved and optimistic that Erich's discussion with his mother will eventually help improve her relationship with the children.

ERICH MAKES THE effort to talk to his mother a few days later, and once he tells Anna how Elsa feels, she is dumbfounded.

"Oh, I don't know what Elsa is upset about. I come here to help, and *this is how I'm treated?* I'm the one who should be upset, *not her!* I look after those children better than she ever did! They even tell me so. It's good that you brought me here to raise them."

Erich looks at Anna and is stunned. *Could this really be true?* He always thought Elsa was a good mother, but if the children believe that Anna is better, then maybe things weren't as good as he thought. "Are you sure you don't spoil them too much?"

"Spoil them? How would I do *that?* There isn't enough money here to spoil them!"

This hits Erich hard, and he looks at her, shaking his head. *Why does she think that money is the only way to spoil a child?* He lets the comment go since he doesn't want to argue the point. Erich believes that if the children actually feel that Anna is better at caring for them than their own mother, then he is glad that she is there for them. *Perhaps Mama is making up for not being a good mother to me.*

THAT EVENING, AS Elsa and Erich get ready for bed, they talk about their day and other private matters since it is the only time they have alone together.

"You spoke to Anna?" Elsa finally asks.

Erich climbs into bed and covers himself. "Yes, and I think you are making something out of nothing. She isn't turning the children against you. She is just raising them the best way she can, and we have to be thankful for that."

Elsa isn't so sure, but she keeps quiet. *Raising them? Anna is here to help, and I am grateful, but raising them? How can she think that? How can Erich think that? I just don't understand you, Erich. You and your mother never got along, and now you seem to be taking her side. What have I done wrong to make everyone turn against me?*

After they turn off the light, Elsa resolves to do her best to spend more time with the children and give them the attention they both need and deserve. *I will win them back, with or without your support.*

Chapter 27: Some Long-Awaited News

IN THE SPRING of 1956, the family once again runs into hard times when Erich is laid off from his job at the steel plant. Although he takes work wherever he can through his association with the Bricklayer's Union, the work hours are inconsistent, and the pay isn't as good as his regular job. This leaves Elsa the one with the stable income necessary to see them through, and it puts tremendous pressure on her.

Erich deals with his work stress by drinking excessively, and he gets outraged and verbally abusive when he is drunk. Elsa tries to hide this from the children, but they are old enough now to realize what is happening. She tells them that their father's drunkenness is his way of handling stress, and they must be accepting of his behaviour to keep the peace within the family. Anna, however, won't admit that her son has a problem. In her eyes, he can do no wrong. Elsa believes she ignores it because deep down she is afraid. *Without Erich, Anna would have nothing.*

With the added financial stress, together with her family issues, Elsa is having trouble sleeping. When she does sleep, it is erratic and plagued by nightmares. Her dreams centre around her wartime experiences and many times, she wakes up in a cold sweat, trying to catch her breath. Erich is oblivious to her sleep issues, and Elsa keeps them to herself because she doesn't want him to think that she is weak and unable to handle her responsibilities.

Elsa's dreams rouse her buried memories, and she once again thinks about her sister, Greta, and her boys. It is the first time in a long while that she has thought about them. *What has become of them? I wish there were some way to find out. Not knowing their fate is the most difficult part. If only I knew what happened to them, I could put these feelings aside and get on with life.* She shakes her head, attempting to clear her thoughts and once again focuses on preparing lunches for the upcoming work day.

ONE SATURDAY AFTERNOON, Elsa is able to take some time for herself to visit with her friend Margrit. They have coffee at a café on King Street, and the shop reminds Elsa of the ones in Germany. The aroma of coffee and the sweet smell of desserts bring back fond memories from before the war, making her a little homesick for Hamburg and the way things used to be.

The two women talk about their lives, and Elsa tells Margrit about her dreams and her difficulty sleeping. She relays the story about her sister, Greta, and her family and about her wish to find out what happened to them.

"Have you ever tried to find them?"

"Yes, shortly after the war. Unfortunately, I couldn't leave my family to go to Berlin to search, so I had to settle with inquiring by mail. It was really disappointing not to hear anything back in response to my countless letters, but I'm sure it was because everything was in such upheaval at that time."

"That's a shame! It must be so terrible not knowing what happened to them."

As they continue to talk, Elsa learns that Margrit has a brother who lives in West Berlin and works for the government there.

"I have an idea! I'll write to my brother, Otto, and ask him to search around and see if he can find out something about your sister. He has several government connections, and I'm sure he can check their records for information. I can't promise that he will be successful, but it's worth a try."

"Oh, I don't want to impose on him," Elsa says, regretting having told her.

"It's no bother! He will do anything for me! So, what do you think? Shall I write him to ask for his help?"

After a few moments, Elsa thanks Margrit and agrees to have her contact her brother to ask for his assistance since she sees no other way to find the information. Elsa tells her friend everything she knows about her sister and nephews so that Otto has some basis for his research.

I'm so fortunate to have a friend like Margrit. Even though there may be no hope of finding any information about Greta and the boys, just knowing that we have tried makes me feel better. I know I shouldn't get my hopes up, but I somehow have a good feeling that Margrit's brother will find out something.

A FEW WEEKS later, Margrit calls Elsa to tell her that her brother has agreed to aid her in her quest. She promises her that as soon as she hears back from Otto, she will let her know. Elsa is both relieved and happy that this man, whom she has never met, will take the time to do this for her. *Regardless of what Otto finds, I will put this behind me and not think about it again. Life goes on.*

Time passes slowly, and Elsa has yet to hear any news of Otto's success or failure. Margrit assures her that he will do everything in his power to find information about her sister, but Elsa thinks that he has probably changed his mind. *I really shouldn't have expected that he would do this for me. I'm nothing to him.*

CHRISTMAS HAS ALWAYS been important to Elsa. Since coming to Canada, she has kept the German tradition of celebrating on Christmas Eve, complete with the opening of gifts. Although she loves the season, it has always been difficult for her because it coincides with the anniversary of her mother's death. Elsa often feels sad at this time and has come to recognize that the unhappiness she experiences is known as depression. It seems odd to her that she would still be bothered by this after all these years but assumes it must be because of the traumatic circumstances that took her mother's life.

The Christmas of 1957 proves even more challenging than usual for Elsa, and she believes this is due to her disappointment with not having received word of her sister's fate. She does her best not to let her emotions take control and loses herself in the plans for the holiday.

On Christmas day, the phone rings at the Kaufmann home and Elsa answers it. "Merry Christmas!"

"Merry Christmas, Elsa. Can I stop by for a quick visit?" her friend Margrit asks.

"Yes, I'd love to see you!"

A few hours later, Margrit arrives with gifts for Frieda and Rudi as well as a bouquet of flowers for Elsa. They thank her for her kindness, and the two women make their way into the kitchen. As Elsa makes them coffee, Margrit tells her she has some news. Turning from the counter, she regards her friend with anticipation.

"Otto finally contacted me with information about your sister and her family," she says with a slight smile. "It has taken him months to find any records, and what he did find was incomplete."

Elsa sits at the kitchen table, preparing herself for the news Margrit is about to tell her. She takes a deep breath and exhales trying to cope with the anxiety she feels. "Okay, so tell me."

"After their arrest in the spring of 1940, Greta and the children were sent to Ravensbrück, a concentration camp for women, about 80 kilometres north of Berlin. They stayed there until July of 1942 when they were relocated to Auschwitz camp in Poland. Unfortunately, that's all he was able to learn."

Elsa looks at her friend with tear-filled eyes. "Thank you, Margrit! Thank you so much! You have made this a happy Christmas for me, despite the sad news. I think, deep down, I have always known Greta and her family were gone, and this finally gives me some closure."

"They could have survived Auschwitz, you know. I've heard that some people were fortunate to live through it."

Elsa shakes her head. "You and I both know the chances of that are highly unlikely, Margrit, but I'm fine with that. I feel much better just knowing what you have told me. I'm sure that if Greta had survived, she would have looked for me."

"I guess you're probably right. I'm sorry, my friend."

Chapter 28: Life's Challenges

AFTER ALMOST TWO years of sporadic work at the steel plant, Erich finally opens his own bricklaying and stonemason business. Elsa is happy with his decision and supports him completely. She is confident that this will ease their financial situation and perhaps help curb his daily tavern visits.

Erich's business starts off slow, but it eventually gets better. He accepts jobs anywhere, even if he has to leave the city for short periods. It is difficult for the family when Erich is away, but they recognize that it is a necessary sacrifice to help ease their financial burden.

THE CHILDREN CONTINUE going to school, but they both detest it, and many days, they just don't bother to attend. Elsa receives a call from the elementary school notifying her of their truancy, and she tells Erich so that he can handle the situation. He confronts them both, and now that they are older, he issues them an ultimatum—either stay in school or learn a trade. He is adamant that both of the children become hard-working, self-sufficient adults. Frieda and Rudi are relieved that their father is giving them this option, but they now face the difficult decision of what to do with their lives.

Because of her love of music, Frieda dreams of making it her career. She talks Erich into allowing her to enroll in guitar lessons, and even though money is tight, he is willing to do anything for her. When she finishes grade eight, at sixteen years of age, Erich signs a form permitting Frieda to quit school so that she can focus on her music studies. She takes her decision seriously and practices the guitar for eight hours every day. Not only does she dream of becoming a famous musician, but she also wants to impress her father as well.

Rudi wants to learn a trade but can't commit to one until he is eligible to quit school with parental approval, just as his sister did. Erich asks him repeatedly about what he would like to do for a living, but he has no idea. Rudi is lazy and a little slow at learning, which concerns Erich. *Perhaps the malnutrition he suffered as an infant damaged his brain.*

One evening, Erich approaches his son once again to talk about his future. "How about learning to be a bricklayer?"

Shrugging and with a complete lack of enthusiasm, Rudi replies, "I dunno."

"Well, you can work with me during the summer to see how you like it."

"But Dad... it's my summer vacation! *Do I have to?"*

"Yes, Rudi. I was working when I was your age, and so did your mama. You don't have a choice in this so you will work for me to gain some experience." Erich realizes he has his work cut out for him to try to motivate his son, but he is determined that Rudi makes something of himself, and he will do whatever he can to make that happen.

EARLY IN 1958, Elsa's health declines and she visits the doctor. After completing a preliminary examination, her family physician believes she has found the cause of her discomfort.

"Your right kidney doesn't appear to be functioning properly, and this is the reason you're experiencing so much pain. You should have come to see me ages ago, Elsa. Why did you wait so long?"

"I've been so busy with work, the family and the house that I just haven't had time. I really thought it would go away on its own."

"Well, ignoring the initial signs of infection may have caused some permanent damage. I want to send you to a specialist for treatment."

Elsa feels the blood drain from her face. "What happens then?"

"Let's get you seen by the specialist and go from there, okay?"

Elsa sees the nephrologist and undergoes various tests. The results aren't promising, and the specialist schedules her for surgery.

The operation is successful, and Elsa slowly feels better, but she is told that her work at the cotton mill is dangerous since it doesn't allow her to take washroom breaks when she feels the need.

"If you don't want to cause further damage to your kidney, you really must quit your job."

On the way home, Elsa tells Erich about the doctor's suggestion. "What do you think I should do?"

"Well, that's a silly question. You have no other choice *but* to quit."

"But—what about the money? We can't afford me not working!"

"No, but we can't afford you getting sick again either. Don't worry, I'll take on extra jobs."

With Erich being the only source of income, their situation is once again strained. He takes on as much work as possible, and although he is a good bricklayer and mason, he is no businessman. Bills pile up, creditors hound them for payment, and now with Elsa's health issues, he once again turns to the bottle as a way of handling his stress.

Anna helps with the children and the household chores and constantly reminds Elsa of everything she does for her and all the sacrifices she makes. Even though she has no problem speaking her mind, Anna still refuses to say anything to Erich about his drinking. Realizing that things are getting out of hand, thoughts of moving out enter her mind. With her pension from Germany, Anna now has some money of her own and concludes that once Elsa has recuperated, she will look for an apartment. *I do so much for them and get nothing in return. They take me for granted. Well, they will miss me when I am gone!*

AFTER TWO MONTHS of recovery, Elsa feels like her old self. It isn't long, however, before the guilt over not being able to work and contribute to the care of her family weighs heavily upon her. *How are we ever going to manage on one income? I wish I could do something to help with the finances.* She ponders the notion of helping Erich with his business and formulates a possible plan that could help it become more efficient and profitable. *I will need to be cautious of how I approach this topic with Erich. If I can get him to agree, I'm sure our financial situation will improve before too long.* She decides to wait until the weekend to speak with him because she knows this is when he is most agreeable.

"How are things going with the business, Erich?" Elsa asks on Saturday morning as she pours him a cup of coffee.

"Things are picking up. I have to go to Orillia for a job that will take most of the summer, and I'm taking Rudi with me."

"Well, that's good to hear. It will be a good experience for Rudi to work with you," she says as she realizes her opportunity has so readily presented itself. Keeping a neutral expression and tone in her voice, she asks, "Who will look after the books for the business and pay the bills while you are away all summer?"

Erich hadn't given it any thought since he has never been away for that length of time before, and he scratches his head but doesn't reply.

"Well, I have a plan if you'd let me tell you," Elsa says carefully.

He looks expectantly at her and nods. "So, tell me about this plan of yours."

Elsa explains how she would take care of the finances for both the business and the house in his absence. She has worked everything out on paper to prove that her idea has merit, and she hands it to him, nervously waiting for his feedback.

Erich takes a few minutes to study her proposal, and he looks back at her with surprise. "You figured all this out *by yourself?*"

Don't look so shocked! I am capable of using my brain. Elsa suppresses her thoughts and replies, "Yes, I did. So, what do you think?"

"This is good. I never thought to do things this way. It makes sense what you have done here." Erich smiles, which to her, seems like the first time in many months, and she smiles back.

"So, you'll let me help?"

"Okay, Elsa, let's try it your way for a while and see how things work out."

She hugs him and feels that she has finally made progress with him and his stubborn ways. "Thank you for trusting me. I won't let you down," she says with conviction. For the first time, confidence and pride envelop her, and she likes how it makes her feel.

Erich looks happily at his wife of sixteen years and can see how much this means to her. *I have to trust her to try to fix the mess I have made with the business. I just hope this works.*

THE SUMMER IS quiet with Erich and Rudi away, but it gives Elsa the time to focus on her business plan. The process proves to be a challenge, but she continues to work at it, adjusting things as necessary to accomplish her goals.

It isn't long before Elsa realizes some success with her ideas for both the business and at home. She is satisfied and happy with her efforts to turn things around and thinks that Erich will be very pleased with her achievements. Elsa now feels in control of her life, and it provides her with a sense of self-worth.

Frieda continues with her music and wins many competitions because of her skill and talent. By the end of the summer, a teaching position at the studio where she has been taking lessons comes available, and Frieda gets the job. She is thrilled to finally be earning some money of her own, and it makes her confident with her career choice. *One day I'll make a name for myself. I'll be just as famous as Les Paul!*

ERICH AND RUDI return home at the end of August after completing the job in Orillia. Working for his father was a terrible experience—one that he hopes will never be repeated. At his young age, Rudi fails to comprehend that the purpose behind the treatment he received was to teach him the skills necessary to survive in the working world rather than a personal attack. *God, my old man is so mean! He treated me worse than the other guys, and I'm his son! He's so unfair!*

Rudi is happy to be home but unhappy at the prospect of having to return to school. He has a very strong-willed adolescent behaviour, like most boys his age, but his laziness and devil-may-care attitude makes raising him even more challenging. He skips classes most days and Elsa receives another call from the school.

Frustrated by her son's apparent lack of interest in anything, Elsa approaches Erich to discuss the issue that evening as they get ready for bed. "I don't know what will become of that boy. He is so lazy. He doesn't want to work or go to school. What are we to do?" she asks with a hint of hopelessness in her voice.

"I will show that boy who is the boss here! He will do as I tell him! He will go to school and learn some trade if it kills me!"

Elsa says nothing because she knows what this means, and although she doesn't entirely agree with Erich's methods, she knows this is how her father would have handled this situation. She feels that there really is no other way to get through to the boy, and she prays that it will help him to change.

THE FOLLOWING EVENING, Erich approaches Rudi to talk, but the discussion soon escalates as Erich's temper flares. He pulls off his belt and puts Rudi over his knee and smacks his backside.

"You *will* do as you are told! You *will* go to school! You *will* learn a trade! Do you *understand*, Rudi?"

Rudi cries out, "Yes, Daddy! I will! *I will!*"

Erich stops with the belt because he feels that this act of discipline has had the desired effect and things will improve. "Okay then, Rudi, wash your face and go to your room. Tomorrow you will go back to school and work hard to learn and do well."

Anger boils within Rudi, not only over his father's treatment but also at himself for allowing his emotions to control him. He stands up gingerly and nods before silently making his way to the washroom.

Later, in his room, Rudi's thoughts run rampant. *Why does he hate me so much? Why can't he just leave me alone?* He knows that if he were to disobey his father, he would have to face further encounters with the belt. He could run away from home, but they would only find him and bring him back, which would have the same result. Rudi figures the best way to handle things is to do as his father tells him, at least, for now. *I guess I have no other choice. I'll just go to school until I'm sixteen and be finished with it for good. Everything will be so much better once I'm done. God, I can hardly wait!*

ALTHOUGH RUDI ATTENDS school regularly and makes a concerted effort to do better, his grades are still below average. It discourages him and makes him hate going even more than before.

Rudi eventually falls back into his earlier routine of skipping school, and this time, Erich and Elsa are called to meet with the principal.

At the meeting, they agree that tutoring would be beneficial to help Rudi improve his grades. The sessions help somewhat, but not as much as everyone had hoped. The tutor reports that Rudi has trouble retaining information and feels there may be an underlying issue. With his learning disabilities finally identified, the principal meets with Erich and Elsa once again. He suggests placing Rudi in a special needs class, and they consent. Rudi then moves from his regular class to one that will provide him with the extra support he requires.

Rudi hates this change and lets his parents know his displeasure. "I'm in the retard's class! I hate this! I'm quitting school, and I don't care what you say!"

Elsa has always had a knack for calming Rudi down when he is upset, and she hopes he will respond favourably to her latest attempt. "Now Rudi, you have to try—you just can't quit! You can do anything you put your mind to—I know it!"

"I don't know, Mom, I feel *so* stupid! I really don't think I can do it," he says, feeling a sudden heat radiate on his cheeks while attempting to choke back his tears.

"Come on now, will you just promise to try your best? If not for yourself, then for me—*please?"* Elsa says. She knows that Rudi will give in to her plea because he always does when using this approach.

He finally agrees, even though he is doubtful of his success. He will give it his best shot, but only because he promised his mother, and he will do anything to avoid letting her down. Rudi can't stand the thought of Elsa being disappointed with him.

Rudi works harder than he has ever done, despite his unhappiness with the situation. This special class is full of children who not only have learning issues but also have behavioural problems as well. Over time, these behavioural issues rub off on Rudi, causing him to become unmanageable.

Many of the children from the regular classes make fun of Rudi and bully him, calling him "Stupid Nazi" and other derogatory names. He gets into many fights and faces discipline both at school and at home.

Outside of school, he hangs around with some of his classmates and gets into trouble with the law. The boys are caught shoplifting and are brought home by the police. After a severe punishment, Rudi concludes that once he is old enough, he will leave home. *I've had enough of this crap! Nobody likes or cares about me! I go to school, and I'm picked on. I stand up for myself, and I'm punished. I can't even have some laughs with my friends. I just can't win!* He swallows his anger and becomes distant with his family.

Erich insists Rudi work with him once again in the summer of 1959. He figures this is a great way to keep him out of trouble, and if he pays him for his work, the money might be an incentive for him to work hard. Rudi realizes he can't turn his father down, so he spends another summer working under his watchful eye, trying to cope with his daily responsibilities.

Rudi likes having the weekly paycheque, but it doesn't seem to motivate him enough to improve his work ethic. His mind is elsewhere, causing him to make silly mistakes. Erich holds in his displeasure because he knows the boy has problems, but this becomes more challenging when he has been drinking.

"What's the *matter* with you, Rudi? How many times do I have to show you? You need to pay attention or you'll *never* amount to anything!"

Rudi knows his father is drunk and tries to ignore his comments, but deep down they play on his mind and fester like an untreated wound. *He's probably right. I'll never amount to anything. I don't know why I even bother to try! I guess what the kids at school say is true—I am stupid!*

Chapter 29: A New Direction

ANNA GETS HER own apartment in the fall, and Elsa is relieved that she has moved out. She knows that Anna has been unhappy living with them for some time, and having teenaged children around can be challenging, especially for a senior.

Elsa is alone when the children and Erich are away for the day, giving her the opportunity to enjoy some solitude, which is a new experience for her. She still works diligently helping Erich with his business, but now that plans have been established, it is only a matter of dealing with the day-to-day tasks and any minor issues that arise.

Erich was surprised by Elsa's ability to manage the business so well in his absence. He wasn't sure she could undo the damage he caused through his neglect, but he realizes that trusting her to take over the business was a good decision. Being free of the administrative function alleviates Erich's stress and allows him to focus solely on the physical job, which is the area he enjoys and where he excels.

FRIEDA HAS BECOME an attractive and popular young woman, going on many dates with men she meets at the Club or at work. She is very independent and motivated to succeed, although, at times, her ambition can be mistaken for selfishness.

Using her hold on her father, Frieda talks him into teaching her how to drive. Once she gets her licence, she also manages to get him to agree to co-sign a loan enabling her to buy a car.

"I don't think this a good idea, Erich. If she misses any payments, we will have to cover them. We just can't afford to do that," Elsa warns.

"Oh, don't worry. Frieda is such a responsible girl, she'll make her payments on time," he assures her.

Elsa's inner voice screams at her, *Don't do this! You'll regret it later!* She swallows her feelings and tries to take it in stride, but the intensity of her intuition continues to gnaw at her, leaving her to struggle with her emotions. Elsa has never been one to ignore her instinct, but she wants to believe and trust Erich's judgement, so she agrees to it.

NOW THAT ELSA has managed to change the financial outcome of the business and the family, she thinks about how much she would like to learn a trade and work for herself. *I know I'm not that young anymore, but even at thirty-five, I still have many years ahead to commit to a career. After helping Erich with his business, I know I can succeed.* As she investigates her options, Elsa decides that she would like to learn to become a hairdresser and the idea of it excites her. The only obstacle she faces is getting Erich to agree to give her the opportunity, so one Saturday morning, she tells Erich about her dream. He sits at the kitchen table silently and listens to her with a neutral expression, making it difficult for Elsa to gauge his reaction to her idea. Once she has finished her proposal, she takes a breath and holds it, waiting for him to respond.

"It sounds like you've done your research into this and that you're really determined to do it."

"Yes, I called the hairdressing school to ask about it. I know it will be difficult going to school and looking after the house, but I managed it when I was working in the cotton mill. I know I can handle this too."

Realizing that Elsa would never consider doing something like this without first making sure they had the finances to cover it, Erich plays the devil's advocate. "What about the cost? Can we *afford* it?"

"Yes, we have enough money to pay the monthly fee. I have worked it all out and can show you on paper if you'd like."

"No, it's fine. As long as you know that the numbers work out." He looks into Elsa's eyes and grins. "Are you sure this is what you want?" he asks, knowing the absurdity of his question.

"Yes, Erich, I want this more than *anything!*"

"Well, then I think you should go ahead and do it, honey." He has learned to trust Elsa's judgement, and he knows she will be successful with this after having proved herself with managing his business.

Elsa hugs him fiercely as her eyes brim with tears. "Thank you! You won't regret your decision. I promise you, I'll do my best." She is astonished by his support and happy at the prospect of being able to do something just for her.

THE FOLLOWING YEAR, Elsa attends hairdressing school in downtown Hamilton and is so pleased with her decision. Although she isn't fluent in English, her marks are high in the theory portion of her classes, and the practical is even better. Elsa has always enjoyed styling her own and Frieda's hair and realizes now that this is her true calling. She loves everything to do with hair and beauty. After finishing school, she writes her provincial exams and does her practical exam, and passes both with honours.

Once Elsa receives her hairdressing licence, Erich surprises her with the news that they will buy a house in an area that allows commercial business, and he will renovate it to include a beauty salon for her. His offer stuns Elsa, bringing her to tears. She doesn't remember ever feeling so delighted. Things are finally coming together for her in ways she never dreamed possible.

They find a suitable house in the city, and Erich purchases it and commences the necessary renovations. A month later, Elsa's Beauty Salon opens to the public, and Elsa works hard to make her business a success. With her unwavering determination, it isn't long before she builds a large clientele to keep her very busy and along with it, a steady stream of income flowing in.

As Elsa's business continues to thrive, it grounds her, giving her a sense of independence, which is something she has never before experienced. Her family is, of course, still very important to her, but with the children now young adults, they no longer depend on her as they once did. Ultimately, the salon is what gives her life purpose.

With Elsa working hard to make her own business successful, she hasn't had time to devote to Erich's business. Although Erich assures her that he can follow her plan and manage it himself, he neglects it and things soon fall apart. He doesn't tell her about the problems because he is too embarrassed to admit to her that he has once again mismanaged his company. Erich is angry with himself for letting things slide, and his alcohol abuse escalates once more.

Chapter 30: The Surprise

RUDI TURNS SIXTEEN in October, and Erich insists that he complete grade eight before agreeing to sign the form allowing him to quit school. After finally finishing in June of 1961, and without any idea of what to do with his life, Rudi reluctantly goes into his father's bricklaying business full time. Erich is happy with his son's decision, although he knows it won't be easy to train him. He feels confident that working full time will limit Rudi's involvement with his friends and help him to mature.

Each morning, Erich drives Rudi to work, and with Rudi's extensive training, they remain on the job site for ten to twelve hours. It is a pace to which the young man is unaccustomed, making it difficult for him to adjust to his father's expectations. Rudi knows his options are limited, and he continues to work to the best of his ability. After the first week, he is so completely exhausted that he sleeps the entire weekend. On Monday morning, he questions his ability to withstand a repeat of the previous week, but he forces himself to get up and start the routine over again.

Erich tries to be patient with Rudi while teaching him the fundamentals required for his job as a labourer. Certain aspects of the work are easy for Rudi to retain while others appear to be out of his grasp. Erich realizes that the boy will never become a certified bricklayer but still attempts to train him as much as possible. Deep down, he feels responsible for Rudi's learning disabilities. He still believes his son's issues stem from him having suffered from malnutrition as an infant, and although this has never been proven, Erich blames himself for not having done more to provide the proper nourishment to aid in his development.

Rudi meets a girl at a dance one Saturday, and he falls head over heels in love. Her name is Mary, and his parents adore her. Erich and Elsa are not sure where this romance will lead, but Mary seems to keep Rudi grounded and happy, and that is important to them. They have noticed a significant change in his behaviour since he has been dating her, and they hope that their relationship will eventually blossom into something meaningful and lasting.

FRIEDA STILL TEACHES music and makes a decent living. She spends much of her spare time going to the Club and has become a social butterfly who loves to drink and party, even though she is still legally underage. Elsa worries about her daughter's behaviour becoming similar to Erich's and feels the need to speak to Frieda and warn her about the possible outcomes of her conduct. *Too many terrible things can happen to a young girl who is drunk.*

One Sunday morning after breakfast, Elsa approaches Frieda to discuss her fears. "I know you enjoy going to the Club and having fun drinking and dancing, but I want you to be careful when you drink so that you aren't taken advantage of. You understand what I'm saying, *don't you?*"

Frieda looks at her mother and laughs. "Oh, *come on*, Mom! You can't be *serious!* I can take care of myself, you don't need to worry!"

"I'm your mother, and I *do* worry. Terrible things can happen to a girl, especially when alcohol is involved."

"I know all about that, and I can handle things on my own. Trust me, Mom, I would never get myself into a situation like that. Besides, all the fellows I go with are gentlemen so don't lose sleep over it, okay?"

"Well, if there ever comes a time when you can't handle things, be sure to defend yourself."

Frieda laughs again but stops once she notices that her mother is sincere. "Yes, Mom, I promise to punch the guy in the nose as hard as I can," she says while trying to keep a straight face.

Elsa is unsure whether Frieda really appreciates her fears, but at least, she has done her best to warn her daughter and prays that she will never find herself in this predicament.

Erich also has a hard time coming to terms with Frieda's behaviour and feels a bit jealous of the men with whom she spends her time. *How can my little girl grow up and forget about me?* Perhaps the difficulty he has isn't so much her conduct as it is the feeling of being slighted by her. *How can this even be possible? It's complete madness,* he tells himself, yet Erich has mixed feelings when it comes to his only daughter. *What's wrong with me? I should be happy and proud that she's growing up and doing well for herself. Maybe it's the thought of getting old that bothers me.* Erich cherishes his time with Frieda but realizes that it won't be long before he has to share her with another man, and this thought disturbs him more than he is willing to admit.

ELSA'S SALON CONTINUES to do well, and she is happy and content with her life, despite Erich's drinking. With the increase in her clientele, she has had to hire someone to assist with small duties like shampooing, cleaning and answering the phone.

Over the past few weeks, Elsa has been ill and worries that she will need to take time off work. Although the thought of it bothers her, she has no choice. After a few days of vomiting, Elsa finally makes an appointment with the doctor and has Frieda drive her there.

"Well, Elsa, what seems to be the problem?" Dr. Walker asks.

Elsa describes her symptoms, and the doctor examines her.

"With what you tell me, I suspect you're pregnant, Elsa, but let's order some blood work to confirm this," she says.

Elsa sits on the examination table in shock. "*Pregnant?* At my *age?* How can that be? I'm thirty-seven years old!"

"I take it this wasn't planned?"

"No, it definitely was *not!*"

"Well, let's get the results of the blood work to confirm things before you get too upset. It will probably take a week, but I'll call you with the results as soon as I have them. Until then, just try to relax, and take one day at a time, okay? I'll prescribe you some medication for the vomiting and nausea, and you should feel better soon."

"What is it, Mom?" Frieda asks with concern when Elsa rejoins her in the reception area.

"Let's go, we can talk in the car."

As Frieda puts the car in gear, Elsa asks her to stop at the lab and pharmacy before they head home.

"Sure, Mom. So what did Dr. Walker say? What's *wrong?*"

"I just need to have a blood test done, and once the results are back the doctor will know more." She doesn't want to tell Frieda what the doctor suspects just in case it is wrong, but the more Elsa thinks about how she feels, the more she believes the doctor may be correct in her assumptions.

"Okay, but did she say what she thinks might be wrong?"

"No, just that I need to have the blood work done. She assures me that it's nothing serious."

On the drive to the lab, Elsa thinks about how Erich will take the news if she is indeed pregnant. *Will he be happy? Maybe the doctor's wrong, but if it's something else, it could be worse.* She does her best to calm her nerves and have the patience to wait for the results.

ELSA TAKES THE medication prescribed by the doctor and feels slightly better within a few days. Finally, after a stressful week, Elsa receives the call she has been anxiously awaiting. Dr. Walker confirms what she has already begun to accept as the truth. *Well, I guess that's it then! It will definitely be an adjustment for us, but I know in the end, we'll be happy.*

After Elsa cleans up the dishes that night, she sits back down at the table. Erich is reading the newspaper and smoking a cigarette.

"Erich, there is something I need to tell you."

He stops reading and looks at her with interest. "Okay, tell me what's on your mind, honey."

"The doctor called me today with the results of my blood test."

Worry lines Erich's face. "Well, what did she say?"

Elsa swallows hard and fights to hold in her emotions. Using every ounce of courage she can gather, she finally says, "I'm pregnant." Feelings of both relief and dread wash over her as she watches Erich's expression.

"You're *what?*"

"I'm pregnant," she repeats.

Erich feels as though he has been sucker punched. He is quiet while the reality of Elsa's words hit him. "Well, I certainly didn't expect *that!*"

"Neither did I, but it's a blessing from God, so we just have to come to terms with it. You know that all things happen for a reason, Erich. Can't you be happy about it?"

"I don't know how I feel yet. Just think of all fuss and trouble having another baby will be, especially at our age, and what about the salon?"

Elsa can see that it will take some time for Erich to come to terms with the situation but knows that he will be happy once the initial shock wears off.

"I can work in the salon right up until the baby comes, and then I'll take a few weeks off leaving Elizabeth to run things in my absence. Once I return to work, I can care for the little one between clients."

"Have you told the children yet?"

"No, of course not, I wanted to tell you first. Besides, because of my age, I think it's best for me to wait until the first three months are over before we inform them. The doctor said there are many risks involved with pregnancies in later years."

Erich nods as he gets up from his chair and approaches his wife. He holds her tightly, trying to provide the reassurance she so desperately needs. "Everything will be okay," he says before going to the fridge to grab a bottle of beer and head to the living room with the newspaper. His thoughts are clearly not on the local news now. His mind is spinning with notions of how different their life will be with a baby in the picture. *A blessing? I'm not so sure.*

ELSA CONTINUES TO work in the salon despite her overall lack of energy. Thankfully, with the use of the medication, her severe morning sickness has finally passed.

Despite her initial shock, she finds herself looking forward to caring for an infant again. Although Erich has yet to accept the idea of having a baby in their lives, Elsa knows that he will eventually come around.

The evening before Elsa plans to tell the children her news, Erich comes home from work in a drunken stupor. She hasn't seen him this drunk in a very long time, and she makes him aware of her annoyance with his behaviour and an argument ensues.

"Why do we have to have another kid anyway? We're getting *too* old to start over again!" he shouts with spittle flying out of his mouth.

"Keep your voice down, Erich. I haven't told Frieda and Rudi yet, and I don't want them to find out this way."

"I wish this whole thing would just go away, so we could go back to normal!"

Elsa is disgusted by Erich's attitude and finds herself trembling. "*Normal?* What do you call *normal?* Is it when you're drunk, and *we pretend to be happy?* I just don't understand you anymore, maybe I never really have." Now that she is aware of how he actually feels, she is shocked that she could be so wrong about her husband. She honestly believed he would come to accept the baby and give her the support she needed.

Without another word, Erich turns away and enters the kitchen. A moment later, the silence is broken by the sound of the refrigerator door opening and the loud clinking of beer bottles.

Elsa goes quietly to the bedroom and shuts the door to be alone with her thoughts and give Erich time to cool down. She lies down on the bed, burying her face into the pillow and weeps.

Erich falls asleep on the sofa and wakes in the early hours of the morning to the sound of Elsa's sobs. He places a pillow over his head to block the painful noise. Even in his drunken state, he realizes how hurtful he was to his wife, yet he can't make himself get up to face her now. *We'll talk in the morning and come to terms with everything—that's what we'll do. Everything will be better then.*

AFTER HER ALARM goes off, Elsa gets up to take a bath and get ready for her day. She cried all night and still finds herself crying as she makes breakfast. *How can I possibly have any tears left?*

When a noise from the kitchen wakes Erich, he gets up slowly and makes his way there. He enters and approaches his wife remorsefully. "I'm sorry, Elsa. I was out of line last night. I should never have said those things. It will be an adjustment to have a baby, but we'll get used to it." He reaches out to touch her arm, but she moves away from him as though he carried an infectious disease.

"It doesn't matter anymore, Erich. You have your wish—there will be *no baby*."

"Don't talk like that. We'll make this work, *I promise.*"

She turns her back to him, allowing more tears to flow freely down her face. "No, Erich, you don't understand. *I lost the baby last night.*"

Erich stands there stunned and at a loss for words. His first instinct is to take Elsa into his arms, so he moves toward her. Sensing his approach, she turns quickly to face him with an angered expression unlike any he has ever seen, and he instantly backs away.

Finally, he says the only words that come to his mind. *"I'm so sorry, honey."*

Elsa nods slightly and once again turns her back to him. She is afraid to say another word because she knows that anger and hurt could cause her to say things she may later regret.

Assuming she wants to be alone, Erich leaves the kitchen. Guilt overwhelms him, and he gets into his truck to go for a drive to clear his head but is suddenly overcome with grief. He actually came to terms with the pregnancy last night and planned to tell Elsa that even with the initial shock, he felt glad to be a father again. *How could I have been so selfish? This is my fault!* Erich pounds the steering wheel in frustration and for the first time in years, he cries.

ERICH AND ELSA don't speak for several days. They are both hurt and need to find their own ways to deal with their grief. Elsa calls Margrit, and upon hearing the distress in her voice, she immediately goes to see her.

"Oh, Elsa, I'm *very* sorry! You're probably going to hate me for this, but *what a terrible man!* How could he treat you like this?"

"He can be difficult to deal with sometimes, but he's still my husband. I have to have faith that things will improve."

"I don't know, Elsa. No one deserves to be treated this way."

"You're right, but it was partly my fault. I shouldn't have argued with him."

Margrit shakes her head. "I care about you, and I think you need to open your eyes and realize that you have alternatives, you know?"

"What *alternatives* are you talking about?"

"If things don't improve, you should think about leaving him."

"*Leaving him?* But that would mean that I have failed in my marriage. No, I could never *leave him, I love him!*"

"Alright, Elsa, you need to do what's best for you. I just don't think I would be able to put up with his behaviour."

When Erich and Elsa finally talk, she tells him that losing the baby wasn't his fault. "This would have happened anyway. It was God's will. Remember that everything happens for a reason, even if we don't understand why." They both cry and the experience brings them closer together.

ELSA DOES HER best to accept her miscarriage, but she can't seem to come to terms with it. Even after six months, whenever she goes into a department store and sees baby clothes, she immediately breaks into tears. If she passes an infant on the street, she is overcome with grief.

Erich insists that she make an appointment with the doctor, which Elsa does, and he goes with her for support. The doctor tells them that the best way for her to heal from this loss is to get pregnant again. Both Elsa and Erich hadn't given that possibility any thought.

"I'm afraid to try again. I don't think I could stand it if I lost another baby."

"Well, think about it. I would have you come in for additional visits to check how things are progressing, but it's up to you."

Erich and Elsa consider the prospect of another pregnancy and finally agree to make another attempt. They both feel confident that they will be blessed with a baby soon, but after several months of trying, Elsa becomes discouraged. *What if I can't get pregnant? What if that was my last chance?* She struggles to push these negative thoughts from her head because she knows they only cause harm, but she finds it difficult. Not knowing what else to do, she visits Dr. Walker again to discuss her fears.

"There's nothing physically wrong with you, Elsa. The only problem you have is that you're trying too hard. Remember it's a natural process. If you are too tense or stressed about it, it may never happen. You just have to learn to relax and let nature take its course."

After getting the reassurance she needs, Elsa informs Erich what the doctor has told her, and finally in April of 1962, they get the happy news that Elsa is pregnant again.

Fortunately, her morning sickness is mild compared to her last pregnancy. Regardless of its severity, however, Elsa would never take Thalidomide again after learning that not only does it cause terrible birth defects but also that it was likely the cause of her miscarriage. Despite Elsa's guilt over the fact that she may have inadvertently been responsible for losing the baby, she realizes that she can't let it consume her. As difficult as it is, Elsa must put it behind her to mentally prepare for the coming months.

FRIEDA SHAKES HER head in disbelief. "Wow, Mom, a *baby?* That *is* a surprise! You mean you and Dad *actually* planned this? What *were* you thinking?"

"Oh, what difference does it make to *you* anyway? I think it's great news, Mom. *I'm happy for you!"* Rudi says.

"This baby was planned and wanted very much by both of us. I know it's a shock to you, but can't you be a little happy about it?" Elsa asks, hoping for some understanding from her daughter. Frieda shrugs her shoulders and silently leaves the room.

"Don't let Frieda's reaction bother you, Mom. You know how selfish she can be! Either she'll get over it or she won't. It's *your* life, and you deserve to be happy. If having this baby makes you happy, then that's *all* that matters," Rudi says, giving his mother a supportive hug.

Rudi's mature attitude surprises Elsa, and she realizes that his girlfriend, Mary, has had a tremendous impact on him. She knows that what he says is right, but it still hurts her that Frieda is disappointed with this turn of events. *All I can do is pray that she will eventually accept my pregnancy and be pleased about it.*

THE FOLLOWING SUNDAY, after church, they visit Anna and tell her the news. She shakes her head but says nothing to Elsa. Turning to Frieda and pointing her finger at her she says, "*You* should be the one having a baby, *not* your mother!"

Frieda squirms in her seat, not knowing what to say and looks over at her mother, waiting to see how she handles the situation.

Elsa is disgusted by her mother-in-law's callousness. She didn't expect her to be happy about the baby, but she never thought she would react in this way. *Anna has some nerve saying that! Who does she think she is?* Elsa wants to say something in her defence, but nothing tactful comes to her mind so she stays silent.

"That's an *awful* thing to say, Mama! I think you owe Elsa an apology," Erich says forcefully to his mother.

"I will *not* apologize! This is a *terrible* mistake. Now you have to live with it! You two are much *too* old! You will be *fifty* when this baby is born—old enough to be a *grandfather!*"

Erich does his best to hold his temper. "We both wanted this, Mama. It's *no* mistake. We're sorry you feel that it is." He then gets up from his chair and turns his back to his mother. "Come on, everyone, let's go home. Goodbye, Mama."

Anna remains seated, with contempt lining her face. "You will see that I'm right! Don't expect me to raise this baby for you like I did the other two because *I won't do it!* I have done more than enough for this family and what thanks do I get?"

This last comment stops Erich in his tracks, and he turns around to confront his mother once again. "*You* didn't raise the other children, Elsa *did!* You were there to help when we needed you, and we appreciate it, but make *no* mistake, Elsa was the one who raised them! In fact, you've *never* raised a child in your life! Apparently, you live in a dream world if you think *you* were the one to raise our children. You are nothing but a selfish woman—*you always have been!*" He then turns to leave the apartment, slamming the door behind him.

Elsa is very surprised by Erich's words. *I was mistaken to think that Erich was against me when it came to his mother and her handling of the children. I just wish I would have known this sooner.*

AS THE MONTHS pass, Margrit visits Elsa frequently to support her and check that her relationship with Erich is a healthy one. Shortly before the expected arrival, she plans a baby shower and invites their German friends to attend. Elsa is surprised and overjoyed by the outpouring of kindness shown to her.

Erich prepares the nursery, and as the due date gets closer, his enthusiasm grows. With his birthday being December 18th, he hopes that because the baby is due just before Christmas, he may be blessed with a special birthday gift. When Erich's birthday arrives, however, Elsa feels no signs of labour.

"Can't you just push it a bit?" he asks.

Elsa laughs and replies, "No, honey, it doesn't work like that. I think this baby wants a birthday of its own."

IN THE EARLY hours of December 20, 1962, Elsa's water breaks and she goes into labour. Erich gets up and prepares to take her to the hospital. It is exceptionally cold, and a thick layer of ice coats everything. He goes out to warm the car, but as luck would have it, it fails to turn over. After repeated attempts, he finally admits defeat. The frigid temperature has drained the battery, and there is just not enough time to arrange to boost it.

Erich rushes back into the house and wakes Frieda. "Mama's in labour and my car won't start. You have to take us to the hospital."

Frieda gets up and dresses quickly to drive her parents there. She drops them off at the front entrance, promising to join them once she finds a parking spot.

In the waiting room, Frieda flips through a magazine while Erich nervously paces back and forth. It has been a few hours and still no news, and he is getting concerned.

Finally, Dr. Walker comes in and approaches Erich with a smile. "Congratulations, Erich. You have a healthy baby daughter. Elsa had a difficult time, but she's doing well. You can see the baby in the nursery, and Elsa is down the hall in room two."

After thanking the doctor, he and Frieda go to the nursery to meet the new addition to their family. The nurse holds the baby to the glass and Erich forms a broad smile.

"Isn't she cute? Just look at how beautiful she is!" Frieda nods but says nothing. "Let's go and see Mama," he says anxiously.

"You go ahead, Dad. I'll see her later. I'm going to call Rudi to tell him the news."

"Hello, Mama! How do you feel?" Erich asks as he enters Elsa's room. She looks pale and exhausted but wears a smile that could brighten the darkest day.

"I'm tired but incredibly happy. Have you seen her yet?"

"Yes, she's beautiful, Elsa!" he tells her proudly as he sits on the edge of her bed and leans forward to kiss her forehead. "I'm so happy that we have her. She will always be there for you and will care for you when you get old."

She looks at him and nods. *What an odd thing to say.* A while later, the nurse enters the room with the baby and places her in Elsa's arms, and she forgets about Erich's words. She looks down at her round face and perfectly shaped features and smiles.

"Have you thought about a name, Elsa?"

"Yes, I want to call her Laura. I've loved that name since the first time I heard it."

"It's a beautiful name for such a beautiful baby!" Erich replies as Elsa hands him his new daughter.

When Elsa and Laura come home from the hospital on Christmas Eve, Elsa places her under the tree. "Look at the lovely gift Santa Claus has left for us!" Everyone laughs—except for Frieda.

Chapter 31: Rudi

RUDI ADORES HIS baby sister and never dreamed he could feel such a strong attachment to her. He takes her out for walks when the weather permits and loves to show her off to all of his friends. "This is my baby sister!" he tells them proudly. Mary is also thrilled when they have a chance to spend time with Laura.

At eighteen years of age, Rudi's thoughts turn to marriage and having a family of his own. He plans to propose to Mary in the spring, but as it approaches, Rudi notices her becoming somewhat distant. He tries to speak to her about it but gets nowhere and fears he may have done something to trigger this sudden change in her behaviour.

"What's wrong, Mary? Did I do something to upset you?"

"No, no. It's not you. I just have some things on my mind. Please don't worry yourself. Everything will be okay."

Rudi isn't sure he believes her, but he is willing to give her the benefit of the doubt, even though it bothers him. *I'm sure once I propose to her, things will be better.*

After he goes to pick out an engagement ring he hopes Mary will love, Rudi tells his parents about his plans. They are thrilled because they realize that Mary's influence on him has been a positive one.

"That's wonderful, Rudi! She's a lovely girl. We're so happy for you both!" Elsa tells him with a smile.

ON SATURDAY AFTERNOON, Rudi picks Mary up to go for a drive and get some ice cream. When they arrive at Stoney Creek Dairy, he takes hold of her hand before they exit the car. Rudi nervously places his hand in his pocket and pulls out the ring box. "I love you so much, Mary. Will you marry me?"

She looks at the diamond ring and tears flood her eyes. Mary shakes her head but doesn't say a word.

Astonished by her reaction, Rudi stares at her. *I really thought she felt the same way I do. I just don't understand this. Why is she rejecting me?*

"You... you don't *want* to be with me?"

Emotion chokes her as she speaks. "I can't talk to you now, Rudi. I'm sorry, but please take me home."

Confused and unsure of what to do next, he quickly puts the car in gear and heads in the direction of Mary's house. They drive in silence as Rudi's mind overflows with a multitude of thoughts, and panic slowly engulfs him. "I'll call you tomorrow, *okay?*" he says when he parks the car.

Mary nods without looking at him and quickly exits the vehicle. Rudi watches her run to her house, taking the steps two at a time, and he remains there too stunned to drive off. *What did I do wrong? Maybe she just needs some time, after all, we've never talked about marriage before. I'll call her tomorrow, and we'll get together to work things out then. I know once she has a chance to think it over, she'll say yes.*

AFTER A RESTLESS sleep, Rudi gets up and goes to church with his family. He doesn't tell his parents about Mary's reaction to his proposal, but Elsa notices that something is troubling him.

"What's wrong, Rudi?" she asks as they drive.

"I'm just tired, Mom. I didn't sleep well last night."

"You're much too young to be having sleep issues. Are you sure there isn't anything bothering you?"

"Everything is fine, Mom. I'm working extra hours, and I just find it hard to sleep because my muscles are sore."

At church, Rudi hardly pays attention to the service and patiently waits for the time he can phone Mary.

Later that afternoon, when Rudi calls her, there is no answer. He continues trying until eventually Mary's mother, Janice, picks up the phone. She informs Rudi that Mary isn't home and doesn't know when she will be back. He senses this is a lie but won't challenge her. *If she doesn't talk to me on the phone, I'll go to her house and not leave until we work things out.*

Standing on Mary's front porch, Rudi opens the screen door and knocks. When no one answers, he hammers on the door, anxiously yelling Mary's name.

After ten minutes, a neighbour comes out on his porch and shouts at Rudi. "They're not home, so stop the racket! If you don't, I'll call the police!"

Disheartened, Rudi gets into his car and drives back home. He can't understand what is happening, and he fights to control his emotions.

TWO WEEKS OF trying to reach Mary has taken its toll on Rudi. He is crazy with worry and eventually gets the courage to go back to her house. He once again stands on her front porch, but this time, he knocks and patiently waits for someone to come to the door. When no one answers, Rudi tries again. The curtain finally opens, and Mary's mother, Janice, peers out before finally coming to the door.

"Hello, Rudi. Please come inside."

"Where's Mary?" he asks anxiously.

"Sit down, Rudi," Janice tells him softly.

"*What's happened?* Where's Mary? I need to speak to her!"

Tears shine in Janice's eyes. "I'm so sorry, dear, but Mary passed away a week ago." She turns to the fireplace mantle and retrieves a letter, which she hands to him. "She asked me to give this to you and to tell you how sorry she was, for everything." Janice gently touches his arm and adds, "I know she loved you very much."

Stunned, Rudi sits there holding the envelope and looks at Mary's mother, shaking his head in disbelief. *This can't be happening. It must be a dream!* Barely able to hear his own voice through the pounding in his ears, Rudi finally says, "I don't believe you! She can't be dead—*she just can't be!*" Suddenly, he gets up and heads in the direction of Mary's room.

Janice reaches for his arm and gently leads him back to the sofa. "Mary was ill with cancer. She just found out two months ago, and when she knew you wanted to marry her, it was more than she could take. She went into a convent in Toronto, where the sisters made her comfortable until the end." Janice stands and looks at Rudi sympathetically. "I'll make us some coffee. Why don't you read her letter while I do that?"

Rudi sits back down and looks through tear-filled eyes at the envelope that bears his name and takes a deep breath. With shaking hands he finally manages to open it. When he removes the letter and unfolds it, he sees the salutation and wipes his eyes.

Dear Rudi,

By the time you read this letter, I will be gone from this earth. I love you with all my heart, and that's why I decided it was best for me to leave you and not tell you that I was dying. I wanted all your memories of me to be happy ones and to think of me as I was. I didn't want you to feel pity for me.

The cancer I have is very progressive, and the doctors gave me only a short time. You're the best thing that has ever happened in my life, and I want to thank you for being my best friend.

I'm so sorry we couldn't make a life together. If I weren't sick, I would have said yes to you in a heartbeat. Please understand that leaving you is the hardest thing I've ever done. Please don't be angry with me for doing it. Always remember how special you are and how much you have meant to me.

I know you'll find another love to spend your life with and that you'll be happy. I wish you the best of everything and will wait in heaven until you're there to join me.

All my love, Mary

After reading the letter, Rudi refolds it and places it in his jacket pocket. While Janice is still busy in the kitchen, he heads to the door and leaves without a word. He gets into his car and drives off, never to return to the house or to see Mary's mother again.

WHEN RUDI TELLS his parents about Mary, they are deeply saddened by his loss. He sinks into a deep depression, hardly leaving the house, except to work, and he drinks heavily. Elsa is very concerned for Rudi and advises him to see a doctor, but he won't listen. After a while, he becomes more withdrawn and stops going to work. Erich views his son's behaviour as a weakness but tries to be patient with Rudi, telling him that the work will help to take his mind off his sadness. Unfortunately, this advice only angers Rudi, and he and Erich argue.

Unexpectedly one day, Rudi informs his parents that he is moving out on his own. Although surprised by this, Elsa and Erich know he is old enough to make his own life choices, and they won't stand in his way.

"Are you sure you want to do this, Rudi?" Elsa asks.

"Yeah, Mom, I'm sure."

"What will you do for money?"

"Don't worry about me, I'll be fine." He kisses his mother on the cheek and shakes his father's hand.

Elsa looks at her son with tears in her eyes. "Well, if things don't work out, you know you can always move back home."

Ignoring his mother's statement, Rudi looks at his parents. "Thanks for everything you've done for me. I may not always have appreciated it, but I just want to tell you that I do now." He grabs his suitcase and leaves without looking back.

"I sure hope he'll be alright," Elsa says.

"Well, there's not much we can do for him. He's got to figure out his life on his own, we can't do that for him."

RUDI LIVES WITH a friend and picks up odd jobs to make money but doesn't appear to care about anything. Living for the moment—drinking and girls—these are all part of Rudi's new lifestyle. He rarely visits his family because it reminds him of his loss, and the failure he feels he has become in the eyes of his parents.

Erich always feared that Rudi would ruin his life, yet he does nothing to try to help his son. He offers no support, emotional or otherwise. "He has made his bed, now he can lie in it," he tells Elsa.

She shakes her head at his comment. *Erich is turning out to be just like my father.* "How can you say that? Have you no compassion? The boy is hurting. Why must you be so unfeeling?"

"He needs to grow up and accept the things that life throws at him. He can never be a man if he doesn't!"

Elsa says nothing more because she knows he won't listen to reason. Her heart is breaking for her only son and vows to do whatever she can for him.

On the odd occasion that Rudi comes home for a visit, he is sullen. Erich has given up on him, and for the most part, he ignores his presence. Elsa tries to support him, although it's apparent that he won't accept her advice. It is painful for her, but Elsa knows there really is nothing more she can do. *He must live his own life and make his own choices. I have to let go of him.* She prays that Rudi will eventually end his grief and come to his senses.

Chapter 32: Frieda

SINCE LAURA'S ARRIVAL, Frieda spends most of her time at her grandmother Anna's apartment. When she does come home, she is cordial but doesn't discuss things that are happening in her life. Both Erich and Elsa are bothered by the apparent distance growing between them and their eldest daughter. Because they have always been close, Erich wonders whether his mother may be to blame for the change in Frieda's behaviour toward them.

One afternoon while working in the salon, one of Elsa's long-time customers and friend, Barbara, tells her something that surprises her.

"You know, Elsa, it's none of my business, but your problem with Frieda is rather obvious to me."

Elsa looks at Barbara in the mirror with interest as she puts rollers into her hair. *"Really?* What do you think it is?"

"Didn't you say that things changed with her around the time you got pregnant, and once the baby was born it got worse?"

"Yes, that's true."

"I'd be willing to bet that Frieda is jealous of Laura."

"Jealous? You really think so? Why on earth would a twenty-year-old be jealous *of a baby?"*

"Well, hasn't she always been 'Daddy's Little Girl?' Haven't you both always doted on her?"

Elsa stops briefly to consider what her friend has said, and although it seems absurd, it would certainly explain things. "That thought never entered my mind, but you might be right about what you say. I just can't understand why she would feel this way—she is an adult after all."

Barbara looks at Elsa's reflection in the mirror and nods. "I've seen this before with my brother and his family, so it isn't that unusual. Maybe you should try talking to her about it."

"Perhaps you're right. I'll give it some thought. Thanks for bringing this to my attention."

BECAUSE OF THE falling out Erich had with his mother after sharing the happy news of Elsa's pregnancy, their relationship with Anna has remained somewhat strained. Even though Elsa hates the thought of contacting her, she reluctantly calls Anna to ask whether she has any idea what could have caused the change in Frieda's behaviour.

"We're very concerned about Frieda," she tells her mother-in-law. "Could you ask her to call me, please?"

"I will ask her, but I can't promise that she will call you back."

"Well, that's *her* decision to make, Anna. Just relay the message to her," Elsa snaps.

Hearing nothing from Frieda, Elsa wonders if Anna actually conveyed her message or whether Frieda just ignored it. Not knowing what else to do, Elsa tells Erich about the possibility that Frieda is jealous of Laura.

"I can't believe that! It doesn't make sense."

"I know, but think about how she's been acting since I became pregnant."

"Well, it was an unexpected surprise, Elsa, but I'm sure that isn't the reason for Frieda's odd behaviour. I suspect that Mama is behind this. You remember how she was when we told her about the baby. Perhaps this is her way of retaliating."

"I don't know, Erich. Maybe it's time we spoke to Frieda to find out the reason she is acting this way."

"That's a good idea. Let's have the family over for dinner on Sunday. Once it's finished, we can approach Frieda and talk about what's going on with her," Erich suggests.

AFTER DINNER THAT Sunday, Elsa asks Rudi to take Anna and Laura for a walk, so she and Frieda can do the dishes. While the three of them are out, Elsa and Erich sit with Frieda.

Erich lights up a cigarette and looks at his daughter. "So Frieda, you're spending lots of time with Oma lately, and you seem a little distant. Did we do something to cause this?"

Frieda shrugs casually. "No, not really. I just wanted to have a change. I can't afford to be out on my own so Oma offered to let me live with her. She said I could stay until I either save up money for my own place or until Christian and I possibly decide to get married."

Stunned by Frieda's last statement, her parents glance at each other. They had no idea she was in a serious relationship seeing that she has never had more than a couple of dates with any man and had never even mentioned Christian before.

"Do you think you *will* marry Christian?" Elsa asks while trying to remain calm.

"I don't know. He's nice and everything, but he's a bit boring. I guess it's because he's so much older than me. I think I'd still like to date some more before getting married. There are just so many men around. I want to be sure about who I end up with."

Elsa understands her daughter's apprehension to settle down with the first man who comes along. Although she loves Erich, had the times been different, she most likely would have dated a couple of men before getting married too. However, the war changed that for women and their options were limited. Elsa figures that even if she had dated other men, she would have still ended up with Erich. She could never imagine loving anyone else as much as she loves him.

"So, you're sure we didn't do anything to upset you?" Erich asks.

"I'm sure. Everything's fine, Dad."

"Okay, but you would tell us if something was bothering you, *wouldn't you*?" Elsa asks as she gently touches her daughter's arm. Frieda looks back at her nods and the discussion ends.

ERICH AND ELSA had hoped that Frieda would be more open about her feelings since she never kept anything from them before, but now the harsh reality that their relationship has changed eats away at them.

"I guess there's nothing more we can do to get her to be honest about what's really bothering her," Elsa says.

"No, I don't think there is. I'm sure she will come around. She's a good girl so we shouldn't worry too much."

It isn't long, however, before they realize that speaking to Frieda only made things worse. Each time Erich and Elsa try to contact her, she tells them she is very busy teaching, providing they can reach her at all. Anna appears to be making excuses for Frieda, and she is never there when Erich and Elsa come to visit. It is becoming evident that their daughter is avoiding them. Erich becomes angered by Frieda's behaviour and his mother's lack of concern for his feelings, and Elsa worries about their daughter and the effect the situation is having on their family.

"If this is how she wants it, then so be it! She's twenty-one—not a kid anymore—she can do whatever the hell she wants!" Erich shouts to Elsa as he opens his sixth beer of the night.

She knows he is only hurt and angry and doesn't mean what he says, but she understands how he feels because she feels the same way.

ONE AFTERNOON, THE phone in the salon rings. Elsa's assistant, Elizabeth, answers it and lets her know that Anna is on the line. Elsa is very surprised that her mother-in-law would phone her about anything, but she excuses herself from her client to take the call. Anna tells her she must speak with her as soon as possible, and Elsa can hear the distress in her voice and immediately gets a knot in her stomach.

"What's wrong?"

"You must come to see me as soon as you can. We can't talk on the telephone." Anna then ends the call abruptly.

After Elsa hangs up, Elizabeth notices that her employer's face has gone pale. "Is everything alright, Elsa? Is there anything I can do?"

"Would you mind watching Laura for a couple of hours and finishing up with Mrs. Smith? I just have to step out for a while."

"Sure, that's no problem at all. Do what you need to do, and don't worry. I'll take care of the salon and the baby until you get back."

Placing her hand on Elizabeth's shoulder, Elsa whispers her thanks and then kisses Laura, telling her to be good while she is away.

The baby smiles from her playpen and waves excitedly to her mother before continuing to play with her toys.

ELSA CLIMBS OUT of the taxi and notices her mother-in-law staring down from her window. Her stomach tenses, and she races into the building to find Anna pacing in the corridor outside of her apartment.

"I'm glad you got here so quickly," she says with some agitation that is so out of character for her.

Elsa's heart beat quickens. "What's going on? Is something wrong with Frieda?"

"She's gone!"

"Gone? Gone where?"

Anna slowly relays the entire story to Elsa, and she sits there quietly listening with her hands clamped together so tightly her knuckles turn white.

"Frieda was fed up with Christian and broke it off with him, and since then, she has been seeing another man."

Elsa attempts to swallow, but her nerves make it almost impossible. Words fail her, so she just continues to listen to what her mother-in-law has to say.

"This man, like Christian, is older. I met him once or twice, and the impression I got wasn't a good one. They spend much time together, and some nights Frieda doesn't come home. She has begun distancing herself from me as well. When she was here the other day, I could tell something was troubling her. I asked her what was wrong, but Frieda denied that there was any problem. I went through her things after she left and found a letter she wrote to this man. From it, I discovered that he is married, and I also learned the reason for Frieda's behaviour." Anna pauses, placing her hand over her heart and takes a deep breath. "She is pregnant with this man's child!"

As the shock of this news sinks in, Elsa trembles, and she covers her face with her hands. Meanwhile, Anna stands by impatiently waiting for her to get control of her emotions. After a few minutes, Elsa finally uncovers her face and looks at her mother-in-law. Taking this her cue, Anna commences with the details surrounding Frieda's departure.

"When I approached her about the letter, she was furious. Frieda told me to mind my own business and then packed her things. She said she loved this man and was going off with him. I don't know where she went." Anna shakes her head incredulously. *"This is the thanks I get for helping her!* I do so much for this family, and it's *never* enough! No one ever appreciates the sacrifices *I* make!"

Elsa looks at her with amazement. "Yes, that's right, this all about *you*, isn't it? *You* do so much for this family, how could I possibly forget that! If it weren't for *you*, we wouldn't be in this mess right now!" *Wow, I can't believe I just said that! I'm so fed up with her arrogant attitude!*

"Sure, blame me for *your* mistakes as a mother! I have done my best to raise the children properly since you were never there for them!"

"That's because I worked to help provide for my family. You never even raised *your own* children. You gave them up at birth because you couldn't stand the fact that they were *boys*. You let your own mother raise them, so don't you *dare* judge me. You are a selfish and heartless woman with nothing better to do than try to control other people's lives!"

"Oh, you don't need to worry. I will be gone from this world soon. I won't live to see another Christmas, and then everyone will be happy!"

Elsa just shakes her head in disgust, and makes for the door, leaving her mother-in-law standing in the middle of her living room. As she exits the apartment, Elsa doesn't look back, she just quietly closes the door. *That certainly didn't go well. Erich isn't going to be pleased when I tell him about this, but hopefully, he won't be too angry with me. This has been building up for years, and I'm glad to have finally put her in her place.*

Chapter 33: The Death of Dreams

ERICH EXPERIENCES A range of emotions over the news of what Frieda has done. He is shocked, hurt, worried, but mostly he is angry. "I just don't understand how she could do this to us," he says to Elsa, trying to make sense of their daughter's behaviour. "Didn't we always do the best we could for her?"

Elsa nods and wraps her arms around him. "Do you think we should try to find her?"

"No, she has made her bed!"

Elsa remains silent since she doesn't want to cause an argument. *Well, isn't that a typical response! He uses this cliché so often, but I realize now that this is his way of coping with his frustration—he can't solve the problem so why get involved?*

Each day is difficult for them. Erich deals with his feelings by drinking heavily, and Elsa loses herself in her work. Baby Laura is the only thing that seems to be keeping them together and brings them what little joy they share.

ONE EVENING, SEVERAL months later, Erich tells Elsa that the bank has been hounding him for payments on Frieda's car.

"Well, just pay what is owed and sell it."

Erich looks down at his feet for a moment. "I... I can't."

"I don't understand. What do you mean you *can't?*"

Erich sighs and finally confesses that he has mismanaged his company. "I've looked over everything. There's just no way I can pay what I owe. The business is... well... it's worthless now. The only solution I see is that it will have to close."

Elsa can feel her face grow hot with anger, and even though she always tries to stay calm and never raise her voice, this pushes her over the edge. "Why didn't you tell me that you were having a problem with the business? You are unbelievable, Erich! How could you let this happen? *How?"* she shouts.

He looks down at his feet once again. "I... I'm so sorry, Elsa. I didn't want to burden you. You've been so busy with the salon and with Laura. I really thought I could handle this myself, but I messed everything up again. I'm just no good for anything!"

"You're sorry! *You're sorry!* After everything we've been through, how could you just let it all go to *hell?"* Realizing that her anger is getting the better of her, she stops to take a deep breath. Once she feels more in control, she continues speaking in an even tone. "You bring me the books, and I'll look them over to see if I can figure a way to avoid losing the business."

Upon reviewing everything and making some quick calculations, Elsa is pale. "We can pay off some of our debts, but you're right, I don't think we have any choice, we need to close the business. We'll go to the bank to arrange a second mortgage on the house and salon to help with the payments, but from now on, Erich, I will be the one in charge of the money. Do we agree?"

Erich nods since he can't seem to find the words he wants to say. He knows she is right and the guilt he feels over his inability to manage his business properly attacks him like a cancer, slowly eroding his sense of self-worth. *What kind of man have I become that I have to have my wife step in and take control?*

THE FOLLOWING DAY, they go to the bank to arrange for refinancing, but the bank manager informs them that due to their poor credit rating, they don't qualify. If they aren't able to make the payments, they will lose the house and with it Elsa's salon. Elsa and Erich sit in the manager's office as the bitter reality of their situation sinks in.

"I'm very sorry, I wish there was something I could do," the bank manager says sadly. "If only you would have come in to see me sooner."

They thank him for his time and leave the bank. Sitting silently in the car, Elsa turns to Erich with tears in her eyes and a look that sends sharp pains into his chest.

"Well, I guess that's it then. I'll have to close my business too, and we'll have to sell the house. It's now up to you to find another job to support the family," she says with emotion choking her words.

Erich looks straight ahead, avoiding Elsa's face because her pained expression is more than he can stand. "I'm so sorry, Elsa," he whispers. Guilt once again chokes him, and he can't think of any way to change the dire situation they now face.

AFTER CLOSING THEIR businesses and selling the house, they are able to pay back a good part of what they owe. They move into an inexpensive rental house in the east end of the city. It is small, dirty and in need of much repair but it is the best they can afford.

Erich works when he can get jobs through the Union, and he gives the money to Elsa to manage, and in turn, she gives him an allowance. She still does hair, but because they live in a residential area, businesses aren't permitted. Any money Elsa earns is "under-the-table" income and, therefore, unreported.

With the dramatic changes to their lives, many of their friends from the Club no longer associate with them. Erich is angered by this, but Elsa takes it in stride. She has always felt that the only reason their friends came to the parties they held was due to the almost limitless supply of alcohol they provided. Elsa's friend Margrit, however, still visits her regularly and tries to help her as much as possible. Whether to listen or provide her a shoulder to cry on, she is there to give her the support and friendship she needs.

Laura, now two years old, demands much of Elsa's attention, and she is happy to spend time with the toddler since it provides a welcome distraction from the stress of her daily life.

Erich and Elsa continue to take Laura to visit her Oma every Sunday. Elsa has made peace with her mother-in-law, mainly for

Erich's sake, and they never speak about Frieda and are civil to each other. Anna's feelings for Laura are lukewarm at best, and although Erich is aware of this, he still insists that they make their weekly visits.

In her times of trouble, Elsa still recalls the words of her mother. *"You must stay strong and take each day as it comes."* She does her best to keep her faith, although it is tested beyond its limits with Erich's drunken and malicious behaviour. She tries not to say anything that will anger him because when she does, they only argue. A few times the arguments are so heated that Erich comes close to being physically abusive, and Elsa knows that she must try to keep the peace for Laura's sake. She realizes this isn't a healthy environment for a child, so she tries to focus most of her attention on the needs of her baby to try to compensate for it.

In addition to the stress of their current situation, Frieda and Rudi remain a constant source of worry and grief for their parents. Hearing nothing from Frieda, Erich and Elsa have concluded that they have lost their eldest daughter for good. They rarely speak about her and try to go on with their daily lives as though she never existed.

Rudi has met a girl, Sandra, and the two of them elope. Erich and Elsa are both surprised and concerned with his choice of a wife because she appears to be much the same as he is—lazy with no ambition. He continues having issues holding a steady job, leaving the newlyweds in dire financial straits. They only visit when they are seeking a handout, and Elsa gives Rudi what she can, but she isn't able to spare much since they are still paying off their own debts. She can only hope that he will get himself a proper job soon, but as time goes on, Elsa doubts that this may ever happen.

Chapter 34: One Step Forward...

AT THE BEGINNING of 1968, Elsa finally manages to pay off all their debts and once again saves what little money she can. Erich still works when possible, and Elsa continues to do hair to make ends meet. It has been a continuous struggle, budgeting and saving, but now with their finances in better shape, Elsa thinks about the possibility of buying the house they have been renting.

When she approaches the landlord to ask if he would be interested in selling the property, to her surprise, he is agreeable. They settle on a price and work out an arrangement where he will hold the mortgage, with the only stipulation being that Erich and Elsa must secure mortgage insurance.

"If something should happen to your husband and you can't make your mortgage payments, you'll end up losing your home, and I hate the thought of that," he tells her.

Elsa consents to this, thinking it is a very smart idea and instructs him to draw up the papers and call her when they are ready. She is thrilled by the prospect of owning a home once again.

"DO YOU REALLY think we can afford to do it?" Erich asks with a hint of excitement in his voice after Elsa tells him the news.

She gives him a confident look. "Do you think I would go to this trouble if I thought we couldn't make this work?"

Erich nods and an uncharacteristic look of joy overtakes his face. He knows his wife is better at handling money than he ever could, so he agrees to the purchase.

Elsa spends much of her time planning for improvements to the little wartime house now that Laura is in school full time. After telling Erich her ideas, he draws her plans on paper, takes the necessary measurements and estimates the cost involved. Erich will do the renovations himself, using discarded building materials from his jobs when possible, to save money. Having lived through the war, both he and Elsa are very resourceful, keeping old things to reuse in one way or another.

With Erich's time being spent on work and remodeling, he has curbed his drinking somewhat, and this pleases Elsa because it allows her to speak to him more freely. Erich seems happier too. He spends a little time playing with Laura, which is something he never seemed to have the chance to do in the past, and she is happy that her daddy gives her the attention she craves.

BY 1970, RUDI AND his wife, Sandra, have two children, a boy and girl. Their financial issues have been made worse with the arrival of the babies, but Elsa continues to help them as much as she can, although she is becoming more frustrated with Rudi's behaviour. *How much longer can we keep giving him money?* At the same time, she thinks about what will happen if they don't help him. *We've already lost a daughter—we don't want to lose a son as well.* She is torn between feeling that they are being used, and feeling sorry for them, and it eats away at her, leaving her emotionally drained.

THE PHONE RINGS early one morning in mid-April 1971, rousing Erich and Elsa from a sound sleep. Erich gets up and leaves the bedroom, staggering half asleep as he makes his way to answer it.

"Hello? Who is this?" Elsa hears him say. She gets up and stands beside him, patiently waiting to learn the identity of the late-night caller. Suddenly, Erich sits down with a stunned expression.

"Erich, what is it?"

He hands the receiver to her without speaking.

"Hello, who is this, please?" After a brief pause, she hears a familiar voice at the other end of the line.

"It's me, Mom—Frieda."

Elsa sits down beside Erich, too shocked for words. She holds the receiver to her ear and waits.

"Mom, would it be okay for me to come home?"

Elsa doesn't answer and hands the phone back to Erich. "She wants to come home," she tells him as all the hurt feelings and anger resurface within her. It has been seven years since they last heard from her, and Elsa shakes her head in disgust. "She has some nerve calling us after all this time!" She walks back to the bedroom, leaving Erich to speak to his long-lost daughter.

An hour later, Erich finally returns to bed. He beams when he tells Elsa that Frieda will be coming to visit them in a few days.

"You're just going to *let her* come back? Don't you remember all the heartache and trouble she caused us?" she says raising her voice.

"She is still my little girl, Elsa! She needs me!"

"Oh, yes. *Your* little girl and *now* she needs *you*—after seven years! I tell you, this is a mistake. She *will* hurt us again, Erich, I promise you. She's just like your mother—selfish!"

Without responding, Erich goes into the kitchen and opens the fridge to take out a beer. Elsa follows him there and watches him take a long pull on the bottle.

"Ah, there you go again, handling your problems with beer!" she shouts, knowing that an argument will ensue, but she doesn't care. This time, she won't be passive. She is primed for a fight. *He's too blind to see what's happening. Well, I won't put up with it—not anymore!*

They both raise their voices, and as they argue, eight-year-old Laura gets up from her bed and enters the kitchen with her hands over her ears and tears spilling from her eyes.

"Mommy, Daddy, stop it! *Stop it!*" she yells, trying to be heard over her parents' shouting.

When they notice Laura standing there, they both stop to look at her, and Elsa rushes over to comfort her. She holds her daughter close and kisses the top of her head before taking her back to her room.

Elsa searches for a reasonable explanation to defuse the situation, but nothing plausible comes to her mind. She finally says, "Mommy and Daddy are just having a disagreement, that's all, but everything is okay." Noticing that this has done nothing to dispel Laura's obvious concerns, Elsa tries a different approach. "I have a surprise for you," she says with a forced smile. "You're finally going to meet your sister!"

Laura looks at her mother wide-eyed, and Elsa can see the excitement take over her young face, effectively making her forget the trauma of her parent's angry words.

"*When*, Mommy? When will I meet her?"

"Very soon. Now, off to sleep with you, young lady! It's very late!" Elsa says, kissing her young daughter before heading to the door. "Goodnight, sweetie."

Laura once again tries to imagine what her sister, Frieda, must be like. Her parents told her that because she lived so far away, she was never able to visit, and the more Laura thinks, the more excited she becomes. *I can hardly wait to meet her!* When she finally falls asleep, she dreams about her big sister and all the fun they will have.

Erich is in bed, smoking a cigarette and staring at the ceiling when Elsa enters.

"Everything will be fine, Elsa. Frieda's sorry for hurting us and things will be different now."

Elsa doesn't reply, she just gets into bed and lies on her side, away from Erich and turns off the lamp on her bedside table. *I have such a bad feeling about this! I wish I could share Erich's point of view, but I just can't. Erich is so gullible, and Frieda knows exactly how to wrap him around her little finger.* She says a silent prayer that everything will indeed be better than it once was.

TWO DAYS LATER, Frieda arrives at their house while Laura is at school. With her are a man and two young girls, whom she introduces as her fiancé and children, aged four and six. She tells her parents that the father of the girls is the man she left with years earlier and explains how he later ran off with yet another woman, leaving her stranded without any support.

Erich and Elsa listen to Frieda's sad story but say nothing until she has finished. Erich is happy Frieda is back, but Elsa remains guarded. She is fearful that Frieda might cause more problems for them, potentially ruining the first bit of happiness they have experienced in many years. Elsa hates feeling so negative toward her own daughter, but she knows that history has a way of repeating itself, and she can't help how she feels.

When Laura arrives home from school, she is so excited to finally meet her sister.

"Laura, this is your sister, Frieda, and her soon-to-be husband, Phil," her father says with a broad smile. "And these are her little girls, Sally and Karin."

She looks at them wide-eyed. Laura never expected her sister to have children, but she tries her best to hide her surprise. "Hi," she says timidly.

Frieda looks at her little sister with indifference. "Well, you've grown since I saw you last. Why don't you and the girls go and play, and let us adults have a visit." She turns away from Laura and continues talking with her parents.

Laura stares at her sister's back, blinking away tears and then looks to her new nieces. *She doesn't like me, and I don't know why. I didn't do anything wrong.* She shakes her head and runs to her bedroom, leaving Sally and Karin in the living room with the adults. *I'm not playing with her girls!*

A few minutes later, Erich enters Laura's room with the girls in tow, his face etched with anger. "Laura, you *will* play nicely with Sally and Karin, *do you understand?"*

Knowing she has no other alternative, she replies, "Yes, Daddy."

ERICH HELPS FRIEDA and her family to find a house and her fiancé find a job. When Frieda marries Phil, he adopts the girls as his own. They come to visit almost every weekend to drink and party, and Frieda pawns the girls off to Elsa to care for while she, Erich and her husband get drunk.

Frieda does nothing to help her mother with making meals or cleaning up, nor does she even offer to buy any food. She treats the children disrespectfully, leaving Elsa to try to make the girls feel welcome. She is angry with her eldest daughter for her treatment of not only her children, but Laura as well. Elsa is also mad at Erich for being part of Frieda's carefree lifestyle. *This is just another excuse for him to drink.*

Laura is wise beyond her years and can see the effect that these weekends are having on her mother. She knows her mother is angry and hurt by Frieda's behaviour, and she is too. *How can she treat us this way?* Laura wonders again while putting on her apron in preparation for doing the dishes on Saturday afternoon.

Frieda comes into the kitchen to get more beer and laughs at her younger sister. "Just look at you! Do you have any idea how ridiculous you look wearing that silly apron?"

Laura is beside herself and glares at Frieda. "Well, at least, I help Mom! What have you ever done to help her? All you do is come here, get drunk, and expect Mom to take care of your kids and wait on you! You should be ashamed of how you treat her!"

Elsa is shocked by her youngest daughter's view of the situation, and she can't help but feel a little gratified. This young one has said what she has wanted to say for a long time.

"Phil! Get the girls! We're leaving, now!"

Her husband rushes up the stairs and takes the children by the hand, heading for the door. Unsure of the reason behind Frieda's need for a hasty departure, Erich follows close behind.

"Wait! Why are you leaving? Has something happened?"

Frieda's face twists with rage. "Ask your other daughter! We won't stay in a place where we're not welcome!" She runs out of the house and down to the street.

Erich rushes out after her. At Frieda's car, he leans into the open driver's side window. "What did Laura say?"

Frieda tells her father what her younger sister said to her and watches with satisfaction as his face turns crimson.

"Please, Frieda, please don't go. She's just a *stupid kid* who doesn't know anything. I promise you, I'll see to it that Laura pays for her disrespect. Just don't leave, okay?"

"Sorry, Dad, but we're going." Frieda drives off, leaving Erich on the road, watching as her taillights fade in the distance.

Erich storms back into the house. "Laura! Where are you?" He finds her in the kitchen and grabs her in a fit of rage, shaking her violently. "How *dare* you! Who do you think you *are?* This is *my* house, and *I* decide who visits, *not* you!" He then raises his large calloused hand and slaps her.

Shocked by her father's attack, Laura holds her cheek, accepting his abuse without a word and her eyes sting with tears. *I should have thought about how he would react to me telling Frieda off. Now I'm paying the price, but I don't care.*

Elsa can't believe her eyes. *Dear God in Heaven, who is this monster?* She pulls his arm attempting to get him away from Laura. "Leave her alone, Erich! She only said what I was thinking and should have said a long time ago!"

Erich moves slightly, allowing Laura the opportunity to escape his reach, and she runs to her mother's side.

Noticing the result of this action, Erich then approaches Elsa and raises his hand to strike her. As he does, Laura screams at him to stop. She knows it is wrong to yell at her father, but she isn't concerned about the consequences, all she cares about is her mother.

Erich looks at both of them and finally puts down his hand, and then without a word, he makes his way to the basement rec room.

Trembling, Elsa gently takes Laura and holds her close, stroking her hair. "Are you alright, sweetie?"

Laura sniffles and with shaking hands, she wipes her eyes and nods. The shock of the incident leaves her looking as though she is under a spell. Elsa leads her into the bathroom and helps her to wash her face, and then the two of them leave the house.

"YOU KNOW DAD loves you, don't you? He just gets very confused when he's been drinking. We have to be very good when he drinks so that this doesn't happen again, okay?" Elsa tells Laura while they sit on the swings at the park a few blocks from their house.

Laura shakes her head, and tears fill her eyes. "I don't think he loves me anymore, Mom. He only loves Frieda."

Elsa looks at her young daughter, so hurt by the actions of her husband, it almost brings her to tears. "Oh, that's *not true.* Dad is very proud of you and cares about you so much, although I know you can't see that right now. You know I would never lie to you, don't you?"

Laura studies her mother's face for a moment and nods back to her without speaking. *I know Mom wouldn't lie to me, but I think she doesn't want to believe that it's true. If he really loved me, he wouldn't treat me this way.* This thought hurts her much more than the slap her father gave her earlier.

Elsa embraces Laura before making their way home. They hope that Erich will still be in the basement when they return because they are both emotionally drained from their earlier encounter with him and couldn't cope with another similar episode. As they walk in silence, Elsa thinks about how much easier life would be without having to deal with Erich's drunkenness. *I just don't recognize this man anymore. Our marriage is failing, and I don't know what to do. Maybe Margrit was right, perhaps it's time for me to think about leaving him, but how will I ever be able to do that?*

IN THE DAYS that follow, Laura tries to talk to Erich, but he refuses to speak to her unless she apologizes for her outburst. She fails to understand why she needs to ask for his forgiveness. She was only defending her mother by telling the truth and putting her sister in her place.

"Why should she apologize, Erich? If you want to hold a grudge over what happened, why not blame me? Laura was only standing up for me, saying what I should have said myself," Elsa says, trying to put an end to his anger toward their daughter.

"Neither you nor Laura has any right to have an opinion here. You're most certainly the root of the problem. It's your fault that she doesn't know how to behave!"

"Okay, *fine!* It's all *my fault*, and I'm sorry. Now can we drop this and get back to normal, *please?*"

"Not until I have an apology from Laura, and I expect her to call Frieda to apologize to her too."

Elsa says nothing more, and she leaves Erich in search of Laura. *I guess this mess is my fault. If only I had stopped Laura from saying those things to Frieda, none of this would be happening now. I really should've said those things myself. My own daughter has more courage than I do!*

Elsa enters Laura's room to find her sitting on her bed hugging her knees to her chest and staring blankly at the wall.

"How are you doing, sweetie?"

She shrugs with indifference. "I'm okay, I guess. Did you talk to Dad?"

"Yes, but I'm afraid it didn't do any good. He won't change his mind. He wants an apology from you and also wants you to apologize to Frieda. I'm sorry, Laura. This is my fault."

"*You* didn't do anything wrong, Mom. This is *so* unfair! It makes me mad! It should be Frieda who apologizes to you!"

"Shhh—I know it seems unfair, but if we want this to be over, you just need to do it. *Please*, Laura."

She looks at her mother with a frown. "Okay, Mom, but can you come with me?"

"Of course, I will."

Even though Elsa agreed to go with her, Laura's stomach tightens with fear at the thought of approaching her father.

"Come on, let's go and get this over with," Elsa says.

Erich is sitting in the living room watching TV when Laura enters with Elsa. He turns and looks at his daughter expectantly.

"*Well?* Do you have something to say to me?"

Laura swallows hard trying to force her fear away, and her voice comes out as a whisper. "I... I'm sorry, Dad."

"*Sorry?* Sorry for what?"

"I'm sorry for yelling at Frieda."

"Fine, now go and call her to apologize—and Laura—don't you *ever* do something like that again—*understand?* This is my house, *not yours!* As long as you're living under my roof, *you will do as I say!*"

Laura nods and stands there quietly, waiting for her father to reciprocate the apology.

"What are you standing there for? Go call your sister!" Erich says sternly, pointing to the phone on the table.

Laura's stomach burns as she picks up the receiver to make the call. It is the most difficult thing she has ever had to do in her young life. When she hangs up, she returns to her room.

Sitting on her bed, Laura has a hard time to catch her breath, and hot tears spill down her cheeks. *Dad really does hate me! Maybe if I were more like Frieda, I could get him to love me too.*

Elsa is upset with Erich's treatment of Laura but will say nothing to cause further tension. *I sure hope that Laura's forced apology won't encourage Frieda to come around again.*

It isn't long, however, before the weekend habit commences once more and things are just as they were. Elsa and Laura keep their feelings and comments to themselves and do their best to ignore the usual routine. *How much longer can we live this way? I really have to do something,* Elsa thinks.

LAURA WANTS SO much to win her father's love and approval that she feels the only way to accomplish this is by competing with her sister for his affection. In her young mind, she believes that because Frieda is good at playing the guitar, she should also learn an instrument to make her father proud of her. Laura approaches Erich to ask for piano lessons, but he tells her that because space is limited in their small wartime house, he can only agree to allow her to learn the organ.

"It's the same as a piano," he tells her. "If you're serious about this, I will talk with Mama and see if we can make this work."

Laura is disappointed that she can't learn the instrument of her choice, but because she wants so much to prove herself to her father and win his praise, she reluctantly agrees.

Erich and Elsa discuss Laura's request for music lessons. "I think we should give her the same opportunity we gave to Frieda," Elsa says.

They borrow money from the bank to purchase an organ and pay for the weekly lessons. Laura takes lessons and practices as much as possible, but after a year, it is evident that she lacks the musical talent of her older sister.

Erich is quick to point out his displeasure at Laura's inadequate musical capabilities. "I spent all that money, and you just don't have the knack!"

Laura's idea to win her father's love and approval falls to the wayside—adding another blow to her self-confidence.

Without warning, Erich gives the organ to Frieda, who has now begun learning to play. Laura is extremely hurt by the insensitive actions of both her father and sister and comes to realize that no matter what she does, her father will never be proud of her or give her the love that she so desperately craves. *I can't believe that Dad gave Frieda my organ! He didn't even give me a chance! Oh well, I never liked it anyway. If she wants it, she can have it. I just don't care anymore!*

Chapter 35: Erich

LAURA IS EXTREMELY shy and withdrawn, so she doesn't have many friends and is frequently teased. Elsa does what she can to try to make her feel better, but her attempts prove unsuccessful.

"Kids can be so cruel. They're just jealous. You're a lovely girl and very mature for your age. That makes you different from the other kids, and they have a tough time dealing with that," Elsa tells her, trying to ease her hurt feelings.

"But I don't like to be *different*, Mom. I just want to have *friends!*" *No one really likes me! Dad doesn't, Frieda doesn't and even the kids at school don't! Mom is the only one who really cares about me and loves me.* Although she loves her mother, it just isn't enough to make her happy.

Elsa strokes her daughter's hair. "Don't worry, things will be better soon, you'll see."

Realizing that Laura's lack of self-esteem is mainly due to Erich's drinking and his relationship with Frieda, Elsa is also aware that she shoulders some of the blame herself for not standing up to him. *I have to talk to Erich, regardless of the outcome. I have to make him see the extent of the damage his behaviour has caused Laura. I just can't stand by and let this continue.*

ONE SATURDAY WHILE Laura is visiting Rudi, Elsa finally gets up the nerve to speak to Erich.

"I'm worried about Laura," Elsa says after they have lunch.

"Why? What's the problem?"

"She lacks both confidence and self-esteem, and I'm worried that she won't have a happy life."

"Now *why* would she feel that way? Isn't it *your* job as her mother to see that she feels good about herself?"

"How can you *not know* the reason for her problems, and how *dare you* blame me? Are you *really* that blind not to see that *your* behaviour is the source of this?"

"My behaviour? What's *wrong* with my behaviour? I've never done *anything* to cause her to feel bad!"

"You are *unbelievable*, Erich! Your drinking and relationship with Frieda are hurting Laura to the point where she thinks you no longer love her. If that behaviour isn't *wrong*, I don't know what is! I sometimes wonder if she isn't right! Do *you* love our youngest daughter?"

Erich is beside himself with rage, and he balls his fists at his sides as he spits out his reply. "How can she think that I don't love her? Didn't I buy her the organ that she could never play worth a damn? She needs to grow up!"

"Yes, *we* bought her the organ. Maybe she didn't play well because it wasn't the right instrument for her to learn, but you should never have shunned her attempt or turned around and given it to Frieda. Don't you realize she's reaching out to you because you've basically ignored her since Frieda's return?"

"So she's *jealous*—she'll need to get over it!"

Elsa shakes her head in disgust. "Jealously is definitely a factor, but you have to ask yourself, who the jealous one really is here. Frieda has been the one with that problem since my pregnancy with Laura."

"Yeah, well, if you hadn't been pregnant in the first place, things wouldn't have turned out the way they did! Frieda wouldn't have run off with that guy, and we would still have kept our house and businesses!"

"You're blaming *me?* As I recall, *we both* wanted a baby, and you were ecstatic when Laura was born. Frieda running off was *her* decision. If it was because she couldn't come to terms with Laura's existence, then that was *her* issue. As for the loss of the house and our businesses, the only one to blame for that is *you!* You were too proud to tell me you screwed things up and because of that, we ended up *here!*"

Erich raises his fist in rage to Elsa, and she stands before him unmoving. "Go ahead, *big man*—hit me! *I dare you!*"

Boiling with rage, Erich turns and slams his fist into the veneer coffee table—smashing it to pieces before storming out of the house.

Elsa remains in the living room, shaking as she picks up the pieces of her coffee table. *Well, I know this did nothing to improve the situation, but I had to try. We can't keep living this way. I hate the thought of leaving, but I just don't think we can put up with anymore.* Once she is calm, she sits down with a cup of coffee and reviews their finances. After doing some calculations and estimates, she works out a plan to save some money in case things deteriorate and leaving becomes her only option.

THE RELATIONSHIP BETWEEN Elsa and Erich is further strained in August 1974 when Frieda gives birth to her third child, a boy. She and Phil name the baby Erik, after her father, but change the spelling. Erich is excited for his namesake, talking only about him and Frieda, leaving Elsa and Laura to watch silently as he drifts further away from them. Elsa knows she can't remedy the emotional damage Erich has already caused Laura, but she will do her best to see that his behaviour doesn't inflict further harm. She continues saving what little money she can and realizes now that things will probably never get better. Although the thought of leaving frightens her, Elsa must think of what is best for Laura.

ERICH HAS SUFFERED from back problems for the last few years, which he attributes to his bricklaying, but lately, the pain has become excruciating. The intensity of it causes him to become very agitated and makes Elsa and Laura's lives even more intolerable. Finally, after months of coaxing by Elsa, Erich finally agrees to see the doctor.

"What did the doctor say, Erich?"

"I have arthritis in my back. He said that if I continue to work, there's a good chance I might not be able to walk."

"I'm sorry to hear that. Is there anything that can be done?" Although Elsa is sympathetic to his health issues, she frowns as she thinks about the impact that this will have on them.

"I just have to try to control the pain with medication and stop working."

"How are we to live if you give up your job?"

"We have our savings. It'll see us through for a while, but once it's gone, I'm not sure what to do."

"What about applying for social assistance?"

"I won't take charity from anyone! I took enough of it during the war and won't take it again—not even from the government! I care for my family on my own!"

Elsa sighs, knowing that he will never allow it, but she fears for their future. "Alright, Erich, please calm down. I was only making a suggestion."

ERICH'S PAIN WORSENS as time goes on, and the medications do nothing to alleviate it. He is miserable and angry all the time. At least before, he was only that way when he was drunk, but it is becoming harder for Elsa and Laura to be in the same house with him. Elsa does her best to keep the peace within their small family by trying to ignore Erich's behaviour.

"We have to be more tolerant of Dad now that he's sick. His pain is becoming hard for him to handle and that's why he's so moody."

"He was moody *before* he got sick, Mom."

"That was different. His drinking caused that, but when he didn't drink, he was fine."

Laura nods reluctantly. *I don't understand why you keep making excuses for Dad's behaviour. He was never fine. He's just an angry, unhappy person despite his health issues.*

The change in Erich's behaviour is so drastic that during one of their weekend get-togethers, he becomes very aggressive, causing him and Frieda to have a huge argument that ends with her and her family leaving. Elsa isn't sure what the argument was about, all she knows is that Erich is adamant that Frieda and her family are no longer welcome in their home. She and Laura are relieved that he has come to this conclusion on his own. *We should have never allowed her back into our lives. Maybe now things can get back to the way they used to be,* Elsa thinks.

Erich detaches himself from everyone and only speaks when he feels the need. It troubles Elsa that he has become so withdrawn, but she knows that there is no speaking to him and resigns herself to doing her best to take care of her family. *Erich reminds me more and more of my father, and I really thought I'd never have to deal with that behaviour again. There's no way I can leave him now that he's sick. I'm stuck here and just have to make the best of it.*

The financial and emotional stresses are almost overwhelming, and Elsa is reminded of how she felt when she had to tend to her father and brother during the war. *I really must be careful not to get sick this time—Laura needs me. I have to take one day at a time. I'll get through this, just like I've gotten through all the other tough times in my life.*

ERICH VISITS THE doctor again in the summer of 1976 after experiencing shortness of breath and severe pain in his chest. The doctor sends him to a specialist for tests, and the results aren't good.

"You have lung cancer, Erich. You've probably suffered with it for the last few years with all the back pain you've experienced," Dr. Shaw tells him.

He looks at the specialist and sighs. "So, I'm *dying?*"

"Well, there has been some significant progress made with treatment for this type of cancer. We can remove the affected lung, and you stand an excellent chance of beating this disease if we catch it early enough."

Erich's stomach clenches at the thought of his own mortality, and he swallows hard. "Okay, let's do it," he says, knowing full well that if he were to think more about it, he would probably not agree to it.

When he returns from his appointment, he sits down with Elsa and tells her the news of his illness.

"You're doing the right thing. It's the only choice under the circumstances. Don't worry, we'll get through this together, honey," she says, wiping a tear from her eye. *Why am I really crying? Deep down I still have some feelings for Erich, but is it because I sympathize with him or because I know now that I can never leave? I just don't know what I feel anymore!*

Together Erich and Elsa go to break the news to Laura. It is a difficult task, but Erich comes directly to the point, leaving his youngest daughter upset and confused.

"I don't understand. How did this happen?"

"The doctor figures it's because I've smoked since I was ten years old. Apparently smoking isn't good for you, only no one knew that back then."

"So after the operation, you'll be okay?"

"Sure I will, Laura." He winks at her and smiles bravely, hoping that he is right.

That night, Laura can't sleep. She closes her eyes, but her brain won't allow her to rest. *I can't believe Dad has cancer. We might not always get along, but it's not fair for anyone to be sick like that. I know Mom thinks that there's a reason for everything, but I just don't understand why this has to happen.*

IN SEPTEMBER, LAURA starts high school, and at the same time, Erich goes to have his surgery. She takes some time from school to support her mother, and Rudi comes by often to drive them to and from the hospital.

"Mrs. Kaufmann? I'm Dr. Shaw. Erich's surgery went well. We had to remove half of his right lung, and he will have to undergo radiation treatments. We'll see how things progress in the next few weeks, but I'm hopeful for his recovery."

"Thank you, Dr. Shaw. When can we see him?"

"He's still in ICU so it may be a while, but the nurse will let you know shortly."

Elsa nods and thanks him again. When he leaves, she waits with Rudi and Laura.

"Well, it sounds promising," says Rudi.

"Yes, but it's still going to be a stressful few weeks."

"Will Dad be coming home after that?" asks Laura.

Elsa takes her daughter's hand and strokes it caringly. "Like the doctor said, we'll have to see how things progress."

After several more hours of waiting, the family is given permission for a brief visit with Erich. His appearance shocks Elsa. At once, all of their past problems mean nothing. *I've never seen him look so pale! Just look at all those tubes and machines! We take our lives for granted until something like this happens. Please God, help him get well.*

It isn't long before Erich feels a bit better, and his colour returns to normal, despite the radiation treatments. This makes him confident that he will be well enough to come home soon.

Relieved by the positive outcome of the surgery, Elsa looks forward to having Erich return home so that they can piece their lives back together. *I'm sure now that he's feeling better things will be better too.*

Finally, a month later, Erich leaves the hospital. He is pleased to be home, and Elsa is happy to have him back. Laura, although thankful that he is getting well, feels somewhat hesitant. *Will things go back to the way they were before?*

ELSA AND LAURA take turns caring for Erich, and he appears to be getting stronger each day, but after six weeks, he falls ill again. Erich has trouble walking, and his skin colour takes on a yellowish tinge. He spends most of his time in bed and needs constant care.

During all this time, Elsa has also been looking after Erich's mother, Anna. She is becoming senile and requires extra attention, and now with Erich being ill as well, Elsa stretches herself to the limit.

One afternoon, while Elsa is with Anna, Laura tends to her father. She brings him his lunch on a tray and helps him to sit up in bed. He stops eating for a few moments and holds out his arms.

"What are you doing, Dad?"

Erich looks at her indignantly. "What does it look like I'm doing? I'm reading the newspaper, *stupid girl!*"

Laura is bewildered. "But you don't have the paper, Dad."

"What do you mean? Of course, I have!"

"Okay, Dad, whatever you say. Please don't get angry. I'll be right back. Why don't you finish your lunch?" Laura goes into the kitchen, trying to make sense of her father's actions. *What's happening to Dad? I have a bad feeling that something is very wrong.*

A while later, as Laura cleans up from lunch, she hears a loud thud and Erich screams. She races into the bedroom to find that he has fallen to the floor.

"Get me back on the bed!"

Laura attempts to lift him, but the moment she touches him, he screams in pain.

"Don't touch me!"

"I don't know what to do, Dad!"

"I need to get back to bed! Do something, *stupid girl!*"

Fear envelops Laura, and she frantically tries to think of some way to lift Erich back into the bed without causing him more pain. Not knowing what else to do, she takes the bed sheet, placing it beneath his frail body and wrapping it around him like a stork carrying a baby. Kneeling on the side of the bed and using all of her strength, she pulls the sheet, trying to hoist her father back up. During this process, the sound of Erich's constant screams cause her to cringe. After several excruciating minutes, Laura's plan is finally successful.

"I'm so sorry I hurt you, but I didn't know how else to lift you."

"Just go away and leave me alone!"

Laura shakes her head but says nothing. She goes back to the kitchen to wait for her mother's return. *Nothing ever changes. No matter how hard I try, I can never do anything right.*

When Elsa finally comes home, Laura tells her about what happened. She goes into the bedroom and notices Erich having a conversation without anyone being present in the room. Her hopes for his full recovery are shattered. *He's hallucinating! This is definitely not good.*

AT THE BEGINNING of December, Elsa calls their family doctor, and he makes a home visit to examine Erich since he is too weak to travel. While the doctor is in with Erich, Elsa and Laura wait patiently in the living room for word on his condition.

"The cancer must have spread. Dr. Shaw wasn't sure whether he caught all of it when he did the surgery. I think it's best that he goes back to the hospital where he can get the care he requires. You can no longer adequately tend to his needs with how much he has declined," the doctor regrettably reports.

They are saddened by the news, but deep down they suspected this was the case. Before leaving their home, the doctor calls for an ambulance to take Erich back to the hospital.

Seeing Erich is emotionally painful for everyone. Rudi helps when he can, despite all of his own personal issues. Frieda, however, has not come around to offer any support at all after learning of her father's illness, and Elsa is happy that she is keeping her distance. To ease their stress, Elsa and Laura take turns visiting Erich.

ON LAURA'S BIRTHDAY, Rudi takes her to the hospital and waits while she goes in to visit their father.

"Hi, Dad, how are you feeling today?"

Erich turns to her with a look of confusion. "What's that yellow truck doing in here?" he asks while touching Laura's yellow sweater.

Laura takes her father's hand as tears stream down her face. "It's only me, Dad, Laura. There is no truck here, okay? It's just me."

"*Laura?* I don't know any *Laura!* Where's *Frieda?*"

Laura quickly removes her hand from her father's as though burned by it and leaves the room sobbing. *Dad doesn't even know me! Even after he told Frieda not to visit anymore, he still remembers her! I knew Dad never loved me.*

Rudi looks up from his magazine and notices Laura enter the waiting room. Her anguished expression sends pain stabbing into his heart. He rushes to her side, immediately putting his strong arms around her.

"What's wrong?"

Laura takes a few deep breaths, and Rudi hands her a tissue.

"I don't think I can visit him anymore, Rudi. I just can't do it!" she cries into his shoulder after telling him what happened.

"It's okay, Sis. If you don't want to visit anymore, you don't have to. Try to remember how Dad used to be, and forget about this. The Dad you know isn't here anymore, he's already gone."

Laura nods but knows she won't ever forget this visit as long as she lives. "I never really liked how he used to be. I just wish I could've worked things out with him and said goodbye before he forgot me, now I'll never get the chance." She always hoped that once she became an adult, she and Erich would finally be able to improve their relationship, eventually helping her to heal and forget the past. *I just don't know if I want to remember how Dad used to be. Part of me doesn't want to remember him at all!*

Rudi understands and appreciates his sister's feelings about their father. He also wishes that he could have somehow made his relationship with him better. *The only thing I can do now is to be here for Mom and Laura and set aside those feelings.*

ELSA IS FRAIL and gets sick often. The doctor advises her to stop seeing Erich and focus on her own needs.

"There's nothing you can do for him now, Elsa. You know yourself that Erich wouldn't want you to suffer because of him."

She reluctantly agrees since she knows the doctor speaks the truth. Elsa feels terrible not being there for Erich, but she just doesn't have the strength to watch his pain. Elsa tells Rudi and Laura about the doctor's suggestion, and they both nod.

"It's okay, Mom. I'll take care of things with Dad from now on," Rudi says.

"Are you sure? I hate to put this burden on you because you have your own life and family to deal with."

He puts his arm around his mother. "Don't worry, Mom. I can handle it."

She looks into his face and can see that he is sincere. "Thank you, Rudi. I'm so grateful to you for taking over the responsibility."

RUDI VISITS HIS father every day. He stays for hours at a time and calls his mother with reports on how Erich is doing. "The doctor says it won't be much longer now, Mom."

Elsa and Laura anxiously await the call that will tell them that Erich's suffering has finally ended. Each time the phone rings, they rush to answer it, but it is never the call they are expecting. Weeks go by, and Erich still clings to life. The doctors have him on morphine to make him comfortable, but they can't understand why this frail man is still holding on.

Finally, at 7 a.m., on January 28, 1977, they get the news they have anticipated for so long. When the phone rings, Elsa answers it immediately. The sound wakes Laura, and she gets up and stands by her mother's side, patiently waiting for the call to end. Elsa holds the receiver tightly to her ear and listens intently to the person on the other end of the line. A few minutes later, she gives her thanks and hangs up before turning to her daughter with a heavy sigh.

"Well, it's over. Dad is finally at peace," she says with tears rolling down her tired face.

Laura says nothing and gives her mother a gentle hug. They stand together quietly as a sense of relief washes over them.

Before Elsa calls Rudi to tell him the news, she looks out the window and notices the snow. She turns on the radio and hears the warnings for a blizzard, predicted to be the worst of the century, and she shakes her head. "This is unbelievable—of all days to have weather like this!"

When Elsa tells Rudi of his father's passing, she asks him to come by the house to pick her up and take her to the hospital. She needs to identify Erich's body and make the necessary arrangements for his funeral. She warns him about the weather, telling him to take his time driving.

Rudi finally arrives at his mother's house at noon, after fighting the heavy snow and traffic. Once he has a cup of coffee to warm up, he and Elsa slowly make their way to the hospital. The funeral arrangements will have to wait since the storm has completely shut down the city.

"MAYBE WE SHOULD stop at Oma's to tell her about Dad," Rudi suggests when they leave the hospital.

"Oh, I don't know. I'm really not in the proper frame of mind to deal with her right now."

"I know, Mom, but I think it would be easier to tell her in person than if you called her on the phone. I think Dad would want that, don't you?"

Elsa lets out a sigh and reluctantly agrees to make a quick visit to her mother-in-law. *I guess Rudi is right, I owe it to Erich to tell her in person. I just hope she won't be difficult.*

When they tell Anna the news, she wails—dramatizing the loss as though it were hers alone.

"Oh, my only son! My wonderful, darling boy! How could this happen? It isn't right that God should take him from me! Whatever will I do without him?"

Anna continues to cry and carry on while Elsa and Rudi sit there quietly watching her performance. After ten minutes, Elsa looks at Rudi and whispers, "Let's get out of here. I can't take this anymore."

Rudi nods and they both get up and prepare to leave.

"You're not going yet, *are you?"* Anna says with her hand over her heart.

"Yes, Anna, we are. Laura is home alone and waiting for us."

"But you can't leave me, I'm much too upset! Laura is fine on her own. I... I just don't think I can be by myself."

"I'm sorry, but we can't stay. The weather is nasty, and we really have to get back home. Don't worry, you'll be okay."

"I always knew you didn't care about me! I don't know what Erich ever saw in you!"

Elsa doesn't respond. She and Rudi do up their coats and walk out the door.

Anna stands at the entrance ranting as she watches them disappear down the corridor. "I should have been the one to die instead—I bet you would all be happy then!"

DRAINED FROM THEIR visit, Elsa sits in the car, staring at the snow as it blows around viciously.

"Are you going to contact Frieda, Mom?" Rudi asks while attempting to drive through the deep snow and near zero visibility.

"No! Your father told me he doesn't want any of us to have any dealings with her, and I won't go against his wishes!"

"Okay, Mom. I was only asking," he says defensively.

Elsa gently places her hand on his arm. "I'm sorry I snapped at you, Rudi. It's just that we don't need any more complications right now—you understand—*don't you?"*

"It's fine, Mom, don't worry about it," he says, trying not to let his hurt feelings show.

Chapter 36: The Tough Road Ahead

AFTER ERICH'S FUNERAL, Elsa and Laura adjust to life without him. They go about their daily routines just as they always have, but the silence within their little home is larger than life. They are both happy that they no longer have to deal with Erich's behaviour, but they miss him just the same.

"Thank goodness the man who holds the mortgage insisted on insurance or we would lose the house," Elsa tells Laura.

Laura is relieved to hear that they won't lose their home, but at the same time, she is shocked to learn it was even a possibility. "Will we be alright, Mom? I mean, do we have enough money?"

"Money is tight, sweetie. Because of Dad's pride, any money we did have is gone. I've applied for widow's pension, and you'll get an orphan's pension. It isn't much, but it should help to get us through," she says, trying to dispel Laura's fears.

It is a struggle for Elsa to pay the bills and care for Laura on the monthly assistance she receives. To supplement the meagre income, she does some sewing for neighbours and even considers returning to hairdressing, but because she hasn't practiced her trade for so long, she realizes this isn't a viable option.

Laura has found a friend at school whose parents invite her to have supper with them at least twice a week, which helps to stretch their limited supply of food. There are many nights where Elsa forgoes eating just so they can make it through until the next month's cheque arrives. She never dreamed that they would have it this hard. *Why did Erich have to be so stubborn? Now we have to pay the price for his stupid pride. I'm so tired of struggling to make ends meet.*

In the spring, Elsa plants a vegetable garden to augment their limited food budget. The garden turns out to be very successful, thanks to the assistance of her neighbour, and she is able to grow a variety of vegetables and fruits. She freezes a great deal so that they will have plenty to eat throughout the winter months.

ELSA STILL CARES for Anna out of respect for Erich, but she finds it extremely stressful having to deal with her dementia.

One afternoon, she and Laura do Anna's banking, and they visit her at the nursing home where she now lives. Elsa gives her mother-in-law the money from her monthly pension cheque that she cashed for her at the bank, and after a brief visit, they make their way back home.

When they arrive, Anna calls Elsa in a tizzy, accusing her of stealing her pension money. Elsa is annoyed with her mother-in-law's behaviour but tries to keep calm since she knows it is mainly due to her condition.

She and Laura go back to the home, and together they search for the missing cash. They finally find it in a trash bag, still in the envelope that Elsa had given to Anna. Elsa cleans the money and returns it to her. After explaining where she and Laura found it, Anna is still adamant that they tried to take her money. This episode, although not serious, increases Elsa's stress level and causes her to lose her composure.

"I did *not* steal from you, nor have I *ever* stolen from you! If you don't trust me, that's okay. I'm done with you, Anna. You'll have to take care of your affairs on your own from now on!"

Elsa grabs Laura's hand, and they make their way to the exit. "Let's go home."

Her mother's reaction stuns Laura, but she understands that the day-to-day pressure Elsa has been under since before Erich's death is to blame.

Even though Laura isn't close to her Oma, she feels sorry for her and turns to look at her one last time. Anna stands in the corridor staring back at her, muttering incoherently to herself when an orderly comes to take her back to her room.

Elsa and Laura don't visit Anna again after that. Although Elsa feels sorry for shirking the responsibility, she is relieved that she no longer has to deal with this senile yet self-important woman who has never been kind and has only ever cared about her own needs. *Forgive me, Erich, but I just can't put up with Anna any longer.*

Elsa later learns, through the family doctor she and Anna share, that Frieda has taken over the job of caring for her. This surprises Elsa but makes her happy to know that her eldest daughter has finally taken on some responsibility for someone other than herself. *It's about time she did something to help this family.*

IN EARLY 1978, RUDI divorces Sandra, and she moves to Alberta, taking the children with her. Rudi later leaves Ontario and goes to Saskatchewan, never to return or see his mother and sister again. He calls Elsa occasionally, and when he does, it is usually to ask for money, which she, of course, doesn't have to give him. After several of these calls, she finally tells him to stop contacting her. *I just can't understand how Rudi could let his life deteriorate like this. At his age, he shouldn't be asking his mother for money, especially when he knows we're struggling too. Has he no pride?*

Chapter 37: A Chance for a Fresh Start

IN NOVEMBER OF 1978, Elsa celebrates her fifty-fifth birthday by going out for supper with Margrit. She can't recall the last time she was able to go out, other than to run errands, let alone to go out for a meal. They go to their favourite German restaurant, The Schnitzel House, and are fortunate to get a table almost immediately when they arrive. Once seated, they order a glass of wine and chat to catch up with each other.

"I received a letter from my brother, Otto, who lives in Berlin," Margrit says. "You remember Otto, don't you? He was the one who found the information about your sister."

"Yes, of course, I remember," Elsa replies before taking a sip of her wine. "How is he?"

"He's getting better. I did tell you that his wife died three years ago, didn't I?"

"*No*, you didn't tell me. I'm very sorry."

"Oh, that's okay. Otto has finally come to terms with it, and he's planning to make the trip to Canada to visit with me over the summer. I'm so thrilled that he's going to come. You know we haven't seen each other for over twenty-five years?"

Elsa nods to Margrit as the server approaches their table to take their order. "Well, I'm happy that the two of you will finally be reunited."

Margrit's eyes light up. "You *must* meet him, Elsa! The two of you have so much in common, and I think it might do you both some good."

"I would be honoured to meet him, but only to thank him in person for all the work he did to find out about my sister, nothing more. If you think that I need a male companion, I'm afraid you're mistaken. I don't want to get involved with any man. I was married for thirty-four years, Margrit, and that was long enough. From now on, I'm staying on my own."

"Okay, I understand what you're saying, and I promise not to push either of you into something you don't want. I'll arrange for you to meet him so that you can thank him, and after that, I leave things up to you, okay?"

Elsa looks at her friend and smiles, shaking her head. "You *really are* something—you know that?"

A sly smile forms on Margrit's face. "*Whatever* do you mean?"

IN JUNE OF 1979, Elsa meets Margrit's brother, Otto, when he comes to stay with her for the summer. The meeting goes well, and they find themselves spending more time together, discovering that they actually do have a lot in common with one another. A few years Elsa's senior, Otto is short with a rounded belly and thinning hair. Despite his physical appearance, he is an understanding, gentle and caring man. He possesses a real knack for getting Elsa to laugh, which is something that she hasn't been able to do for a very long time. Even though Erich has only been gone less than two years, Elsa is surprised how at ease she feels with Otto and finds herself having feelings for him. While she enjoys their time together, she is afraid to let their relationship get too involved. *He's only here for the summer and then he goes back to Berlin.* Not only is Elsa fearful of getting hurt, but she also worries about what Laura will think.

One evening after supper, Elsa sits down on the sofa beside Laura, who is engrossed in a novel, and asks her if she can take a few minutes to talk.

"Sure, Mom, what's going on?"

"What do you think of Otto?"

"He seems really nice, and he certainly can make you laugh, that's for sure."

Elsa smiles as she recalls the jokes Otto has told her. "Yes, that's true. Does it bother you that I spend time with him?"

"No, I'm glad you have someone to talk to and hang around with."

"Okay, I just didn't want you to be upset about it. Promise me that if something ever bothers you, either about Otto or anything else, you'll tell me."

Laura nods and smiles at her mother. "You know I will. Stop worrying, and enjoy your time with Otto. He's going back to Germany soon, isn't he?"

A slight frown forms on Elsa's face. "Yes, he leaves at the end of August."

"Well, then you should be with him whenever you can because I know it makes you happy."

"Thanks for being so understanding, sweetie."

IN MID-JULY, Otto and Elsa plan for a day trip to Niagara Falls. Elsa prepares a picnic basket and packs other necessities to make their day complete. When they arrive at the falls, the place is packed with tourists, and it takes them over an hour to park the car and find a suitable spot to have their picnic. After setting things up, they sit on a blanket and enjoy the summer sun. The mist from the falls reaches them and provides a refreshing, welcome break from the heat of the afternoon.

"I love this place," Otto says. "I've never seen anything quite like it anywhere I've been."

Elsa nods and takes a bite of her liverwurst sandwich. "I like it too. This was the first place we visited when we came to Canada in 1951, and it holds many fond memories for me."

Otto looks at her but says nothing. His gaze then shifts toward the magnificent view of the falls and he listens to the thundering roar of the water as it makes its way down to the river below. A while later, he turns back to Elsa and takes a deep breath.

"Elsa, I enjoy our time together and like to believe that you do as well," he says rather nervously.

"Yes, I do. You've made my life much happier than I ever dreamed it could be, since losing Erich."

"You have made me extremely happy too. I was so lost when Gertrude died, and I never thought I'd find joy again—*until I met you.*"

They both sit in silence, pondering their admission to one another. After a few minutes, Otto once again turns to Elsa and pulls something from his pocket. His eyes shine with tears as he looks into her face. "I know this is sudden, but we aren't getting any younger. I know there are many things we must work out, but my dear, Elsa, would you do me the honour of becoming my wife?"

Speechless, Elsa looks at the ring Otto holds between his fingers and inhales deeply. As the shock of the proposal sinks in, she is finally able to form a reply. "Oh, Otto, this *is* very sudden. I *never* expected this, and I really don't know what to say. Could you give me a little time to think it over?"

"Certainly, Liebling. There is much we need to discuss, and I want you to be sure of your decision."

Throughout the afternoon, they consider the issues facing them, and the plans to be settled before beginning their new life together. Because Otto and his wife never had children, Laura is at the forefront of their conversation. The other obstacle they face is being from different countries, and Elsa has already made it clear to him that she won't leave Canada to live in Berlin.

When Otto brings Elsa back home, he unloads the car and helps her to carry things back into the house.

"Where is Laura?" Otto asks.

"She is spending the day with a friend. I think they were going to the beach."

"Well, it's good for her to get out and have some fun. I had a lovely day, Elsa, but Margrit is expecting me, so I have to leave now. Please think about what we discussed today, ja?"

Elsa smiles. "I had a nice time too. You can be sure that I'll be thinking of everything we talked about."

Otto kisses her tenderly before going to his car. "I will call you tomorrow, Liebling."

THAT NIGHT, ELSA isn't able to sleep as her thoughts run wild with different scenarios of what her life will be like to married again. *What should I do? Don't I have a right to be happy? Haven't I always put everyone's needs before my own?*

Not being able to stay in bed any longer, Elsa gets up and goes into the kitchen to make herself some tea. As the kettle heats, she stares out the window to the back yard and is once again lost in her thoughts. When the kettle whistles, it shocks her out of her trance, and she goes over to pour some water into her cup.

"Mom, is something wrong?" Laura asks, rubbing her eyes as she gets accustomed to the light.

"Oh, Laura, I'm so sorry I woke you."

"That's okay. Are you alright?"

"Sit down, sweetie. I want to talk to you."

Elsa tells her about Otto's proposal and about everything the two of them discussed that afternoon. When she finishes, she looks at Laura, trying to gauge her reaction to the news.

Laura looks away from her mother, feeling tightness in her chest, and she rubs her hands over her face. "Would you still live here, or are you planning to move to Berlin?"

"I've told Otto that I won't leave Canada since I have ties here, so he's willing to immigrate."

"What do you want to do, Mom?"

Elsa shakes her head. "Well, I... I'm not really sure. I don't want to do anything that would upset you or change our relationship. You're all I have left."

"I know that. You're all I have left too, but I won't be here with you forever, you know. You have to think of the long term, Mom. You deserve some happiness in your life," she says, even though her feelings are choking her. *I do want her to be happy, but I'm really not sure how I feel about this. How can Mom think that this won't change our relationship? Everything will change if she marries Otto.*

Elsa is amazed by her young daughter's mature response. She thought for sure she would be against her marrying Otto, but after learning otherwise, she feels relieved and happy. Elsa smiles and gives her a hug. "I love you, you know."

"I love you, too, Mom," Laura replies before making her way back to her room. It is now her turn to have trouble sleeping.

AFTER A FEW days of thinking and discussing the details, Elsa accepts Otto's proposal. He cuts short his stay to go back to Berlin to begin the process of immigrating to Canada and to settle his affairs there before he and Elsa can get married in Hamilton. Otto asks her to come with him, but she refuses to leave Laura by herself, so on August 5th, he boards a plane that will take him back to the country of his birth.

Margrit is thrilled with her brother's decision and couldn't be happier to have Elsa as a sister-in-law. Laura puts on a brave front with her mother because although this is difficult for her to accept, she really does want her to be happy.

Elsa misses Otto much more than she anticipated. *This really is the right thing for me to do! Otto and I belong together because we make each other happy. I hope you understand and are pleased that I'm finally moving on with my life, Erich.*

Otto calls Elsa every other day to stay in touch and discuss the progress with the arrangements that will bring them closer to their wedding. By mid-August, however, Otto's calls stop. After several days, Elsa tries calling but has no success in reaching him. She contacts Margrit to ask whether she has heard from him, but she hasn't either. Fear seeps into Elsa's veins. *Maybe he's changed his mind. Maybe he doesn't want to marry me, so he's avoiding my calls.*

ELSA'S HEART SINKS when she opens the door and notices Margrit's expression. After a week of worry, her emotions are raw.

"What is it? Tell me. It's Otto, *isn't it?"* Elsa whispers.

Margrit nods, taking her friend's hand into her own. She blinks away tears and chokes out her reply. "There's been an accident. A week ago, Otto was driving from the city when a truck hit his car. He was killed instantly."

Elsa sits silently as shock sweeps over her, and she trembles. "How can this *be?* I don't understand, Margrit. We were *so* happy. We were going to get *married.* How can this *happen?"*

Overcome by emotion, Margrit embraces her friend. "I know—*I know.* It isn't fair that this should happen, but like you always say, all things happen for a reason, even if we don't understand why. We just have to have faith and trust in God that this tragedy somehow has meaning. You know we'll always be sisters-in-law in our hearts."

Elsa shakes her head, unable to believe that Otto's death serves some ultimate purpose. *Why? Why did this have to happen?* In her grief, she suddenly questions her faith. She has been through so much heartache in her life, and just when happiness is within her reach, something happens to take it away. Elsa knows she shouldn't think this way, but she can't help feeling sorry for herself. *What have I ever done to deserve this much misery in my life? Am I such a terrible person that God feels the need to punish me?*

SEVERAL DAYS LATER, Margrit and Elsa fly to Berlin to make the funeral arrangements and stay for the burial while Laura remains at home. It is the first time in her life that she has been alone, and although she likes having her independence, she misses her mother terribly. *Mom is going to need my love and support to help her deal with this. I just hope I can do it.*

Chapter 38: Coming to Terms

AFTER ELSA'S RETURN from Berlin, she and Laura live each day the best they can. Elsa spends time doing menial chores around the house to keep her mind off her grief, and she and Margrit get together often to help each other deal with their loss.

One day, Elsa receives some unexpected news from Margrit that once again distresses her. She learns that her best friend must move to Arizona due to her husband's ill health.

"I'll miss you so much, Elsa. We must promise to visit each other when we can."

Elsa nods back with a slight smile, but she knows it is a trip she can never afford to make. "I'll miss you too, and I hope we'll be able to visit, but if not, we can still write and call each other to keep in touch."

LAURA IS STILL plagued by a lack of confidence, although she has learned to hide it well. Elsa tries to encourage her by telling her how proud she is of her, but it never seems to improve Laura's attitude about herself. Elsa can't help but feel responsible for this. *Could I have handled things differently? Perhaps if I had stood up to Erich earlier, I could have limited the damage his behaviour caused.* The more Elsa thinks, the more she has feelings of self-doubt, not only about Laura but also about other aspects of her life. *Could I have changed the outcome with Frieda and Rudi?* Now that she doesn't have Margrit to discuss her feelings with, she ruminates about her own failures repeatedly.

She continues to analyze her thoughts, and Elsa shakes her head in frustration. *Why do I blame myself? The past is the past and can't be changed. I only did what I thought was best under the circumstances—didn't I?* She digs deep into the layers of her mind and comes to understand the cause of these feelings.

Even after all this time, she can still hear her father telling her that any problems in her marriage are her own doing. Although she is now a widow, Heinrich's words haunt her. *Maybe this memory from so long ago has done more damage to me than I thought. After years of guilt and blame, could it be that I also suffer from low self-esteem? Could it be that subconsciously I've always known this?* Elsa sits and reflects on this for some time. *What can I do to change things?* She finally decides the best way to deal with this is to confront her feelings about the past. *But how do I go about doing that?*

After considering this for a while, Elsa takes a notebook and slowly writes down her thoughts. As she does this, she finds her past transferring smoothly from her mind, through the pen, and down onto the paper. Once she has written a few pages, she stops, and for the first time in her life, she feels like a heavy burden is being lifted from her. *Could this be the outlet I need?* Elsa believes she is on the right track and continues to record her memories. During the process, she finds herself forgiving her father for his treatment of her and forgiving herself for allowing the past to have such an influence on her life.

IN JUNE OF 1980, Laura graduates from high school—the first one in her family to achieve this goal.

Elsa is bursting with pride at her little girl's accomplishment. "Dad would be so proud of you!"

"Oh, I don't know about that. Nothing I ever did was good enough in Dad's eyes. He only cared for Frieda—not me—*and don't try to deny it.* But it's okay, Mom. Even though it still bothers me, I've come to terms with it and so should you."

Elsa is saddened by this, yet at the same time, she knows there is truth in what Laura says about her father. *Isn't this the same realization I came to myself about my own father not too long ago?* She looks at her daughter again and is amazed how she was able to deal with her feelings about the past so much earlier than she could herself. The act of forgiving those people in your past who have hurt you, and forgiving yourself for things you did or didn't do is part of the healing process. It allows you to live your life to the fullest, without regrets. Elsa knows now that she has succeeded in raising her daughter, despite the hardships they endured while she was growing up. Her pride swells within her again as she looks at the young woman standing before her.

Laura's application to the community college is accepted for the fall semester, and she is excited about the prospect of accomplishing another first in her family. Elsa worries about how she will afford her schooling, but Laura assures her that she can manage. She has a summer job lined up and has been approved for a student grant and loan from the government. Although her daughter's initiative delights her, Elsa is sorry that she couldn't provide her with the money needed for her education. *If only things had been different. I would've done anything to give my little girl what she needed for a good start in life. Oh, why do things always have to be so difficult? Well, I can't change the past. I guess the only thing I can do is be here when she needs me and pray that she'll be happy and successful.*

Part Three: A New Understanding

Chapter 39: Accepting the Past

I PUT THE notebook aside for the first time in hours and get up to stretch and rub my burning eyes. I look over at the clock and see that it's close to 7 a.m. *So much for getting any sleep! I wonder how long it must have taken Mom to write all this down.* After finishing the journal, my admiration for her has grown more than I thought possible.

I knew some of these stories, but many of these hardships she never shared with me. I realize now that Mom began writing this as a method of therapy, except I wonder if she ever thought of its significance, not only to me but also to future generations. This piece of the past is too important not to share with my children and eventually them with theirs. *My mother is a living history book. It's such a shame that she can no longer recall these stories herself. Nevertheless, maybe it's a blessing that she has forgotten these things.* I'm so thankful she took the time to record her thoughts and memories.

I take the notebook upstairs with me to the kitchen and make some coffee, and as I turn to take a mug from the cabinet, my husband, Jack, enters.

He walks over to me and rubs my shoulders. "You didn't stay in bed last night."

"No, I just tossed and turned, so I got up because I didn't want to disturb you. I spent the night reading that notebook over there on the table. My mother wrote it—a journal of sorts I guess you could call it."

"You never told me your mom kept one."

"Well, to be honest, I almost forgot about it. I found it when I was packing Mom's things from the house and just threw it into a box. I remembered I had it last night when I was thinking about what to tell Mike for the eulogy."

Jack sits down and takes the notebook in his hands. "Can I look through it?"

"Sure, go ahead."

He continues skimming it while I make breakfast, and suddenly the silence of our Saturday morning ritual is shattered by the ringing of my cell phone. I look at the caller ID and see that it's Mike, so I quickly answer.

"Mom, you need to get here now," he says anxiously.

"Okay, I'm on my way," I say and end the call. I tell Jack that I need to go back to the hospital, and he insists on driving me. I'm thankful to have his company and think it's probably better that I not drive considering how exhausted I feel.

MIKE AND CATHY sit beside Mom's bed, and Cathy holds her hand. They notice me and attempt a smile. Words are unnecessary. I go over and stand beside them, giving each of them a gentle squeeze on the shoulder. This small sign of affection overwhelms them both, and tears flood their eyes.

I look over at Mom and feel an overwhelming tightness in my chest. Her eyes are closed, and she breathes shallow breaths through her open mouth. It pains me to see how much she's deteriorated in a few short hours.

I go close to her and take her bony hand in mine. After a few minutes, her eyes flutter open ever so slightly, and I bend down toward her.

"How are you feeling?" I ask, not expecting a reply.

She looks at me with deep concentration. "Oh, Laura, you came to see me. I'm so glad," she whispers.

My vision suddenly blurs with tears. It's the first time in over a year that my mother has recognized me. "I'm here, Mom."

She winces as she tries to swallow, and I gently stroke her hand.

"I knew you would come—I told him so," she says finally.

"Who did you tell, Mom?"

"Dad."

I nod and smile at her while trying to control my emotions. "Did you see him, Mom?"

"Yes—he's taking me home soon—he promised."

She gradually shifts her gaze to a corner of the room, and she smiles warmly. "I'm ready to go now, Liebling."

Suddenly she lets out a breath and is gone. I look at her peaceful expression and smile through my tears. I release her hand and stand as Jack, Cathy, and Mike approach me, and we share comforting hugs.

"She's finally free," I say.

AFTER WE RETURN home, I hand Mike the notebook. "You wanted more facts about Oma's life for her eulogy. I want you to read this. It should make the process a bit easier."

Mike looks at the notebook and quickly flips through the pages. "Did *Oma* write this, Mom?"

"Yes, a long time ago. It pretty much covers her life up until about 1980. Once you've read it, I can fill you in on her life after that if you'd like."

Mike nods to me and opens the notebook.

"I'd like to read it too, Mom," says Cathy.

"I want you to, and I'm sure Oma would want you to as well."

Cathy smiles as her eyes shine with tears. "I'm going to miss her, Mom."

"Yes, I know. We've already been missing her for a long time, but at least, we know she's now at peace."

I watch Mike's expression change while he reads, and every so often he stops to make notes. He focuses intently on the task he has ahead of him, when suddenly, he stops and looks up at me and shakes his head. "Jeez Mom, some of this is hard to imagine."

"I know, but it's all true. Oma had written this well before she had Alzheimer's, and many of the stories she told me when I was growing up are in there too. She did it as therapy to help her deal with her past. After so many years of trying to cope with her memories, she needed a release. I believe this was the only way she could think of to accomplish that."

Later that evening, he finally puts the notebook down on the table. "Wow, Mom. You never said your dad treated you and Oma that way."

"I never wanted to say anything negative about him to you. Looking back now, I can appreciate that his drinking was an illness, just like his cancer, neither of which were really his fault. Could he have handled stress better? Sure, of course, he could have, but I don't blame him. I forgave him a long time ago. My childhood memories aren't especially good, but there are some happy ones. Like summer vacations spent at cottages, or waiting anxiously for Dad to come home from work and hand me his lunch pail. I always looked forward to opening it and finding he had saved me his cookies or cake as a treat. I don't know whether he told Oma to put in extra just for me, and although it seems corny, it meant everything to me. I guess that's why your dad and I always tried to make your childhood special so that you would have plenty of good memories instead of just a few."

Mike nods and stands up, grabbing the notepad. "I'm going to the den to start writing."

LATER ON, I'M left alone with my thoughts. I think about my father and the difficulty Mom had dealing with his behaviour. She did what she thought was best at the time, and I'm amazed that through it all, she never once said anything derogatory about him to me or to anyone for that matter. The fact that Mom had stood up to Dad was a surprise to me. I always thought he intimidated her since she was always so passive, but I never blamed her for it. She only wanted to keep the peace within our home and trying to avoid confrontation was her way of doing that. I can now understand that her experience with her own father was responsible for how she handled her later life. I'm glad she finally had the courage to challenge Dad about his reckless behaviour, even though it did nothing to change the outcome. Perhaps doing so helped her more by making her realize that, for once in her life, she was her own person—not to be controlled by anyone but herself.

I go into the basement and pull out the old photo albums. I smile as I go through the pictures. *Wow, was I ever really that young?* As I continue to look, memories explode from the depths of my mind, like a cork popping from a bottle of champagne. I'm amazed at the power these photographs have to help me unlock the past. Even subtle things that I probably would never have been able to remember suddenly resurface. They say a picture is worth a thousand words, but I believe a picture is worth a thousand memories.

Cathy comes down to where I am on the sofa and sits beside me. "Is that you?"

"Yes," I tell her, and she looks from me to the photo.

"You look so geeky!" she says while giggling at my expense.

I thank her for her brilliant observation, and we chuckle as we continue to flip through the pages. A while later, we come upon some pictures of me from college.

"Is this you and Dad?"

"Yes, that was shortly after we met."

"Wow, he had hair!"

We laugh again, relishing the moment. It's so good to have a joyful release despite the sadness we feel.

The photographs are in chronological order, so it's easy to follow the progression of time. We look at my wedding photos, and even though Cathy has seen them before, she still enjoys looking at them.

"Was Oma sad when you and Dad got married? I mean, she was all alone then."

"No, Cathy, she wasn't sad. She was happy for us and happy for herself too. She was finally on her own, free to do what she wanted, as opposed to what other people expected from her."

She nods and reflects on what I have told her. "It still must have been hard for her."

"Yes, but Oma was finally able to save a bit of money, and after a couple of years, she could afford to travel, which was something she was never able to do before. She was sixty-three years old when she went on her first Caribbean cruise."

"Wow, that's amazing! Who did she go with?"

"Well, that's the amazing part—she went on her own—not knowing a soul."

"That's pretty gutsy for someone her age! Heck, that's pretty gutsy for anyone, at any age!"

"Yes, that's true. Oma knew what she wanted and realized that if she didn't go on her own, she probably would never end up going."

"She did quite a bit of travelling, didn't she?"

"Yes, the church arranged regular trips abroad, and she never missed one. She travelled to Egypt, Israel, Jerusalem, Turkey, and Greece with the group and she loved it. I was jealous of all the travelling Oma was able to do."

"I guess that's where I inherited *my* travel bug!" says Cathy. "I remember she also went on a few trips back to Germany. Didn't she even go back and visit Hamburg?"

"Yes, that's right. Your Opa had a cousin still living there, and Oma was able to make contact with her and go for a visit. She went to Hamburg on her very last trip when she was eighty years old, and it amazed me that she was still able to do that trip solo. I was happy that Oma was able to go back and see the city where she was born one last time. I hope to make the trip there myself one day."

As my daughter looks at me, I can already see her mind working.

"We should go visit Hamburg together, Mom! Let's do it! *Please?*"

"Well, maybe. We'll see how things go in the next while and perhaps we can make some plans," I say with a smile.

Just then, Mike comes downstairs and sits with us.

"How's it going?" I ask.

"It's coming along." He suddenly looks at me and frowns. "I know you aren't close with your sister and brother but are you going to contact them to tell them about Oma?"

"I haven't given it much thought. They've never really been a part of my life, as you know, and they haven't been a part of Oma's life for almost forty years. I wonder whether it would even matter to them."

"You haven't talked to either of them in all that time?" Cathy asks.

"My brother contacted me about five years ago after he tried to call Oma and found her phone was no longer in service. He wanted to know where she was, but I believe he thought she had died, even though he never actually said that. Once I explained that she had Alzheimer's and was now in a nursing home, the next thing he asked me was 'What about the house?' I knew then, what Oma always knew—all he was ever interested in was money. I told him I had to sell it to pay for her care and that there was none left. It really irked me that he had the nerve to ask," I say, feeling the old anger stirring within me.

Both Mike and Cathy look appalled by this. "Wow, what a guy! How could he possibly expect that there would be anything for him?" Cathy asks resentfully.

"I guess Rudi figured since he was her son he was entitled to some inheritance, even though he did nothing to help her in the latter part of her life."

They both shake their heads, trying to understand how someone could possibly think this way.

"What about your sister? Have you heard anything from her?" Mike asks.

"Not directly, no. About a year after Rudi called me, I received another call from him, asking if it was okay for him to give my phone number to Frieda. I was shocked by this and questioned whether he had told her about Oma's illness. When he confirmed this, I wanted to know if she requested my number before or after learning about Oma. Once Rudi said that she asked for it afterward, I knew then that she was probably only looking for a possible inheritance as well. Why else would she want to contact me after that length of time? Frieda wasn't interested in me, and she certainly wasn't interested in Oma, since she never attempted to contact either of us before that. I told him under no circumstances was he to give out my number to her. I thanked Rudi for calling me to ask, and I haven't heard from him since," I say, trying to put the past behind me.

"Well, I guess you really don't owe them anything, so why should you go out of your way to tell them?" says Mike.

"You should think more about what Oma would have wanted you to do," says Cathy.

I look at both of them and nod. "That's the dilemma I'm faced with, and I'm not sure what to do at this point."

"Why don't you wait for awhile before making that decision? You have a lot on your plate right now. I'm sure that even if you choose to tell them, it's not likely that they would attend the funeral anyway, so why rush it?" Mike says.

"You're both right," I say. "I'll think it over and make that decision when I'm ready."

I really appreciate that I can talk with my children and that our relationship is a solid one. I think about how difficult it must have been for Mom to have to come to terms with not having any contact with two of her three children for so many years. Although she never said much about it to me, I'm sure that it must have been almost like losing them to death. It's difficult for me to understand why they drifted apart, but I respect my mother's decision—it was her life—only she could know the reasons for doing so. Perhaps because of everything Mom went through in her life, she couldn't deal with their behaviour and thought it easier to end the relationship than having to cope with the added stress of it. This is the only explanation that seems to have any merit to my way of thinking. *Would Mom have wanted them to know of her death, especially considering she cut the ties with them so long ago?* My kids are right, I need to get through the funeral first and not make a hasty decision that I may later regret.

Chapter 40: The Tribute

THE DAY OF the funeral we head over early to prepare a fitting tribute to a very special woman. We set up displays of Mom's favourite things and a slide show of photographs, starting with one of her at five years of age.

I know she took these pictures from her father's apartment when they left Hamburg, and although there aren't many, I'm still amazed that despite everything she went through, she was able to save them.

As we sit in the chapel waiting for the service to start, Mike holds the eulogy he has written and fidgets beside me. He always does this when he's nervous, so it isn't unusual. I turn to see that the chapel is about half full. Most of the people who have come to pay their respects are friends of Jack's and mine. I recognize some people from my mother's church and others who were her neighbours. Many of her friends have long since passed away, but I guess that's one of the drawbacks of living a long life—you outlive many people you care about. I'm thankful to those who came to say a final goodbye to her. I know it would have made Mom incredibly happy.

When it's time for Mike to make his speech, he goes up to the podium with an air of confidence that makes me proud despite the nervousness I know he feels. I haven't read his eulogy, so I'm not sure what to expect, but I know he'll pay a fitting tribute to his Oma.

As he speaks, the room is so quiet you can hear the ticking of the clock in the hall outside the chapel. Turning back to watch the crowd, I can see that Mike has captured his audience's attention. Listening to his words, there are times we smile, times we laugh, and times we cry. Mike has had quite an effect on us all. When he is finished, he sits down beside me, and those around us whisper their praise for his words. I'm so happy that my son wanted to do the eulogy because not only did he do a great job, it forced me to finally read my mother's journal, allowing me to learn about her experiences and gain a greater appreciation for the woman she once was. I know Mom would have been so proud to hear how Mike was able to express her life in such a way. She would never want anyone to feel sad for her, and his speech left everyone who heard it feeling more admiration for her than sorrow.

After the service, many people come up to us and comment on Mike's ability to express the details of Mom's life so well. Some are shocked to learn about the hardships she endured.

"I thought you never knew much about your mother's past, Laura," my dear friend, Joan, says after giving me a supportive hug.

"I didn't—until just recently that is. I found a journal Mom kept when I packed up her things from the house. Back then I just tossed it in a box and forgot about it. The night before she died I suddenly remembered I had it and stayed up to read it."

"Well, I think it's a great story, one I'm sure others would like to hear. Maybe you should consider writing a book."

I look at my friend and laugh. "You can't be *serious! Me?* Write a *book?*"

"Why not? It's a story worth telling, and who better to tell it than you? Besides, it would be a nice way to honour your mom's memory."

I now realize she's sincere, and a familiar feeling of insecurity washes over me. "I don't know, Joan. I've never written anything before. What makes you so sure that I can do it?"

"Let's just say it's intuition. Promise you'll think about it, okay?"

"Okay, I'll consider it," I say with a shrug, and Joan embraces me once more and leaves.

While we pack Mom's things, I think about all the people I spoke with and about Joan's suggestion. *Should I dare even contemplate writing Mom's story?*

"What do you think about Joan's idea? Do you want to try to write a book?" Jack asks, as though reading my mind.

"I don't know. It seems like such a daunting task," I say with the usual self-doubt flooding my thoughts.

"Oh, come on, Mom. Joan is right, you know. It's such a great story, and I bet others would like to hear it," Cathy says.

"As I told Joan, I'll think about it. That's all I can do right now."

THAT NIGHT I'M once again unable to sleep. *Should I contact Frieda and Rudi to tell them about Mom? Should I attempt writing a book? Can I even do it?* Like Mom, I believe there is a purpose for everything that happens in our lives. Perhaps the reason I remembered about the notebook wasn't only to help Mike with the eulogy, but also that I'm supposed to undertake the writing of her story.

"What should I do, Mom?" I whisper in the darkness of the bedroom. "Help me to decide." *Wow, now I'm talking to someone who isn't here!* I think the stress of the last few weeks has taken its toll on me. I laugh at myself and yawn as sleep suddenly finds me.

I don't wake until almost noon the next day and can't remember the last time I slept so late. When I get up, I feel refreshed and happy because I've finally made some decisions.

In the kitchen, Jack pours me a strong cup of coffee. "How did you sleep?"

"Great, once I was able to fall asleep," I say while having a good stretch. "I think I'll try writing a book as a tribute to Mom. Even if no one else reads it but family, it'll be worth the effort."

Jack nods as if he already knew that I would come to this decision. He's known me for over thirty-five years, so I'm sure he had a good idea of what I would do.

"I've also decided against contacting my siblings. I really don't think Mom would want me to."

"I believe you've made the right choices, honey."

Chapter 41: The Next Chapter

I SIT DOWN in front of my computer with Mom's notebook in my hand and try to formulate my thoughts. I make notes and plan out how I will go about telling Mom's story, but self-doubt attacks me once again. *Can I really do this? Where do I begin?* Placing my hands on the computer keys, I slowly type my thoughts. It isn't long before my fingers sail quickly across the keyboard. I watch my words become paragraphs, and the paragraphs turn into pages, and I'm surprised how much I enjoy the process.

As I continue writing, I realize that the research for my book is incomplete. I go online in search of some information about my heritage and stumble upon the website of the International Tracing Service (ITS) located in Bad Arolsen, Germany. It peeks my interest since the organization was set up after the war to track missing persons and provide care and repatriation services to survivors. I learn that through its archives, the ITS aids those searching for relatives lost during the war at the numerous concentration camps around Europe. *Perhaps by contacting the ITS I can learn the fate of my aunt and cousins.* The idea excites me, and since I wasn't able to find any helpful information using online research, I decide that I will travel to Hamburg and include a visit to Bad Arolsen.

I discuss my plan with Jack, and he is supportive. He understands how important this is to me and only wants me to be happy. When I tell Cathy, she is excited about the idea, so I invite her to come along, providing she can take time from work to join me on my quest. *Even if I can't find any records or information, I'll be close to where my family history began and if nothing else, it will help me to organize my thoughts and feelings.* I'm very eager to make the trip, regardless of the outcome, and Cathy is overjoyed when her two weeks' vacation is approved, enabling her to assist me with my research.

IN HAMBURG, WE become detectives, visiting many churches and government archives to hunt through records looking for information about my family. The research is challenging, not only because of the language barrier but also because so many documents were destroyed during the war. Regardless, both Cathy and I remain hopeful that we will eventually uncover something. Finally, after almost a week of searching, we are lucky to find some information. We are surprised to learn that the apartment complex where Mom grew up is still standing.

Cathy and I take a taxi to the address, and we pause for a moment to look at the building before making our way there. As we stand across from it, a shiver overtakes my body. *My mother walked on this very street when she was a child! My grandparents did too!* The excitement I feel is electric—my senses heightened—sounds and colours become more vivid. I can't ever recall feeling this way.

We walk to the building and climb the front steps. As I try to imagine what it was like during the time my mother lived here, a man in his thirties walks up beside us and smiles.

"Guten Tag, you look like you're lost. Can I be of assistance?" he says in perfect English.

I'm surprised he could tell that we don't speak German but feel relieved to be able to easily communicate the reason for our visit. After listening to my story, the man nods.

"My great-grandmother lives in the building and has lived here all her life. I'm just on my way to see her. Perhaps she can help you with your search for information. Her memory is still clear as a bell."

"Oh, we don't want to impose on her," I say.

"It's really not a problem. She loves having company and enjoys talking."

I look over at Cathy questioningly, and she nods back to me.

"Thank you, Herr..."

"Kemper. But you can call me Lothar."

"Well, Lothar, I'm Laura Fraser, and this is my daughter Cathy. It would be fantastic to talk to your great-grandmother, and we would appreciate anything she can tell us."

Lothar leads us into the apartment. The place is small and stuffy. It hasn't been redecorated in some time, but it adds to the picture I'm forming in my mind about what it must have been like when Mom lived here. The living area has a small, well-worn sofa with a table, an armchair, and a TV on a stand against one wall. The living room leads into the kitchen, and there appears to be two bedrooms, and one bathroom in the apartment.

"Is that you, Lothar?" an old voice croaks from one of the bedrooms.

"Ja, Uroma."

The old woman comes into the living room pushing a walker, and Lothar introduces us and explains the reason for our visit. She smiles and looks at me intently. "Please, come and sit, ja?" After a moment, she turns to Lothar and instructs him to make us some coffee.

"So, your mama used to live in the building, ja?"

"Yes, that's right. She lived here until she got married in 1942. Do you think that you may have known her?"

"What is your mama's name?"

"Elsa Kaufmann," I say, and suddenly the old woman's expression changes and tears shine in her eyes.

"She was born *Elsa Schumacher?"* she asks anxiously.

Excitement slowly overtakes me. "So, you *knew* my mother?"

"Ja, your mama and I were best friends..."

Cathy and I are so stunned to meet someone from Mom's past that we hardly know what to say. A few seconds later, my brain suddenly makes a connection.

"Petra?" I ask.

A look of surprise overtakes her. "How do you know my name?"

"My mother mentioned you in her journal."

Petra studies my face and smiles. "You look like your mama."

I manage a nod and do my best to keep my emotions in check.

When Lothar returns with the coffee, Petra begins reminiscing about her past. I tell her that Mom came back to Hamburg after the war searching for her, but when she arrived at her apartment, no one answered the door.

"*Ja?* Well, we left for a few weeks in 1947 to care for my grandparents in Munich. My cousin, Gunther, stayed here while we were away so that we would still have a home to come back to. It was terrible at that time. So many people without a proper place to live. If Gunther weren't here, it would most certainly have been taken over by someone else. Maybe he was just too afraid to open the door when your mama came looking for me."

We are amazed at this woman's ability to remember the past as though it only happened yesterday. I'm overcome by pity and thoughts of how unfair life can sometimes be. *I wish Mom could have been this way.*

As we continue talking, Petra gets up with difficulty and retrieves a photo album from her bookcase. She goes through it gradually, having trouble turning the pages with her arthritic hands. Finally, she finds the page she is looking for and turns it to us.

"This is Mama and me. And here, this is my cousin, Rudi and some of his friends. This is your papa—you see?"

Petra tells us stories in her broken English about herself and Mom, and we ask her many questions. She is able to answer some of them, and we are so grateful that she has allowed us into her home and taken the time to share her memories.

When we are ready to leave, we hug Petra and thank her for her hospitality. She thanks us for the visit and hands me a picture of her and Mom. "You take this, ja?"

I place it in my bag and thank her once more. Just as we are about to go, Petra stops us and turns to her great-grandson.

"Lothar, I want you to take Laura and Cathy to the Danninger's apartment. This is where Elsa and her family used to live."

He agrees to take us, and both Cathy and I are thrilled to have the opportunity to actually see the place where Mom grew up.

We climb the stairs and enter the hallway. Suddenly, I'm covered with goosebumps, and my imagination works in overdrive. I can visualize my grandmother standing in this very corridor, speaking to my aunt. I see her instructing Greta to come back if Arthur hasn't returned home so that arrangements can be made for her and her boys to stay with her twin sister, Ida, in Berlin. That was over seventy years ago, and although the hallway looks somewhat updated, the wooden trim and apartment doors appear original. As we stand here, I can physically feel my mother's presence, and it fills me with emotion—I miss her *so* much.

After thanking Lothar for his kindness, we make our way out of the building.

"I can't believe our luck, Mom! Isn't it awesome to have met Petra! I mean, what are the odds that she would still be alive, much less live in the same apartment from her youth!"

Although I know that many families pass down their apartments to surviving relatives, I share her sentiments. "I guess everything really does happen for a reason." I find myself believing this more than ever now. It makes me feel that writing Mom's story is meant to be, and I will do my very best to see that I tell it in a way that adequately conveys my mom's experiences.

WE LEAVE HAMBURG on a train bound for Bad Arolsen, and we feel elated. Not only are we excited by the information we have already gathered, but also by the prospect of finding out about my mother's sister, Greta, and her family after they left for Auschwitz in July of 1942.

Once we arrive, we spend many hours combing through computer files, microfiche data, and printed materials hoping to find the answers we seek. Our inability to adequately translate and understand the documents hampers our efforts, so we enlist the assistance of an interpreter.

After another day of digging, and just as we are about to lose all hope, Martha, our interpreter, shows us a document and explains that it is a record of adoption. Cathy and I look at one another with confusion and turn to Martha to wait for clarification.

"It's a record of adoption for a ten-year-old boy from Auschwitz called Franz Schweiger. His birth mother is Greta Schweiger, who is listed as deceased, and father is unknown. The record shows Franz was adopted by a German woman named Hilde Kreutzberg, who at the time of the adoption, lived in Berlin."

"Wow, Mom, wouldn't he be your cousin?"

"Yes, that could be true," I admit. "But Greta had twin boys. Is there any adoption record for his brother, Gerhard?"

Martha searches through the adoption records a while longer and looks up at us. "I'm afraid there is no other record, I'm sorry."

"Well, thank you for looking. At least, we know that a boy named Franz Schweiger lived through Auschwitz, and even though there is no record of Gerhard, this man could very well be my cousin. Maybe we can try to locate him." I do the math in my head. "Franz would be close to eighty now, so it's possible that he's still alive."

"I will do a search for him under both Schweiger and Kreutzberg and see what I can find," Martha says.

It isn't long before she happily announces that she has found an address for a Franz Schweiger, who lives in Berlin. She writes down the information and hands it to me.

"Thank you so much for all your help, Martha," I tell her, shaking her hand. "We would never have been able to find this without you."

"I hope he's the person you are looking for. Good luck to you."

AFTER TRAVELLING BY train for just over four hours, we finally arrive in Berlin. We hail a taxi and give the driver the address, and we're there in less than ten minutes. I ask the man to wait for us should this Franz not be the one we're searching for.

We cross the street to the apartment building and head up the steps. Looking at the row of buzzers by the front door, I scan the names until I find the one we want and push the button. As we wait, I can feel butterflies in my stomach. *I haven't had this sensation since I was a kid.*

"Ja, who is there?" an elderly man's voice asks in German.

"Herr Schweiger, I don't know if you understand English, but my name is Laura Fraser, and I'm here with my daughter from

Canada doing some research into my family history. Are you the Franz Schweiger adopted by Hilde Kreutzberg after the war?" I ask, hoping he understands what I have said.

A few moments pass, and the door clicks, allowing us to enter the building, but before we do, I quickly send Cathy over to pay the taxi driver. Once she rejoins me, we make our way to the elevator and up to apartment 306.

When we arrive, an old man with thick gray hair and a wispy mustache stands at the entrance, watching us make our approach.

"Herr Schweiger, I'm Laura Fraser, and this is my daughter, Cathy. We're very pleased to meet you," I say, trying to hold in my enthusiasm.

"Come in, ja?" Herr Schweiger tells us in his thickly accented English before leading us to the living room.

We sit down and observe our surroundings, patiently waiting for our host to speak. As I survey the room, I notice many photos. Most depict a younger Franz with a woman, who I can only assume is his wife and some that show the couple with a smiling child. My eyes finally come to rest upon an old sketch of two young children hanging on the wall. Herr Schweiger notices me looking at the picture and nods. After a few minutes, which to me, seems like a lifetime, the old man finally speaks.

"That is my brother and me. Mama drew it when we were at the camp. I don't know how she was able to keep it, but she gave it to Frau Kreutzberg, who, many years after the war, gave it to me. She was a wonderful woman who took care of me after Mama died," he says with pain in his voice. "I don't know what would have happened to me if she hadn't taken me in."

"I'm very sorry to bring up your painful past, Herr Schweiger, but I believe your birth mother and mine were sisters. Was her name Greta?"

Tears well in his eyes. "Ja, Mama was called Greta."

"You also had a twin brother—Gerhard, am I right?"

He inhales deeply and looks at the sketch once more. "Ja, ja, Gerhard was my brother." A moment later, Franz turns to me, "Dear God in heaven, *you are my cousin!*"

I smile warmly, placing my hand on his. "Yes, I believe so. Can you tell me, Herr Schweiger, what happened to your mother and brother?"

The old man loses himself in his memories, and the pain of the past manifests itself on his wrinkled face as he contemplates what to say. Although I want to learn the details of my aunt's fate, my heart goes out to him.

To live with my own past is one thing, but to have someone else live with it as well seems cruel. Perhaps this is why I have never told anyone the details of my early life. Should I finally break my silence and if I do, how much should I tell this stranger? After wrestling with his thoughts, Franz clears his throat and slowly commences his story.

"We were sent to Auschwitz in the summer of 1942 after being at Ravensbrück. Gerhard and I were separated from Mama when we arrived there. It was one of the most terrible experiences of my life," he says with a shake of his head. "All those children being forcibly torn away from their mothers—I can still hear the screaming." He stops for a minute to pull himself together. "We never saw Mama again, but a woman who was on the train with us, and later worked at the camp infirmary, relayed messages to us from her. That woman was Frau Kreutzberg. My brother and I lived for those messages each day, and I'm convinced it is the reason we never lost hope of our survival."

Franz is silent again and stares at the picture on the wall. "We learned that Mama got sick and later died in October of 1944. After that, Frau Kreutzberg took care of Gerhard and me, but sadly, I lost my brother two months later. In January of 1945, when the Nazis gathered all prisoners for evacuation, Mama Hilde and I hid to avoid the March. That decision saved our lives. Finally, once the Red Army came in and liberated the camp, we stayed there briefly before making our way to Berlin. Mama Hilde took me in and later adopted me. I owe her my life."

Cathy and I sit there silently, trying to absorb what we have heard, and I reach out once again and touch Franz's hand. "I'm so sorry for your loss, Herr Schweiger, but I'm so glad to finally find you."

He nods, and his cracked lips form a slight smile. "Please, Frau Fraser, call me Franz, ja?"

I smile back at him and reply, "Okay, Franz, then you must call me Laura."

I pull out the old photos I have of my mother and her family. To my surprise, Franz recognizes the photograph of our grandmother, Frieda, and we both seem to feel a connection we didn't earlier. It was as though looking at her picture brought us closer together in a strange way that neither of us could understand nor explain. Franz identifies my mother from the photos and tells us about the fun he and his brother, Gerhard, had with her when they came to visit Hamburg. It brings a smile to my face to know that this man has a warm remembrance of my mother.

At the end of our visit, I leave Franz our contact information so that we can keep in touch. He walks us to the door, and I hug him tenderly.

The old man smiles warmly and takes my hand. "Dankeschön, Laura, for visiting me and telling me about my family. It means so much to learn that I still have some other living relatives. You have made me very happy."

WHEN CATHY AND I return home to Canada, my mind is reeling with the information we were able to obtain. I can't believe how fortunate we were to meet Petra and to find my cousin Franz. I went to Germany without much hope or expectation that we would be successful in our quest to learn about my family history, let alone meeting anyone who actually lived during the time my mother lived there.

Our visit to Germany has certainly helped to make Mom's story more genuine to me. I look through the copious notes I took while we were away and begin the process of piecing the story together with a new perspective and with much more feeling and insight.

It takes months, but I finally have a rough draft of my manuscript complete. It's been a labour of love, and the time has come for me to read and do revisions. There are so many people eager to read what I've written. Part of me is afraid of what others will think when they do, yet another part is happy to have the feedback. Regardless of what others may think, the knowledge that I've done my best to honour a very special person is what's most important. To me, the accomplishment of that makes the whole exercise worthwhile.

Chapter 42: Laura

AFTER REVISING MY manuscript, I'm finally ready to have someone read it. I print three copies, one for Jack, and one for each of my kids.

"Okay, here it is. Now read it, and be brutally honest about what you think. Jot down any comments you want to make. I want you to be critical—it's important. I'm a big girl, and I can take it," I tell them truthfully. I want to have their input before I think about letting anyone outside the family see it.

"Wow, Mom! I can't wait to read it!" Cathy says with a smile as she hugs her copy to her chest.

"It's been a long time coming, but you've finally done it. I'm proud of you," Jack says.

I look at him and blush a little. I never did this to solicit compliments. I did it for Mom, I did it for my family, and lastly, I did it for myself.

Cathy is the first one to finish reading my rough draft, and she gives me a big hug. "I think Oma would be so happy and proud of what you've done. You did an excellent job!" she says giving me back her copy of the manuscript.

I take it and quickly flip through the pages. I can see that Cathy has gone through it carefully, judging by the number of comments and corrections she's made. I'm thankful that she has taken the time to be critical and comment on how she feels I could improve my story. I value her opinion greatly because she's an avid reader and can easily recognize the elements that go into making a good book.

"Please don't be insulted by my comments, Mom."

"Don't be silly! I wanted your honest opinion. I would be upset if you hadn't made them."

Jack and Mike finish their copies a few weeks later and give them back to me with comments as well.

"I'm not an expert, but you know I read a lot. Although I don't usually read stories like this, I think it's really quite good for your first attempt at writing," Jack tells me.

Mike also says he enjoyed reading it, which amazes me since he never seems to stick to a book long enough to complete it.

I BEGIN THE daunting task of reading all the comments and making notes based on them. Many of the points are good ones, and I work to incorporate the thoughts my family has provided me. As I write, I see the roughness of the story being smoothed into shape. I feel like a potter creating a delicate piece of art from a lump of clay—I mold and rework it until it comes out just right.

After a year of hard work, it's finally complete. It gives me an overwhelming sense of pride and accomplishment to know I did my best to communicate what a truly remarkable woman my mother was. I don't think I've ever felt quite like this in my life. Perhaps it's because I've finally come to realize that through the process of writing Mom's story, I've actually lost my deep-rooted feelings of insecurity.

It is my hope that Mom's story will make those who read it not only appreciate how fortunate we are today but also recognize the profound influence our past can have on our daily lives—if we let it. For me, learning to effectively deal with my past, rather than ignoring it, is the key to living a happy life. I realize that not everyone may agree with this. We're all different and handle things in a manner that suits us best. It doesn't mean that one person's way is better than someone else's. We should never pass judgement on how a person handles their life since we haven't lived through their experiences.

Mom's story has become a part of my life and now that it's complete, I undergo what I can only describe as a sense of loss. This is something I never expected to feel. *Perhaps subconsciously this story has kept Mom alive to me, and it's only now that I feel the real impact of losing her.* Although this could be a valid explanation, my mind dismisses the idea. As I continue thinking, an unusual feeling suddenly overtakes me. *Could it be that I have finally found something I really enjoy doing? Maybe writing is what I'm meant to do?* The revelation astounds me and once again, a familiar phrase enters my thoughts—*Everything happens for a reason.*

Author's Note

Although this is a work of fiction, there are certain aspects of the story that are based on truth.

Kristallnacht or Night of Broken Glass is an actual event that took place November 9–10, 1938. The Nazis claimed the pretext for the attacks were retribution for the assassination of a German diplomat, Ernst Vom Rath, in Paris by a German-born Polish Jew named Herschel Grynszpan. In truth, however, plans for attacking the Jews were already in the works before the assassination.

The attacks left 91 Jews dead and over 30,000 arrested and sent to the newly formed concentration camps around Germany. In the months that followed, 2000 to 2500 had died, and the rest were eventually released on the condition that they leave Germany forever.

The fire bombings of Hamburg are factual. The attacks, code-named *Operation Gomorrah* by the Allies, began July 24, 1943, and continued for ten days.

The early morning of July 28th saw the worst of these bombings. A 300-metre-high cyclone of fire, with winds of up to 240 kilometers per hour and temperatures of close to 820°C destroyed more than 20 square kilometers of the city. The attacks caused the deaths of 43,000 civilians, injured approximately 37,000, and left 1 million homeless. In the wake of the bombings, over two-thirds of the population fled the city. While this chapter is fictional, it is based on real-life accounts from that time.

The wireless broadcast announcing the death of Hitler is a rough translation of the original made in German on May 1, 1945, the day following Hitler's suicide. It was adjusted slightly for purposes of the story. The actual broadcast was made at approximately 10:30 p.m.

The International Tracing Service (ITS) is a real organization located in Bad Arolsen, Germany. For further information, please visit their website: www.its-arolsen.org

Glossary

Ach du Lieber Gott: Oh dear God

Auf Wiedersehen: Goodbye

Dankeschön: Thank you

Fröhliche Weihnachten: Merry Christmas

Führer: Leader, in reference to Adolf Hitler

Gnädige Frau: Madam

Guten Abend: Good evening

Guten Morgen: Good morning

Guten Tag: Good day

Heil Hitler: Hail to Hitler

Ja (pronounced "Ya"): Yes

Liebling: Darling

Mein Herr: Sir

Mein Schatz: My Sweetheart or Sweetie

Nein (pronounced "Nine"): No

Pfennige: The former German penny until the introduction of the euro in 2002.

Sicherheitsdienst (SD): Security Division of the SS in charge of foreign and domestic intelligence and espionage.

Schutzstaffel (SS): A major paramilitary organization with several branches overseeing the enforcement of Nazi policies, policing, combat units, and concentration camps.

Sturmabteilung (SA): The original paramilitary organization of the Nazi Party. It was responsible for carrying out the attacks known as Kristallnacht. The group was later dominated by the SS and by 1939, considered of little importance to the Nazi Party.

Vielen Dank: Many thanks

Wehrmacht: German Armed Forces

Wunderbar: Wonderful

Acknowledgements

Many thanks to my family and friends who supported and encouraged me during the process of writing this book. I couldn't have done it without you!

Special thanks to my loving husband, Fred, for putting up with the numerous hours I spent in front of the computer, often ignoring him and the clock.

To my wonderful daughter, Sara, who spent many hours reading and editing my manuscript, only to do it over again several times—without complaint.

I would also like to express my sincere gratitude to my dear friend, Patti, for providing me with many helpful suggestions to smooth out the rough edges of my story and bring substance to its characters.

About the Author

Debbie Volf's passion for history, particularly that of the Second World War, was instilled at a young age. Listening to the numerous first-hand accounts of her parents' experiences in war-torn Germany planted the seeds that later grew into a need to learn and understand more about the era and its effects on those who survived it.

When she isn't writing, Debbie spends time reading both historical fiction and mysteries, looking for inspiration for new stories and losing herself in the creative experience. She also enjoys living a healthy lifestyle, travelling and continually learning new things.

She lives in Hamilton, Ontario, Canada with her husband, and they have two grown children.

66224143R00163

Made in the USA
Charleston, SC
13 January 2017